Reasonable Insanity

A Dr. Olivia C. Maxwell Novel

By Cynthia Freeman Gibbs

BROWN GIRLS BOOKS

Houston, Texas * Washington, D.C.

Reasonable Insanity © 2018 by Cynthia Freeman Gibbs

Brown Girls Books LLC www.BrownGirlsBooks.com

ISBN: 978-1-944359-68-3 (ebook)

ISBN: 978-1-944359-69-0 (print)

First Brown Girls Publishing LLC trade printing Manufactured and Printed in the United States of America

DEDICATION

Daddy,
I miss you more than you know. I feel your presence
encouraging me along the way. This book is dedicated to you,
Robert Rochell Freeman. Thank you for believing in me, praying
for me, and for trusting me to write for you.
I love you and will continue to make you proud.
Love, Cynthia NiHot, Pokey Slow, #3.

ACKNOWLEDGMENTS

First, I thank God and Jesus Christ, my Lord, for all of the amazing blessings each day. God, you said in your Word, Philippians 4:6-7 "Be anxious for nothing, but in everything by prayer and supplication, with thanksgiving, let your requests be made known to God; and the peace of God, which surpasses all understanding, will guard your hearts and minds through Christ Jesus."

From my heart to:

My loving husband, J Maurice Gibbs, for being my encourager, sounding board, shoulder to cry on, friend to laugh with, and for taking care of everything, so I could focus on allowing my creative mind to flow. I still feel like a newlywed after nine years of marriage to you. I love you forever.

Mom, Merilyn Freeman, you are my nurturer. You are such a strong inspiration to me. I admire your artistry in your ministry of music, cooking, and making jewelry. You are a walking encyclopedia, avid reader, and Scrabble master, which made a world of difference when you offered me your feedback on my writing. Thank you for taking the time to proofread my work. I love your laughter, the way you care for our family, and for others with your whole heart.

Mommy, Barbara Gibbs, you are an amazing mother-in-law. Thank you for raising J Maurice to be the man that he is. The things you instilled in him as a child are evident today in the way he is in our marriage. I love you for your sense of humor and your caring spirit.

My dearest siblings: Chevelle Freeman, Dion Freeman, and Jamille Freeman Hunter. Y'all are all crazy, and you know it! I can't imagine growing up without the three of you. You have all poured into my life in so many ways that I can't even begin to express it. Thank you for your laughter, listening ears, and your support during my writing journey and throughout my life. I appreciate the time you took to proofread and provide your feedback from your creative brains. I know, as the middle sister, I rule the world!

The best brother-in-law and sister-in-law, Damon Hunter and Vicky Freeman. I thank God for the love you have shown my siblings and to all of us over the years. Y'all are both crazy too and fit right in!

My sorority sister/daughter, JaLeesa Gibbs. I thank you for celebrating with me along the way.

My beautiful nieces and nephews. I know you are all going places and doing big things. You know that Auntie Cynthia is proud of each of you. You are all my favorite!

I appreciate the love and support I have received from my aunts, uncles, cousins, and so many family members. I can't name all of you because I would leave someone's name out. Thank you.

Brown Girls Books – ReShonda Tate Billingsley and Victoria Christopher Murray, you are both amazing in all you do. Thank you for sharing your expertise. Thank you for choosing me!

To my friends who served as readers, editors, mentors, and more. The time you took from your busy schedules meant the world to me. Thank you: Dr. Betty Harris, Brucetta Williams, Christa McDuffie, Iuliana Foos, Jan Kilby, Attorney Jason Pulliam, Lauren McCadney Williams, Dr. Phillip Williams, Michelle L. De La Garza and the Tobin Writers' Group,

Attorney Stephanie Brown, Treyla Lee, and Tricia Mayes. You saw my work in the raw stage, and I thank you for sticking with me to see this project through to the end. Christa, I can't thank you enough for brainstorming with me on story ideas and making sure I knew when it didn't make sense.

My webmaster, the incomparable and unstoppable, Andre Green. #KeepCalmAndLiveOn #TeamDreBrain.

San Antonio Alumnae Chapter of Delta Sigma Theta Sorority, Incorporated. My sorority sisters have been there to encourage and lift me up. It meant the world to me to have you there at the Arts and Letters Committee and Delta REaD Book Club event where Brown Girls Books announced I was their newest author. Thank you for true sisterhood for a lifetime.

Resurrection Baptist Church Family (Redland Oaks and Schertz campuses) – Thank you for your prayers.

Carver Page Turners Book Club – Thank you for inviting me to read to your Book Club in 2016 when I didn't have a physical book. Thank you for inviting me to return with my books.

My sorority sisters who are authors I adopted as mentors: Cynae Punch Brown, Meme Kelly, and Ruth P. Watson.

Finally, I thank all of you who have given me words of encouragement during this awesome journey to become an author to write books for the world to enjoy.

PART 1

RUNNING AWAY

PROLOGUE

San Antonio, TX - 2011

"Savvy." Olivia's raw throat barely allowed a raspy whisper to slip through her cotton-dry mouth. "It's me."

The illuminated phone offered little light in the wooded area where she hid underneath the twilight sky. *Oh no. Why do I only have two percent of my battery power left? Shoot. It hasn't been plugged in to charge since yesterday morning. Doggone it. I gotta get out of here before it goes dead.*

Insects communicated loudly in a swell and fall of harmonized choirs. *I can't hear myself think over the sound of these bugs. Why are they making so much noise?* Olivia slapped her bare arms and face more than necessary to ward off the pests. *These mosquitos are killing me. What if I get the West Nile virus from these things biting on me?*

The crunch of dead leaves with each hastened step she took echoed and seemed to come from someone other than herself. *Is somebody following me? What if they're coming to get me?* A sudden rustling in the trees above her head made her cringe with paranoia of unseen creatures or people lurking around. *What was that? Please don't let a critter jump out at me. There could be coyotes or mountain lions out here. No one will even know what happened to me.*

She jumped wildly at the sound of an owl's hoot and

8

scraped her forehead against a tree branch. "Ouch," she cried. She rubbed her face and felt the roughness of broken skin.

"Olivia, speak up. I can't hear you. What's wrong with your voice? Why didn't you call me back last night?" Savvy chastised through the phone.

Exhaustion from being on the run for seven hours caught up to her once she heard Savvy's voice. Her stomach growled loudly reminding her it had been a day and a half since she'd eaten anything. Vodka. She remembered drinking lots of it in that time-frame, and her body now resented her. *I may need to look for berries and nuts out here to survive. What if I starve or die from dehydration before I find my way out?*

Sharp, radiating pains in her lungs forced her to stop moving and bend over to attempt to breathe. Her chest rose and fell rapidly in her soot-covered shirt with her desire for air. She swooned from the stench of gasoline wafting through her nostrils.

"Savvy," she whispered louder, despite the agony of speaking. "My house has burned down."

"Olivia. What are you talking about? I can't hear you very well. Hold up. Let me increase the volume on my phone." Olivia grew impatient listening to the sound of Savvy fumbling around. "Okay, I'm back. Now, what did you say?"

Olivia hacked, trying to clear her throat and had second thoughts about telling Savvy what happened. Shivering from the coolness of the air made her wish for a jacket. She clutched the phone in her trembling hand and held it close to her mouth to amplify her whisper. "My house burned to the ground." Her words came in short spurts, and her stomach lurched at the memory of her husband. "Malcolm has the kids."

"Did you say your house burned down?" Savvy's voice screamed through the phone. Olivia pulled it from her ear, which hurt from the piercing shriek. "What happened? Where are you?"

Olivia frantically crept around the wooded area trying to find her way out. "I can't talk right now. That's all I can say because I don't want to incriminate you." Tears tumbled from her eyes and onto her phone. "I'm so sorry," she continued, lowering her voice even more. "I can't believe my kids almost died today. Please tell Christian and Simone how much mommy loves them. God knows I would never hurt them. You've been the best friend ever. I love you, Savvy." A siren blared in the distance. Olivia froze as if they could see her if she moved. She ended her call, afraid of being found.

Without the light from the screen, the darkness elevated Olivia's fear in her chest. She began hyperventilating, and the short inhalations of air made her dizzy. She stumbled to a boulder and fell on it to catch her breath. Her lungs burned and struggled to open to receive whatever oxygen they could. The sunrise would be her only saving grace.

My mother is right. I'm not good enough, and no one loves me. Failure is my middle name, and my life is as good as being dead. Who cares that I'm an educated psychologist. People will think I'm a crazy woman if they find me hiding in the woods. The doctor said I wasn't bipolar. What's wrong with me? How did I end up like this? "God, help me," she cried into the night and clenched her head to silence her thoughts. "Please, Lord."

PART 2

A ROSE IS STILL A ROSE

CHAPTER 1

Tallahassee, FL - 1989

"Have you ever hitchhiked?" Olivia asked Savvy.

"Huh?" Savvy's thinly arched left brow raised. She eyeballed Olivia like she was crazy. "Savvy" and "hitchhiking" didn't' even belong in the same sentence.

The girls were introduced earlier in the evening at a gathering in the dormitory of their mutual friend, Lil' Bud at The State University of Florida (TSUF). They instantly connected around a love for the R&B group, New Edition, as well as a passion for shopping. After hanging at the get together for a few hours, they decided to head to a party thrown by Omega Psi Phi Fraternity at Florida A&M University (FAMU).

Savvy was a first-year student at FAMU, and Olivia planned to transfer her credits from Tallahassee Community College there next year in order to earn her Bachelor's degree in Psychology. Hopes of meeting the men of their dreams at the party filled their conversation, which led to the idea of traveling across town from TSUF.

"Hitchhiking, you know, catching a ride standing on the side of the street with your thumb and your leg stuck out," Olivia said.

"Girl, no," Savvy exclaimed. "I know what hitchhiking is and I don't do dangerous stuff like that. Why would you ask something so ridiculous?"

"I always thought it would be fun." Olivia's light brown eyes glowed with excitement.

"Well, it happens to be crazy and reckless."

"You have to live a little, right?"

"I'm confused," Savvy said. "You have a car. Why would you need to beg for a ride with strangers?"

"I don't need to. I want to. Don't be a dud like my other friends," Olivia pleaded. "Plus, I don't have any gas to get all the way to FAMU. We wouldn't have to worry about parking either.'"

"Hold up. I thought we were on the way to your apartment to pick up your car. Are you thinking about bumming a ride to FAMU tonight?" Savvy stopped walking, put her hands on her hips, and stared at Olivia like she'd lost her mind. "Oh no. We're by Frenchtown and you know it's the rougher side of Tallahassee. I ain't willingly letting someone snatch me."

Olivia twisted her lips in disappointment. They started to walk again toward the edge of campus to Tennessee Street, one of the main roads in front of the university. Next thing Savvy knew, Olivia stood on the curb, hiked up her already-short red dress even more, and raised her thumb and stuck her leg out as a silver SUV approached. At five feet, ten inches, she was easy to spot on the side of the road underneath the street light.

Savvy grabbed Olivia's arm and yanked her back from the curb. "Have you lost your mind? You've got to be kidding me."

Olivia laughed. "Oh, come on. We're in college, and this is when we're supposed to have fun. It won't be dangerous."

Savvy shook her head in disbelief as Olivia stuck her leg out and raised her thumb again. A bright purple, lowrider slowly approached. 2 Live Crew's, "Me So Horny," blasted from the window. The car stopped in front of Olivia on the busy street.

A striking man leaned out the passenger side window, studying Olivia from head to toe and asked, "Whassup baby? Whatchu doing standing out here?" He smacked his lips like he would if he were eating a piece of fried chicken. "Girl, you got me thinking about a dark, chocolate, Hershey Kiss. You need a ride somewhere?"

Savvy stood back with her arms folded and rolled her eyes in disgust. *Surely, Olivia would back away from this ghetto lowrider, especially with his tacky, Hershey Kiss line.*

Olivia acted like she'd hit the jackpot, and ran to the vehicle. "Yeah. We're trying to catch a ride to FAMU for a party tonight since we don't have any gas in my car. Can you give us a lift?"

Savvy couldn't believe Olivia was serious about hitchhiking a ride from these thugs in this ugly, purple machine.

"Anything for you baby. We're rolling that way to handle some bizness." He smiled, revealing a gold grill in his mouth across his front teeth, and opened his door to get out. His car might have been tacky, but this man was anything but tacky. All six-feet-two-inches of him was fine, especially his creamy, mocha latte colored skin. He kept running his incredibly long tongue across his full lips, making them unbelievably juicy like one of Savvy's favorite rappers, LL Cool J.

She couldn't help but notice his fresh, high-top fade haircut. Stonewashed jeans made his firm booty tempting to touch. His perfectly fitted Miami Dolphin football jersey accentuated his muscled, tattooed arms.

"Why is your friend standing back there acting like she's your parole officer?" he asked looking over every inch of Savvy's curvy shape. She tugged at the hem of her miniskirt and tried to disappear into the ground. The last thing she wanted was for this dude to see her lusting after him.

14

Stepping back, Olivia laughed and grabbed Savvy's arm. "This is Savannah, but we call her Savvy. Come on, girl, let's get to this party before it ends. We have a way to get there now."

Savvy shook her arm free from Olivia's grip and glared at her. "Girl, puh-leeaze. You're not for real, right? I know you don't think we're about to get in there with these strangers. My mom and dad would kill me if they even thought I'd do something this stupid. Now come on, let's walk back to Lil' Bud's place," she yelled above the ear-piercing music.

"Oh, loosen up, Savvy. There's nothing wrong with these guys. You know this ride is custom made so we'll ride in style. We won't even be in there for long. Come on," Olivia pleaded.

Savvy peered at the guy and noticed how he appeared ready to devour her like a lion eating a wallaby. Her cheeks flushed from him undressing her with his stare. For some strange reason, her body tingled, and goosebumps popped out on her arms.

"Yeah, come on, baby. Come hang with us. We can all go party together," he said, flashing a seductive smile.

"This is crazy, Olivia. I don't even know you well enough since we just met tonight. Not to mention, we don't know anything about these people." Savvy planted her hands firmly on her hips.

"I'm not getting in and you better not either." Savvy began to walk away.

"Hey guys, hold on a minute, and we'll be right back." Olivia's heels tapped on the sidewalk when she darted after Savvy. "Hey, wait up."

Against Savvy's better judgment, she let out a loud sigh and turned around to face Olivia. "What?"

"I promise you. This will be fun. You have to trust me and not worry about these guys. I mean, come on, see how cute he

15

is? His friend looks good, too. Only this one time. I Girl Scout Promise you, I'll never ask you to do this again." Olivia held three fingers in the air in commitment.

Savvy side-eyed Olivia and shook her head. "I don't know why you want to do this. My gut doesn't feel good about them at all."

"You don't have to worry." Olivia used her most soothing voice to convince her to change her mind. She looped her arm through Savvy's and tugged gently on it.

The excitement on Olivia's face was starting to overshadow the voices of her parents telling her to use common sense.

Against her better judgment, Savvy let Olivia lead her to where this random stranger opened the back door like a limo chauffeur. "I'm telling you, I don't like this," Savvy warned through clenched teeth.

"See, I'm the perfect gentleman," he said, extending his hand to Olivia to help her slide into the rear seat. He stuck his hand out to Savvy who huffed and brushed past him to scoot in next to her.

Once he closed the door, Savvy noticed a funny smell in the car. She couldn't quite recognize the odor. It mingled with the scent from the stack of Christmas tree air fresheners hanging from the rearview mirror. She nervously inspected her surroundings and noticed a 40-ounce bottle of Olde English in the driver's cup holder.

The driver turned around to check out the girls. He wore a Miami Heat hat pulled low on his face, almost covering his eyes. He flashed a bright, white, Colgate smile at Savvy and said, "Girl, you sho' look nice in your short blue dress. I see you with your curves in all the right places. You know you got some cute dimples. I would love to put my tongue in your dimple." Savvy didn't reply as she turned and looked out the window.

16

"Ladies, welcome to party central. Let's get it started," the other guy said and cranked the music to the point where it made Savvy's liver quiver from the woofers in the back trunk. The whole car shook from the bass in the music, which could break the windows from being louder than necessary.

The driver showed off the hydraulics on his lowrider by raising and dropping it several times. Savvy's head hit the ceiling from the jolting car. She grabbed a strap above the window to hang on with one hand and tried to soothe the top of her head with the other. She thought the bouncing around would make her sick or she would surely go deaf from the loud music.

Seeing Olivia with a huge smile, made her want to slap it from her face. She couldn't believe her excitement about being with these guys. Olivia bopped her head to the music as if she did this every day.

Scared to death, Savvy fastened her seatbelt, then gripped the seat in front of her to keep her head from hitting the ceiling again. Her eyes opened wide in fear when she mouthed at Olivia, "We need to get out of here."

Olivia mouthed back, "Chill out and relax," and kept moving her head to the music. She swung her Janet Jackson waterfall hairdo back and forth as if she were on stage performing.

The driver finally stopped playing with the hydraulics. He crept along the street slower than the speed limit. Savvy noticed how people driving past them stared, some in awe and others in anger because of the loud music and slow pace.

Okay, okay. I've got to calm down. Maybe, Olivia's right. I'm probably worrying for no reason. Savvy's heart stopped racing, and she began to relax slightly after taking a few deep, shaky breaths. She decided to do her best to enjoy hanging with these good-looking guys if she could convince herself it wouldn't be bad

17

after all.

Olivia smiled at her and gave her the thumbs up when she calmed down. Savvy opened her mouth to ask Olivia about the party when the cute guy pulled out what appeared to be a funny shaped cigar.

He lit it with a cigarette lighter at the same time he puffed softly with his luscious lips. He held the smoke in his chest before leaning his head back to exhale. He took a deeper, slower drag before passing it to the driver who did the same thing and gave it back to him.

The funny smell Savvy noticed faintly earlier, now filled the air and made her dizzy. The cute guy turned around in his seat with the cigar in his right hand after taking another drag. He started talking and held the smoke in his chest. Puffs of smoke swirled from his mouth and nose. "Hey ladies, y'all wanna hit this blunt?"

Savvy's eyes bugged out and shouted above the music, "What's a blunt? I don't smoke nothin'. Plus, I have asthma and your stuff stinks." She coughed from the smoke, which made her chest hurt.

Olivia laughed and yelled, "She knows what a blunt is. We don't wanna hit it right now though. Y'all go ahead and enjoy it between the two of you. We're good."

The cute guy gazed at them with half-closed bloodshot eyes and shook his head. He blew the smoke out slowly through his lips before he took another long drag on the blunt and passed it to the driver. He took a big swig from the 40-ounce bottle and wiped his mouth off with the back of his hand.

Savvy whispered to Olivia, "What's a blunt?"

Olivia whispered back, "Marijuana."

Shaking her head several times in disbelief, Savvy exclaimed, "Marijuana? You mean like weed? I don't do drugs. Get me outta this car."

Olivia pleaded with Savvy. "Will you chill out Savvy? Just chill."

I'm going to die in this car from choking to death. Savvy lowered the window and the wind whipped through her hair. She stuck her head out to capture deep gulps of air into her choking lungs. Olivia tugged to pull her back in. "Chill out, Savvy," she said firmly.

Savvy reluctantly rolled her window to the top and flopped back on the seat. She drew in short breaths to limit the smoke getting into her lungs.

The driver lowered the volume of the music when they passed Frenchtown. "Hey Doobie, pass me the Glock from the glove compartment."

"Here you go, Smack." Doobie passed a gun to the driver. He pulled out another weapon and started loading it with bullets.

"You know these cats usually hang out right here on this corner, man. We gotta be ready," Smack said and took the gun when they approached Adams Street.

"What the hell?" Savvy yelled. *Oh, Lawd. We're about to die. My mama and daddy are going to hear on the news that their baby girl was involved in a gang drive-by shooting. I'm going to be dead.*

"Keep cool, Savvy," Olivia had crazy excitement on her face. "It's gonna be fine. Ain't nothing about to happen in here."

"Yeah baby, listen to your friend," Doobie said and scanned the area. "We have some bizness to handle. Quit stressin' and relax, baby."

"Oh no. I'm not the one to be in a car where y'all passing guns around like you're about to shoot up someplace. Get me the hell out of here," Savvy yelled, reaching for the door.

Olivia grabbed her arm, pulling her toward her. "Don't you know you're about to jump out of a moving car?"

Savvy's eyes showed her terror, and she continued to grip the door handle. "You got us into this mess, and you'd better get us out. Otherwise, yes, I'm jumping."

"All right, fine. We're by the bus station, and we can get them to drop us off to catch the bus the rest of the way." Olivia shook her head in disappointment. She tapped Doobie on the shoulder. "Hey, thanks for the ride. We're gonna get out here. Can you drop us off?"

"Let you out? I thought y'all wanted to party?" Doobie turned around and fixated on Olivia. "Y'all scared of guns or something?"

"Hell yeah. I'm scared of guns. I'm not trying to die tonight," Savvy yelled.

Olivia laughed. "Naw. We ain't scared. We figured we don't want to miss the party. There's a bus leaving from here we can ride to FAMU. Y'all go handle your business, and we'll catch you later."

Doobie said something to Smack, and he pulled to the station.

Olivia took out a piece of paper and a pen from her purse and wrote out her phone number. She leaned across the back of the seat and handed it to Doobie. She batted her eyelashes and told him, "Call me, and we can get together sometime."

Olivia opened her door and gracefully exited. Savvy scooted across the seat, frantically trying to scramble to freedom. Savvy's heart beat rapidly making her body weak and barely able to stand.

"All right baby, have it your way." Doobie leaned out the window and licked those lips again. "I'll call you later." They drove off, turning on a street in the opposite direction of

FAMU.

"I'm done with you right now," Savvy yelled at Olivia and stomped her foot on the pavement. Her hands clenched into fists to the point her nails dug painfully into her palms. "You could've gotten us killed tonight."

Olivia laughed until she had to hold her stomach to keep it from hurting. "You're hilarious."

"There's nothing funny," Savvy shouted. "What the hell is funny to you?"

"I wish you could've seen your face when we were in the car." Olivia continued to laugh. "You were scared. I can't believe you thought something bad would happen."

"What's wrong with you?" Savvy asked with disbelief. "Didn't you see they were passing marijuana cigars and guns around and saying stuff about handling business with someone? They were about to do a drive-by or something. I think they were drug dealers."

"No, they weren't. Now your imagination is getting the best of you." Olivia stopped laughing and peered at Savvy. "They had guns for their protection and knew we were going past a bad part of town. I'm okay, and you're okay."

Savvy shook her head. *Where in the world did Lil' Bud find Olivia? Her head ain't screwed on right or something.*

"Look, I know this seemed crazy but, you have to admit, it woke you up. Right? Doobie is C-U-T-E. Cute." Olivia snapped her fingers and tap-danced on the sidewalk.

Savvy had to admit he was a cutie pie. Still, she shouldn't have pulled her into this mess. Something about Olivia's enthusiasm for adventure made her feel a twinge of excitement amidst her anger.

"Girl, don't you ever do this to me again. I'll never go

anywhere with you for the rest of my life," Savvy snapped at Olivia.

"Don't worry. Now I can check hitchhiking off my list of things to do in college. Let's catch this next bus heading to FAMU. We can still make the party."

Savvy sighed and couldn't believe her ears when she said "Okay," and followed Olivia to the bus. *Who is this Olivia and what am I getting into by hanging with her?* Her friends often teased her about being dry and boring. She knew she had to stay out of trouble and uphold her family's name. *Perhaps Olivia is the kind of friend I need to get some excitement in my world. It couldn't hurt, could it?*

CHAPTER 2

Olivia chuckled as she thought about the events of last night. Savvy would be fun to go to parties with if she loosened up.

The Omega party turned out to be fun, and they had a good time. Olivia and Savvy had given their phone numbers to a couple of fine Ques. They stayed out until after three in the morning, and she barely made it to class by ten o'clock. She'd had to struggle to focus on her professor for two hours.

Now, she had an appointment with her psychologist, which she'd decided to see after dealing with her family issues. This visit would be her third time since she moved to Tallahassee.

After parking her car, Olivia took her time walking into the building. She knew that this appointment was long overdue, especially with the way she was bordering on a breakdown.

Olivia liked coming to Dr. Hughes' office. The whole environment was warm and inviting. Colorful, African paintings hung on the orange walls. There were huge, Kente cloth pillows on a cream-colored sofa and chairs in the reception area.

Shortly after the receptionist checked Olivia in, the nurse escorted her back to wait in Dr. Hughes's office.

"Dr. Hughes will be right with you. Feel free to check out the magazines on the table," the nurse said before leaving the room.

Olivia searched through the stack of *Essence, Jet, Travel,* and *Reader's Digest* magazines. She found *Ebony* magazine and began flipping through it until Dr. Hughes opened the door and greeted her with a smile.

"Hello, Olivia. It's good to see you again."

Olivia stood to hug her. She towered over the doctor's short, petite frame. "Hi, Dr. Hughes. Thank you for getting me in on such short notice. I feel kind of down and needed to talk to someone before I lose my mind."

"Have a seat and tell me what's going on." Dr. Hughes had the kindest eyes, which showed concern when she focused on Olivia.

Olivia sank into the soft sofa. "Today would've been my brother's birthday." She took a deep breath, fighting back tears. Whenever she talked about Noah, she had to struggle to keep it together. But she knew she had to get this off her chest.

"Oh, tell me about him," Dr. Hughes said, sitting down in the chair across from Olivia.

"My brother committed suicide at age twenty-two," Olivia paused and took a deep breath before continuing. "I heard my Mom and Dad talking about the fact that he was bipolar and schizophrenic, but he refused to take his medication. I remember him telling me he heard voices in his head. He got mad when he couldn't make them go away. We had a great relationship when he used his medication."

A single tear wet her cheek.

Dr. Hughes reached over to pass her a tissue. Olivia crinkled it in her hand and dabbed her face. "It's okay. I see he meant a lot to you," Dr. Hughes said.

The single tear found friends and began a cascade down her face. "I loved him more than I love myself." Olivia cried. "My mother acted like she didn't believe his diagnosis and thought he would grow out of it eventually. She treated him so harshly as if he could change if he tried hard enough. He never did because he couldn't. If only she realized he needed more help." Olivia's sadness turned to anger.

Dr. Hughes waited patiently to allow Olivia to work through her emotions. "On New Year's Eve in 1985, my mother found him hanging in his bedroom closet with the belt she gave to him for Christmas. He killed himself, and it's all her fault," she cried.

Olivia stood and paced the room. "But you know, he's not the only person in my family to commit suicide." She stopped mid-step and thought pensively.

"My grandfather also committed suicide right after my mother celebrated her sixteenth birthday. He set their house on fire to kill my grandmother, my mom, aunt, and uncle. All of them were in it. He ended up being the only one who died. The rest escaped unharmed."

"It's tragic to have other family members who have taken their lives. I can see why you are having difficulties regarding these incidences Olivia."

"Dr. Hughes, it isn't even everything. My parents fight all the time and often threaten to kill each other or themselves. When this happens, Mother grabs a vial of my brother's cremated ashes from her dresser and holds them in my dad's face. She threatens to end her life the same way my brother did. Dad tells her to do it and don't make a mess in the house. Can you believe that?" Olivia asked incredulously.

Dr. Hughes nodded her head. "What concerns do you have when you think about this type of behavior in your family?"

"I wonder if this is hereditary. I mean, am I going to be someone who commits suicide instead of dealing with problems in my life? If so, what do I need to do to keep this from happening?" Olivia plopped back into her seat and closed her eyes, stressed out from the thought.

"Olivia, the act of suicide is not hereditary. It is a choice made by your brother and grandfather. There are some studies

25

which show bipolar disorder and schizophrenia tend to run in families. Researchers believe there may be a genetic disposition for this disease," Dr. Hughes said. "You do not have either of these disorders."

Olivia hesitated, letting the doctor's words sink in. "Thank you for telling me I'm okay today. I tell you, Dr. Hughes, my family is enough to make anyone batty." Olivia sighed. "Do I have time to tell you some of the other crazy stuff that's happened in my family?"

"Yes, we have plenty of time. What else is on your mind?"

She leaned forward, anxious to share stories she hadn't shared with anyone else. "So, I have this sister, Sheree. She has got to be the worst person ever, other than my mother. There's no doubt in my mind she's mentally ill. We've never gotten along, and she always picks fights with me. My parents accuse me of being the agitator, and I'm the one who gets punished. Not her." Olivia talked through clenched teeth.

"They treat her like a queen, and me like I'm the runt of our family. Do you know my parents never came to any of my track meets? I was the anchor on my high school relay team. I was a star athlete and popular because I was the fastest runner. They never saw me run during those four years. Never even acknowledged the trophies and medals I brought home. They were too busy putting Sheree in beauty pageants and going everywhere with her instead." Olivia's nose flared. She hated the hate that she had for her sister, but it was very real.

"Why do you think your parents treated you differently?"

"Well, for one thing, Sheree is light-skinned and has long brown hair and green eyes. She looks like a younger version of Vanessa Williams. You know, the one who used to be Miss America? Whenever a dark-skinned person appeared on TV or in a magazine, Sheree would point out they were dark and ugly, like me. If they were light-skinned, she said they were pretty, like her." Olivia sighed and gazed out the window.

"I think my parents feel the same way. They always tell Sheree she's beautiful and how much they love her," Olivia said, not bothering to hide her sarcasm. "They hug and kiss her all the time. With me, they only pat me on the head and never tell me I'm pretty or they love me.

"I used to think my dad would stand up for me, but my mother has complete control over him. He is spineless and does whatever she tells him to do. I know she hates me for not fitting in with the rest of the family, as if it's my fault." Olivia paused. "I'm alone because they choose not to pay any attention to me. I moved to Tallahassee to get away from them. I don't even think they notice I'm gone. The only time my mother calls me is when she wants something."

Tears welled in Olivia's eyes again. "I know this is crazy. Everyone else tells me I favor movie stars and models, but that's only because I'm tall. I'm not pretty enough to get a boyfriend, but, I don't consider myself to be ugly. Although I guess with my skin looking like black patent leather, my parents think I'm unattractive compared to my sister. Sometimes I think that maybe if I was a little lighter, they'd love me."

"Olivia, let me reassure you, you are a beautiful, African-American woman. Do not let anyone tell you otherwise. Not your family, friends, boyfriends, anyone," Dr. Hughes stated firmly. "Sometimes, people have a shallow way of thinking when it comes to skin complexion. They are ignorant of the fact that beauty comes in all shades. So, do not let anyone define you by the color of your skin. Do you understand me?"

"Yes, Dr. Hughes. I understand."

"Now, I know today is rough for you considering your brother's suicide. You cannot let this date paralyze you and get you into a funk. I want you to put an activity to do on your calendar every year on his birthday. Go hiking, travel somewhere, plant a garden or a tree in his name. Do something to show how you can keep living and honor him. Will you do that Olivia?"

Without hesitation, Olivia said, "Yes, I can and I will."

"Very good. Unfortunately, we are out of time. I would like to have another meeting with you next month if you think you need it."

"I may need to see you again. If I find myself slipping into darkness, I'll call to get an appointment. Thank you, Dr. Hughes. You always know what to tell me." *When I become a psychologist, I want to be exactly like Dr. Hughes. She is such an angel.*

"You're welcome, Olivia. You can come to see me any time." Dr. Hughes escorted Olivia to the door where she hugged her.

On the way out, Olivia glanced at her watch, saw she was going to be late for work and sprinted to the parking lot. She jumped in her car and quickly sped onto the street as her mind shifted back to thoughts about her family. She failed to tell Dr. Hughes about her own bad behavior in high school.

Olivia had discovered she could get the attention she desired from her mother by bringing things home to her. It started off with Olivia picking flowers from a field on her way home from school. Her mom's eyes widened with joy when she handed her the bouquet of colorful, wild blossoms. She patted her on the head for being thoughtful.

Next, Olivia began taking school supplies from her classrooms. She progressed to stealing the scarves and hats other kids stored in their lockers. She earned a hug or two after giving her mother the presents.

At sixteen, Olivia started working at a fast food restaurant. On the days she had the responsibility to work in the drive-thru station, her mother pulled to the window. Olivia piled burgers, fries, pies, and chicken sandwiches into bags to sneak out to her.

Her mother encouraged her to get another job working in an upscale restaurant. She presented her with gifts of stolen salt and pepper shakers, glasses, silverware, and plates. The happiness expressed toward her thrilled Olivia, although her mom knew she pilfered everything.

Once Olivia started college, she often sent packages back home to Illinois filled with items stolen from various places. Stealing became a great way to build a relationship with her mother.

After she sent a package, her mom would call and express gratitude for being a good daughter and thinking of her. *Maybe I'll tell Dr. Hughes about this next time I have an appointment. It may be time to stop stealing. Maybe.*

The restaurant appeared empty when Olivia arrived and changed into her uniform. She had to work at the front register. Sleepy from her long night out, it wasn't long after taking her post that Olivia became lost in thought. She leaned on the front counter with her head on her arms, waiting for customers to enter.

Savvy strolled into the restaurant. "Hey, Olivia. Wake your butt up," she barked.

Olivia jumped in surprise and raised her head from the counter. "Hey, Savvy. I didn't even see you come in." Olivia said with a smile once she noticed her friend. "What are you doing here?"

"Remember I mentioned I got a job here, too? I live in the apartment building right back there." Savvy pointed toward the window.

"That's right. I forgot about that," Olivia exclaimed. "Welcome to The Sloppy Burger Spot. You're going to love this job."

"Yeah, I figured I could get some hours in here and work at the Civic Center. I can see all the concerts there for free. My friend got me that job, and it's fun," Savvy said.

"Girl, I want to work there, too. TSUF plays basketball at the Civic Center, and it would be awesome to see all of the fine men shooting hoops on the court." Olivia's eyes lit up. "Please see if you can get me a job there."

"All right, all right. I'll see what I can do. In the meantime, let's talk later after I meet with the manager and find out if I'm working on the register or the fryer."

"Cool. I'll walk you to her office. Don't worry; you'll like her," Olivia said and led her to the manager. "Good luck on your first day." The girls hugged, and Olivia returned to the front counter.

A woman with pink rollers in her hair with two dirty-faced kids entered the restaurant. Olivia was disgusted at the sight of the nasty-looking kids who seemed like they hadn't had a bath in weeks. "Welcome to The Sloppy Burger Spot," Olivia said and put her hand to her mouth to stifle a yawn. She couldn't wait to get home and go to sleep.

CHAPTER 3

"Thank God, it's Friday. Did y'all see those cutie pies in line to get in here? I know we'll each meet someone tonight." Olivia led Savvy and her other friend, Andrea into Club Faces. Andrea was her conservative friend who had to be convinced to hang out. Her Dad threatened to make her move back to Miami if her grades slipped from partying too much, so she never wanted to leave the dorm.

The small nightclub's big dance floor had a DJ booth onstage with turntables spinning the latest hits and mixes. Music blared from the huge speakers, which sat on each side.

Cocktail tables surrounded the room, and college students crowded the bar to get the Happy Hour 4-for-1 Zombies drink special. Steam covered the mirrors around the club from the heat. The room smelled musky with sweat and cologne from people dancing as if their life depended on it.

"Sounds good to me. There are some fine specimen of men in here." Savvy squealed at the number of guys in the packed club.

"I had no idea this place is the spot to be on a Friday night," Andrea said. "This is worth me getting in trouble with my Dad for. I've been missing out."

"See, Andrea. You gotta have a good time during your college years. I figured we'll start here. Afterward, we'll head to The Moon to dance the rest of the night away. That's where everyone goes to keep the party going." Olivia pumped her fist in the air and yelled above the music. "Come on ladies. Let's hit the dance floor."

Savvy and Andrea followed Olivia as she danced her way through the club. Greetings of "Hey, pretty young thing" and "I know I can get a dance with you later" and "Let me buy you a drink, baby" filled their ears when they squeezed through the crowd.

Savvy grabbed Olivia and Andrea by their arms and stopped dead in her tracks. "Oh my gosh. I think I must've died and gone to heaven," she screamed.

"What? What's wrong?" Olivia yelled.

"Nothing is wrong. I just saw Carl Greer. Oh my gosh. I can't breathe." Savvy fanned herself frantically.

"Who is Carl Greer?" Andrea asked.

"He's only the cutest guy at FAMU and the star on the track team. I think I'm in love with him." Savvy seemed to swoon and hung on tightly to her friend's arms.

"Where is he?" Olivia glanced around the room.

"He walked past us and smiled at me. I can't see him anymore." Savvy gazed through the crowd hoping to spot him again.

"Well, next time you see him, grab him and give him a big, sloppy kiss on the lips," Olivia yelled and started trekking through the room again with the girls in tow. "Come on; I love this song." They got on the dance floor and three guys jumped in with them.

Bodies were bumping and grooving to the combination of go-go, bass, reggae, and house music the DJ played. When he put on the song, "Da Butt" by E.U. from the movie "*School Daze*," everyone ran to the dance floor and began grinding their butts on each other. The harmony of people singing the lyrics filled the air.

The DJ kept the club jumpin' by spinning album after album on the turntable. By the time the girls got off the floor, their wet hair stuck to their foreheads, and Andrea's afro puff grew bigger from the perspiration and heat. They laughed at their messed-up hairdos and drenched clothes.

"If I look anything like you two, I'm in trouble," Savvy said to Olivia and Andrea. Her big waterfall bangs were now flat on her head. She carefully fixed her hair by fluffing it out with her fingers. "Y'all are soaking wet."

"Well, I guess you're in trouble since you're wet like someone dunked you in a river," Andrea yelled above the music.

"I think all of my makeup melted off." Olivia dabbed her face with a cocktail napkin.

"Well, even with your makeup sweated off, there's a fine guy, and I mean F-I-N-E, on the other side of the room who can't keep his eyes off of you," Savvy informed Olivia and nodded back toward the dance floor.

"Are you kidding me?" Olivia yelled. "I seriously doubt anyone is thinking twice about me while I look like a wet dog."

"Well think again. He's heading this way right now," Andrea squealed.

The DJ changed the pace with the slow song, "I Want To Be Your Man" by Roger. Sweaty bodies locked together at the hip. Olivia peered in the guy's direction and noticed him working his way across the room with his eyes focused on her.

When he approached her, she noticed his beautiful, golden, desert sand colored skin glistening with moisture from dancing. Chiseled was the perfect word to describe him. Olivia focused on the perfect V-shape from his broad shoulders and chest to his narrow waistline, accenting his six-pack that looked more like an eight-pack. He had to be about six-feet-four-inches tall with arm muscles which bragged on their own.

"Hey," he said as he reached for Olivia's hand, "would you mind slow dancing with me?" She stared at his full lips in a hypnotized state.

The three girls stood together with Olivia in the middle, mesmerized by his fineness.

"I don't mind at all," Olivia said. She smiled at her friends with her eyebrows raised in surprise when he led her away from them.

As they danced, Olivia peeked at Savvy and Andrea, whose mouths gaped open in awe. He put on quite a show and began to sway his hips in a sexual healing kind of way. His movements had her imagination in overdrive, thinking about what he could do off the dance floor to a woman. More specifically, to her.

He stared seductively at Olivia with his onyx colored eyes locked on hers as he rocked her body with his to the music. He put his hands on her hips and pulled her closer. They danced, connected in rhythm. Olivia stretched her arms around the back of his head and ran her fingers through his curly, black hair. She inhaled and nuzzled her nose in his neck. The scent of her favorite cologne, Polo, filled her nostrils. She pressed her cheek to his shoulder, closed her eyes, and exhaled.

He pulled back and grazed his lips on her ear. "You sure are beautiful. What's your name?"

Olivia's skin tingled, and goosebumps raised on her arms although heat from dancing bodies filled the room. "Olivia. What's yours?"

"I'm Dwain," he said softly and flicked his tongue back and forth in her ear. "Come on, let's get off this floor and let me holla at you for a minute."

Olivia held onto Dwain's hand, and he led her off the dance floor. "Okay, I'm game."

CHAPTER 4

After several slow songs, the DJ increased the pace and played "Back To Life," which got everyone jammin' on the floor again. A couple of guys asked Andrea and Savvy to dance. They partied for a couple of hours before being ready to go to The Moon. They searched the club and didn't see Olivia anywhere.

"Do you see her on the dance floor?" Andrea yelled to Savvy. With Olivia's height, she would've been easy to spot.

"No, I don't see her. I already checked the bathroom, and she isn't there either." Savvy started to worry.

"Let me go ask the DJ to page her. She'd better be in here." Andrea stomped off to the DJ booth.

"Hey, party people," the DJ called out. "We need Olivia Maxwell to work her way to the front door. Olivia Maxwell. Your friends are looking for you."

Andrea met Savvy at the entrance. They waited for thirty minutes, and Olivia never showed up.

"This is ridiculous," Savvy said. "I can't believe she left and didn't say anything."

"Let's go see if her car is still out front," Andrea said. "I don't think she would leave us behind."

Unfortunately, Andrea underestimated their friend. The parking space where Olivia's green Honda Accord had been was empty.

"No way. I'm gonna kill her," Andrea screamed, running

around the lot looking for Olivia's car. "This heffa left us, and now we have to find another way to get home."

"That's messed up. We can't even go to The Moon now." Savvy shook her head in disgust. "My feet hurt in these 4-inch heels and I can't walk all the way across town without breaking my neck in these shoes."

"I'm pissed off right now," Andrea said.

"Me, too."

"Hey, isn't that Lil' Bud a few rows away?" Andrea pointed to another section of cars in the parking lot.

Standing at six-feet-five-inches tall, Lil' Bud was easy to spot. There was nothing little about Lil' Bud, whose real name was Buxton Davis. He had a muscular body built like a wrestler and his hi-top fade, shaped in an asymmetrical pillar, added another three inches to his height. He sported his African, leather medallion, hand-braided necklace with a black shirt, buttoned to the top, and baggy black pants.

"Yes, it is. Let's see if Lil' Bud can give us a ride." Savvy pulled off her shoes to run through the cars toward him. Despite rocks in the parking lot poking her aching feet, she ran at top speed.

"Lil' Bud," Savvy and Andrea yelled simultaneously.

"Hey Savvy and Andrea. My girls. Whassup?" Lil' Bud seemed surprised seeing them charging toward him.

"Olivia left us hanging. Can you give us a ride home?" Savvy gulped as she tried to catch her breath.

"What? Y'all know I got you. Tell you what, let's stop by The Moon first and hang. We'll go home afterward. I'm too fly to be done partying this early." Lil' Bud put his hand to his chin and struck up a model pose for the girls.

"Bet. That'll work. Wait 'til we find Olivia. I'm gonna hurt that girl." Andrea pounded her hand into her fist.

—

"She left with some dude about an hour ago," Lil' Bud recalled. "He took off in a black Saab, and she followed him in her car."

"I'm done with her. I betta not see her." Savvy put on her shoes and climbed into the front seat of Lil' Bud's Jetta. Andrea jumped in the back seat and slammed the door, still mad.

"Look, let's keep the party going. I got y'all covered," Lil' Bud said. "Besides, I have VIP at The Moon. I can get y'all in for free, and you don't have to stand in line. You're hanging with the Big Dog now."

He put a Public Enemy cassette in the tape player as he drove them to The Moon. They jammed all the way there.

Cars with FAMU or TSUF stickers were parked bumper to bumper in the club's parking lot. Lil' Bud turned into the lot and, Savvy spotted a green Honda Accord parked at the end of an aisle.

"Hey. Lil' Bud. Go through this row. I think I see Olivia's car," Savvy said.

Lil' Bud drove to the car, and Savvy and Andrea opened their doors to jump out. They ran to the Honda where the windows were all steamed up. Sure enough, the back of Olivia's head lay pressed against the glass.

Andrea pounded the window until Olivia lowered it. She raised her left eyebrow in surprise to see her friends.

"Are you serious?" yelled Andrea. "You're not actually sitting out here in the parking lot getting your slob on with that guy from Club Faces."

"I can't believe you left us hangin' like that," Savvy shouted at Olivia.

Olivia flashed her famous smile of pearly white teeth and laughed. The guy from Club Faces sat in the passenger seat with a smirk on his lips.

"Y'all know I wasn't going to leave you hanging. We wanted to get away for a minute, and get to know each other better," Olivia said.

"You couldn't let us know you were leaving?" Savvy asked in disbelief.

"We were being totally spontaneous. I promise you; I planned to go back to get y'all in a few," Olivia said. "I didn't see y'all on the dance floor, and figured y'all weren't ready to leave yet."

Dwain leaned across Olivia from the passenger seat. "Hey ladies, sorry to cause any trouble. I felt completely taken in by this exquisite woman. I had to ask her to follow me to The Moon for a minute." The girls rolled their eyes at his tired explanation.

"Yeah, this is Dwain, and he plays football and basketball for TSUF. His teammates are coming here. I promise you; I planned to head back to get y'all and bring you here to meet them," Olivia said apologetically.

"Whateva. You're too much." Andrea pointed her finger at Olivia. "We were scared something happened to you."

"Well, you can see, I'm fine. Actually, I'm super fine now that I met Dwain," she giggled.

Dwain laughed and turned her chin to kiss her. They started passionately kissing like Savvy and Andrea weren't standing there.

"You know what, forget you, Olivia," Andrea said. "We're going inside with Lil' Bud."

"Don't worry about us riding home with you. We'll catch a ride with Lil' Bud since you're obviously occupied." Savvy shook her head in disgust and walked away.

"Don't be like that y'all. I'll be in soon, and you can meet his teammates." Olivia raised her window and turned her attention back to Dwain.

"Unbelievable." Andrea stomped off toward Lil' Bud's car. She and Savvy opened the doors to get in.

"I can't believe she took off with a complete stranger and left us," Savvy seethed.

Lil' Bud drove them to the front of the club. "Ladies, don't worry about Olivia. I know Dwain, and he's cool. He's probably going to be a Heisman Trophy winner one day." Lil' Bud tried to calm the girls down.

"I don't care who he is. I'm mad she would leave us like that," Andrea said.

"Me too," Savvy exclaimed.

"Well, we know where she is now. Let's get inside and have a good time," Lil' Bud said.

"We can't even get in now. Do you see how the line is wrapped around the building?" Andrea huffed.

"Girl, please. I told you, you're rolling with the Big Dog. I'm a VIP, and we're going to valet my ride, and step right into the club," Lil' Bud laughed. "Stick with me, and I'll take you places."

Sure enough, they walked right into The Moon and bypassed the long line. DJ Vince played "I'll House You" by the Jungle Brothers, and everyone filled the dance floor. Savvy, Andrea and Lil' Bud danced their way through the crowd to get to the middle of the room.

Despite Olivia leaving them, she kept her promise and entered the club later. She found Savvy and Andrea on the dance floor and reluctantly, they followed her off to meet Dwain's teammates.

It turned out to be a fun night after all with several big, strong football players hanging with them. They forgave Olivia quickly.

Savvy enjoyed the attention from the guys and figured she'd

keep Olivia around for a while. She smiled at one of the players who focused his eyes on her before asking her to dance.

CHAPTER 5

"Girl, I never get to see you since you hooked up with Dwain. You don't have time to talk to me anymore." Savvy teased Olivia on the phone. "Is it official yet? Are you his girlfriend?"

"Well, you know it's only been ten days since we met," Olivia said, drawing her words out.

"And? And? Come on. Tell me, Olivia," Savvy screamed.

"Yes. It's official," Olivia squealed. "He asked me last night when we were at his place watching movies."

"Oh my gosh. You know you'll be the most hated person in Tallahassee. There'll be a lot of people who are jealous of your relationship. I mean, he's TSUF's Point Guard on the basketball team, who also happens to be the quarterback on the football team," Savvy exclaimed.

"I know. I love it, and I'm lucky to be with him. Can you believe he's choosing me over all of the girls he could be with?" Olivia asked in disbelief.

"How could he not choose you? You're gorgeous, and he's the one who's lucky."

"That's right. He's the lucky one," Olivia agreed.

"So, tell me. What do you like the most about him? Let me live through you right now. I never see you anymore except at work. I know he's been keeping you busy."

Olivia thought about her friend's words. That was a hard

question to answer because there were so many things she liked about Dwain.

"Well, after we met at Club Faces, Dwain began wooing me with flowers, teddy bears, and he even writes love letters," she said. "He actually confessed his love for me."

"No way. He already told you that he loves you? I guess he's a true romantic."

"Not only that, he takes me out to the best restaurants in town, and everyone treats him like a celebrity."

"Wow. Tell me more," Savvy begged.

"Dwain is a real gentleman, and I feel like a queen when he opens the door to his Saab for me. He holds my hand whenever we hang out and doesn't hesitate to kiss me in public."

"Public display of affection. There is a God. You've made it to the Promised Land, girl. He is definitely a great catch," Savvy said.

"None of the guys I've ever dated treated me this good. Now, I know what it means to be in love." Olivia smiled and released a sigh of relief.

"Well, I'm happy for you, and I hope he has a friend to introduce me to," Savvy laughed.

"I'm sure he can hook you up with someone. By the way, he gave me tickets for you and Andrea to go to a football game. We can all cheer him on. These seats are right behind the team's bench on the 50-yard line. Can you believe it?"

"Now, that's what I'm talking about. Hook-up is alive," Savvy cheered.

"Oh shoot. I gotta go. Dwain pulled up. I'll call you later."

"Okay, have fun. Bye."

Dwain and Olivia made plans to go for a drive to Tom Brown Park. The lazy Sunday afternoon presented the perfect day for an intimate picnic.

Olivia ran out the door to meet Dwain in the parking lot. She carried a picnic basket containing two chicken salad sandwiches, chips, freshly washed strawberries, and grapes, homemade brownies, and sparkling cider.

"Hey, baby." Olivia grinned from ear to ear.

"You look nice, baby." Dwain kissed Olivia and opened the passenger door for her to get in.

Olivia wore her favorite short, denim skirt, which accentuated her long, toned legs. Her flat abdomen showed in her crisp, white, sleeveless, button-front halter top tied above her belly button. She'd pulled her hair into a ponytail with sunglasses positioned on top of her head.

"I like what you have on sweetheart," Dwain complimented her, which made her beam with confidence about her appearance.

The warm weather allowed them to lower the windows and let the breeze flow through the car. "It feels good out here." Olivia stuck her arm out to ride the wind like a wave.

"Yeah, baby. It's the perfect day to be at the park." Dwain put in a cassette tape. The smooth, relaxing sound of Najee playing his saxophone filled the air.

Dwain had on knee-length khaki shorts with a white polo shirt hugging on his waistline and muscular chest. The Air Jordan tennis shoes he sported, were brand new without any scuffs on them. They were one of many pairs he owned.

"Babe, look. There's a spot underneath that big oak tree." Olivia pointed out after they'd been driving slowly around in the park. The secluded area had one other couple in it, sitting at a picnic table about 100 yards away.

Dwain parked underneath the tree and kept the music on in the car for their listening pleasure. He removed the picnic basket from the back seat, along with a red and white checkered blanket, which they laid on the plush green grass.

Dwain twisted the top off the sparkling cider and poured it into a couple of red cups. Olivia removed the fruit from the containers to place onto the plates she'd packed.

The shade from the tree created a cool space for them on the grass. Olivia kicked off her sandals and laid back on the blanket. "Aaah," Olivia exclaimed. "This is heavenly. I love it. What a magnificent day."

Dwain sat with his eyes locked on Olivia, then brought her close to him to begin kissing her passionately. They took turns feeding each other fruit in-between sipping on the sparkling cider.

Olivia removed the sandwiches and chips from the basket and placed them on the plates. She couldn't wait for him to taste her made-from-scratch chicken salad.

"Babe, I hope you like this food. It's a labor of love." She took a big bite of her sandwich and gazed at Dwain, who suddenly had a strange expression on his face.

"What's wrong, babe?" Olivia asked. "Is there something wrong with the food? Do I have food on my face?" She grabbed a napkin to wipe her mouth.

"No, no. Babe, the food is fine, and you don't have anything on your face," Dwain replied.

"But you haven't even taken a bite yet. Why were you looking at me like that?" Olivia asked.

"Like what?"

"Like something's wrong."

"Liv, I guess I need to let you know, something has been bothering me since we started dating." Dwain sighed.

"What is it?" Olivia bunched her eyebrows together in worry and laid her sandwich on her plate. She was bracing for the worst.

"Well, don't take this the wrong way. You know, by dating me, image is everything. I mean, everyone watches us all the time. People are looking at what we wear, how we look, what we say. You know?"

"I understand which is why I bought a new wardrobe," Olivia laughed. "I've used all of the extra money from my job."

"Yeah, I know, and your clothes are great." Dwain sighed again. "What I'm concerned about is, you could stand to lose a few pounds. I see you have some fat in your stomach area and your legs could use some toning up." He reached toward her and tapped her belly where it showed.

"Excuse me?" Olivia responded in shock and slapped his hand away. "Dwain, you know I weigh only 135 pounds, and I'm five-ten. I run every day, and I'm in excellent condition. Most black men want a woman with some meat on her bones."

"Baby, you're taking this all the wrong way." Dwain reached out to trace her face with his fingertips. "You have a pretty face for a dark-skinned girl. You'd just be better if you dropped about ten pounds."

"Ten pounds?" Olivia exclaimed. "Do you see how skinny I am? You want me to lose ten pounds? You're kidding me, right?"

"Ten or fifteen. I think you'd be even better than you are now. Trust me, I have your best interest in mind, and I want you looking your greatest." He had the nerve to smile like he had given her some news to help her live her best life.

"How do you expect me to do that? I eat healthy, and I've always been in shape. I ran track in high school, Dwain." Stunned at his request, she chewed her lip to keep it from quivering. *I'm not going to cry. He can't possibly be serious right now. He sounds like my mother back when she used to say I was fat, black, and ugly.*

45

"Well, you probably shouldn't have put chips and brownies in the picnic basket. You could've left the bread off the chicken salad sandwiches. I mean, did you even use low-fat mayonnaise?" Dwain evaluated the food. "Look, I didn't mean to upset you. Forget I mentioned it." Dwain took a bite of his sandwich.

"How can I forget that you mentioned this?" Tears pooled in her eyes.

"Baby, forget I said anything and enjoy your sandwich," Dwain said.

"I thought you loved me the way I am," she cried.

"Hey, hey, hey. Don't cry, Olivia. You're messing up your makeup." Dwain put his sandwich on the plate and hugged her. "I'm a fool to hurt you by suggesting you need to lose weight."

"I want you to be happy with me." Olivia sniffled and used a napkin to blow her nose.

"I'm happy with you. Forget it. Okay? I love you," Dwain lifted her chin to gaze at her in the eyes. "Stay exactly the way you are."

Olivia's bruised heart made it hard for her to stop crying. She hiccupped to try to keep the tears from flowing. Dwain reached over with a napkin and wiped her face.

Of course, she lost her appetite, and even if she hadn't, she wouldn't be able to eat due to the knots of despair in her stomach.

Dwain continued to eat. "Baby, this has to be one of the best chicken salad sandwiches I've ever eaten. It's good."

Though his words tore at her heart, she resolved at that very moment to find a way to drop the fifteen pounds to make him happy and look perfect the way he wanted her to be. *There's no way I'll allow myself to lose my man due to being overweight. He's telling me this because he truly loves me and wants us to be together forever. I know exactly what I need to do to get skinnier for him. It worked in high school and it can work now.*

CHAPTER 6

School and work were hectic, which prevented Savvy and Olivia from seeing each other outside of their job in weeks. They decided to hang at the mall to shop and chat about what they had going on in their lives.

Olivia drove to Savvy's place to pick her up. The moment Savvy got into the car, she noticed Olivia appeared to be losing weight. Her skin sagged, and her collarbone protruded sharply. She looked sickly.

"You know, before we do any shopping, I've got to get something to eat. I'm starving." Savvy said once they walked into the mall.

"Me too," exclaimed Olivia. "Let's go to the Soul Food restaurant here. It's better than eating in the food court. They have delicious, down-home cooking."

"Sounds good to me," Savvy responded. They made their way through the mall to the restaurant and requested a table.

Once seated, they read the menus to figure out what to order. A waitress in a blue and white checkered apron stopped by the table with a basket of steaming hot cornbread. The delicious aroma filled their nostrils when she placed it in front of them.

"Hi girls. Here's a fresh basket of our famous cornbread with butter. Are you ready to place your order?"

"Yes, we're ready and hungry. Let me get the baked chicken plate with collard greens and rice. I'll stick with water and lemon to drink. That'll do it for me," Savvy said and folded the menu.

"Sure. And for you?" The waitress directed her attention to Olivia.

"I want the 2-meat plate with fried catfish and fried chicken. For my sides, I'll have mac n' cheese, candied yams, and potato salad. Also, I'll have an order of hush puppies and onion rings for an appetizer. Bring those out right away. Oh, and can you bring out some more cornbread? I would like a big, red Kool-Aid and a piece of peach cobbler with vanilla ice cream. You can bring the dessert out along with the rest of my food." Olivia nonchalantly handed the menu to the waitress before she grabbed a piece of bread and slathered it with the butter.

Savvy's mouth popped open in surprise. "Girl. You weren't kidding when you said you were hungry."

"Oh, it's nothing. I've always been a big eater, and I haven't eaten anything for breakfast. I'm ready for a serious meal. Plus, their food is scrumptious here." Olivia took several bites of the bread, devouring it before grabbing another piece.

"Wow. I don't know where you put it. I wish I could eat like you do and not gain a pound. I don't see how you do it." Savvy began munching on a piece of bread.

It wasn't long before the server returned with their food and placed everything on the table before walking away to another customer.

"Excuse me." Olivia frantically waved her hand in the air to call her back.

"How can I help you?" the waitress asked as she headed back over to their table.

"These hushpuppies are nasty. Do you see this?" Olivia poked at the food with her fork. "They're fried too hard."

"Oh. I'm sorry. Let me get those from you. I'll ask the chef to prepare another order. Is everything else okay?"

"No, it's not," Olivia spat. "This chicken is not seasoned right, and my potato salad is bland. I can't believe you guys got my whole meal wrong."

"Here, let me take the food to the chef and we'll handle it. Again, I'm sorry." The server removed the plate from the table. Her cheeks flushed from the embarrassment of Olivia yelling at her.

Olivia's rudeness shocked Savvy. Olivia was generally the nice one of their group.

"Can you believe that? I mean, what kind of place does this to your food?" Olivia snatched another piece of bread and began to chew furiously.

"Well, hey, don't worry. They're bringing out your food soon, and I'm sure they'll have the problem fixed. It'll be fine, Olivia," Savvy said.

"I'm sorry I snapped like that. I guess I'm loopy from starvation. They're probably spitting in my food in the kitchen right now since I sent it back."

"Yuck. I doubt it. I'm sure they want to get it right."

"Well, they better."

Thankfully, the food arrived quickly, which satisfied Olivia. The girls ate in a feeding frenzy until their plates were almost licked clean. Despite the fact Savvy had less food, Olivia devoured hers, including the dessert, almost before Savvy finished.

Baffled, Savvy looked over Olivia closely. How in the world did her stomach even hold all the food Olivia had just eaten?

Olivia wiped her mouth on her napkin and jumped from the chair. "Sit tight. I've got to go to the bathroom. I think I drank too much Kool-Aid and it's running right through me." Before

Savvy could respond, Olivia ran toward the restroom.

Savvy shook her head, wondering what might be happening with Olivia. She didn't seem her usual self.

Olivia returned and frantically grabbed her glass of water from the table and guzzled it down. Her dark skin appeared flushed and sweaty.

"Are you okay?" Savvy asked with concern in her eyes.

"Yeah, girl," Olivia reassured her. "I had to go to the bathroom bad. I'm good now."

"Okay, if you say so." Savvy kept her eyes on her friend as Olivia plopped back into her chair.

"So, tell me what do you and Dwain have going on this weekend?" Savvy asked.

Olivia's face lit up. "Tonight, we're going to a banquet for the athletes. I hope my dress fits me right."

"Well, that should be fun." Savvy clapped her hands together in excitement. "Wait a minute. Why are you concerned about your dress fitting?"

"Oh, it's nothing. I haven't worn this one recently and want it to be perfect on me," Olivia said. "Let's get the check. It's time to go shopping." Olivia raised her hand and motioned for the waitress to come to the table.

The server brought the check and apologized again about the food. After the girls paid their bill, they headed out of the restaurant. They decided to shop for swimsuits for the "Black Beach Party," a popular event in Daytona Beach every year.

They walked through the mall and found a store with swimsuits on sale for five dollars. Savvy's stomach protruded slightly from eating too much. She worried if it would stick out in everything she tried on. Olivia didn't seem full at all despite the fact she ate a lot more.

"Girl, check out this bikini. This is hot." Olivia pulled a ruffled, yellow bikini off the rack.

"That'll be great on you, Olivia. What do you think of this blue one with the flowers? I can't believe these are only five dollars." Savvy stood in front of a mirror holding the swimsuit to her body.

"Come on, grab some and let's go try them on." Olivia picked out several and Savvy did the same before heading to the fitting room. The girls acted like they were on a runway each time they exited their rooms wearing the different swimsuits. They struck model poses in the mirror and laughed at their silliness.

Olivia's skinny appearance got Savvy's attention when she tried on a turquoise bikini. She could see Olivia's ribs and bony shoulders.

"That's a great color on you," Savvy exclaimed.

"I like the color although it makes my stomach poke out," Olivia said. She turned to the side, looking at her profile in the mirror as she pinched the side of her stomach.

Savvy's mouth dropped open. "Are you serious? You don't have an ounce of fat on you at all. How much weight have you lost?"

"Just a few pounds. Nothing significant." Olivia continued examining herself in the mirror.

"Naw, I think you've lost a lot more. I can see your rib bones. Don't you see that?" Savvy asked, pointing to Olivia's side.

"I've always been skinny. You haven't seen me in a swimsuit before. It's no big deal," Olivia explained. "Now go put on the red swimsuit. We can see if it'll be a hot number for the beach."

Savvy paused in disbelief about Olivia's denial regarding her weight loss. Shaking her head, she walked back into her fitting room to put on the red one-piece swimsuit. When she opened the door to exit, Olivia stepped in front of her and had her clothes on.

"Are you done trying on swimsuits already?" Savvy asked.

"Yeah, I'm done. Let me in. I want to show you something," Olivia said.

Savvy opened the door wider to let Olivia into her fitting room. She walked in, closing the door behind her. She had a wild expression on her face which caught Savvy off guard.

"Why are you looking crazy right now?" Savvy studied Olivia.

Olivia slowly lifted the bottom of the blue top she wore. Underneath, she had on the turquoise swimsuit.

"Um, why do you have your clothes on top of the swimsuit?" Savvy asked.

"Shut up, Savvy," Olivia whispered and put her hand on Savvy's mouth. "Someone might hear you."

Confused, Savvy pulled Olivia's hand away from her mouth and whispered loudly, "What do you think you're doing?"

"I'm going to see if I can steal this swimsuit," Olivia answered.

"What do you mean? They're five dollars!"

"I don't care," Olivia said.

"You've lost your mind," Savvy said, her voice rising.

Olivia put her hand to her mouth again. "Don't worry; we won't get caught. There aren't any security cameras back here. I already checked it out."

Savvy pushed Olivia's hand away. "We? I don't have anything to do with this." Savvy spun around to grab her purse. She pulled out her wallet and counted six one-dollar bills. "Look, I have enough to buy it for you. So, quit trippin', go take it off, let's pay for these swimsuits, and leave."

"No. I want to see if I can get away with it," Olivia said with a weird expression on her face, which frightened Savvy.

"You know what? Get out of my dressing room. Now," Savvy yelled. "I don't want anything to do with you. Get out."

The store attendant knocked on the door. "Are you girls okay in there? I thought I heard you calling for me. Do you need for me to bring you a different size?"

Savvy started to say something, and Olivia quickly covered her mouth with her hand again. "No, we're fine. My friend feels embarrassed about showing me the swimsuit she tried on. I had to make her let me see. You probably heard us laughing about it," Olivia explained.

"Okay, let me know if you need anything," the attendant said and walked away from the door.

Savvy glared at Olivia and slapped her hand away. "If you ever put your nasty hand on my mouth again, I swear I'll bite you."

"You need to relax and not worry about this," Olivia said, pointing to the swimsuit underneath her blouse.

"I have nothing to do with what you're thinking about doing, and I'm not going to be seen with you." Savvy quickly took off the red swimsuit to put her clothes on.

"Don't worry, you can leave first, and I'll come out later." Olivia opened the door and exited the fitting room.

Savvy couldn't believe what Olivia was about to do. Her heart began to race, and her palms became sweaty. She didn't want to go to jail for a stupid five-dollar swimsuit. Shoot, she didn't want to die for a five-dollar swimsuit because her parents surely would kill her.

Savvy put her shoes on, opened the door to her fitting room, and scurried out with the red swimsuit in her hand. Olivia sorted through clothes on the racks in the back of the store.

Savvy marched to her and whispered, "You took that thing off, right?"

Olivia shook her head and didn't even turn toward her. She kept browsing through the clothes.

"I told you, I have enough money to buy it for you. It's my gift to you." Savvy grabbed Olivia's arm to get in her face to glare at her.

"Girl, I'm good. Okay?" Olivia whispered back with the strange wildness in her face again. "You go ahead, and I'll catch you in a minute after I finish shopping."

Savvy huffed in disgust and turned away from Olivia. Her heart still pounded rapidly from anger. Fear of what might happen replaced the desire to purchase her swimsuit. She put it back on the rack.

Looking anxiously around, Savvy noticed it had become crowded with a lot of shoppers. The attendant assisted a mother and daughter on the other side of the store.

Savvy bumped into clothing racks and nervously worked her way into the mall. She maneuvered blindly past several stores and accidentally ran into a woman with a baby carriage.

"Hey. Watch where you're going," the woman yelled and checked on her baby.

"Oops, I'm sorry," she apologized.

Finally, she spotted the red letters on an exit sign. She stumbled out the door onto the sidewalk. The sunlight met her eyes and made her squint.

Her stomach hurt with pain from the knots of anger. She sat on a bench to catch her breath.

Just a few minutes later, Olivia snuck up behind her. "Hey, Savvy."

Savvy jumped from her seat. "Hey, nothing," she yelled and glared at her. "Get away from me."

"Why are you worked up?" Olivia shrugged. "I finished browsing around in the store and said goodbye to the sales attendant. I made my way out here without the security alarm going off. See. Nothing happened."

"But it could have," Savvy exclaimed in dismay. "I can't believe you even tried to involve me in your escapade."

Olivia laughed, causing Savvy to glare at her in disgust.

"You are a common thief, and I don't want anything to do with you anymore." Savvy walked cautiously backward, away from the bench. "I'm not getting in the car with you to go home. I'll ride the bus."

"Savvy, you need to be calm and lower your voice," Olivia said slowly. "As you can see, no one is coming after us. They won't even miss it."

Savvy's anger made her eyes well with tears. "Why did you have to steal it? You have a job, and you have money. I even told you I would buy it for you."

"I know. I know. I simply wanted to see if I could get away with it," Olivia explained. "It's fun when you see how easy it is to steal a few things."

"This is what you do for fun?" Savvy asked in astonishment. "If so, we have nothing else in common. There's no reason for us to associate with each other ever again.

"Really?" Olivia's eyes widened and her eyebrows raised in surprise. "So, it's like that?"

"Really." Savvy stomped away from Olivia toward the bus stop. She scowled over her shoulder and shouted, "It's like that."

CHAPTER 7

The wheels on Olivia's Honda Accord screeched and left black tread marks on the street. She quickly turned into her parking space at her apartment.

She jumped out of the car and briefly thought of Savvy. "Savvy is straight trippin', and I will have to deal with her later," she mumbled to herself. Right now, she didn't have time to think about her.

Olivia hurried to fumble through her keys to find the right one to open the door to her apartment. Dwain wasn't coming to get her for another three hours, which gave her plenty of time to handle business.

She headed to the kitchen and pulled a big bag of potato chips, a two-pack package of Hostess lemon cupcakes, and a big Snickers candy bar from the pantry. She opened the freezer and removed a pint of strawberry ice cream.

Olivia found one clean spoon in her silverware drawer before sitting at the kitchen table. Frantically, she ripped open the bag of chips and shoved handful after handful into her mouth. The sound of her crunching and the crinkling of the bag were the only noises in the room.

After wiping crumbs from her face with the back of her hand, she grabbed the cupcake package. She fought to pull open the cellophane with her fingers, which were slippery from the greasy chips. In frustration, she pulled at the flap in the middle until it popped.

The sweet smell of lemon wafted to her nostrils causing her to inhale deeply. She pulled one cupcake out and licked the frosting off the top. *Oh, this is so good.* She broke it in half to lick the cream filling from the middle. The moist cake seemed to melt in her mouth. She barely took the time to chew and devoured the second one quickly, after which she burped loudly.

Taking a deep breath, she opened the Snickers bar and her teeth sunk into the chocolate. "Umm," she said with her mouth full and her eyes closed. Caramel and peanuts stuck in her teeth from chewing the candy, bite after bite, until she finished it.

Olivia took the lid off the ice cream and licked a drip from the side of the container where it had started to melt. Digging in deep with her spoon, she ate rapidly. "Ouch. Oww." She cried out and held her head from the brain freeze. After shaking it off, she continued to eat until she hit the bottom of the box.

She stuffed the empty wrappers and chips bag into the ice cream container to throw away. Olivia leaned back in her chair, moaning and rubbing her tight and queasy stomach. She heard it grumble loudly from the quick intake of sugary and greasy food.

A juicy sounding belch slipped loudly from Olivia's mouth. She stood from her chair and ran up the stairs two at a time to the bathroom. She lifted the toilet seat and stuck her finger in her throat. Immediately, she began gagging, which finally led to throwing up everything.

The residue from the food combined with stomach acid filled her mouth when she wretched in the toilet. The taste and smell of throw up repulsed her, causing her to puke more.

Her abdomen began to hurt from repeatedly contracting until she couldn't get anything else to come out. She flushed the commode and closed the lid to keep from seeing the nasty mess. "Ugh. This stuff smells horrible," she muttered. She grabbed the lavender air freshener and sprayed a choking amount to get rid of the stench.

Olivia turned to the sink to rinse with mouthwash and wipe her face with a washcloth. Not satisfied, she pulled out a box of laxatives and popped a single pill out of a foil pack. She threw her head back and swallowed it dry.

Next, she searched in the bathroom drawer to find her enema suppositories. After inserting one carefully and washing her hands, she was ready for a bowel movement in less than two minutes. She completely emptied her belly and ignored the painful cramps in her stomach.

Relief flooded her emotionally once she finished the ritual she started the day after Dwain told her to lose weight.

He seemed pleased with her progress, which encouraged her to stay the course. He often reminded her of the importance of her looks and how awesome she was for trying to be smaller.

To help her achieve her goal of being perfect for Dwain, Olivia increased her running to five miles every weekday morning before class and fifteen miles on Saturdays and Sundays. She ended each day dead tired and weak most of the time. Yet, she began an exercise routine at night after work before going to bed.

The first couple of weeks were a big success. Olivia started with fasting on liquids only and took diet and water pills. Now, with her new plan, she ate whatever she wanted and threw it back up.

Olivia removed her clothes and examined herself in the full-length mirror. "I see exactly what Dwain means. My stomach is flabby. I can't believe my thighs are like cottage cheese," she mumbled. She turned around and peered over her shoulder at her reflection from the back. *Who wants a girlfriend with a butt this big and love handles?* She held her arms out to her side and imagined they shook back and forth.

Overwhelmingly frustrated, she flopped onto her bed. Olivia had to figure out a way to lose even more weight so that Dwain would love her forever. She let out a sigh and popped a diet pill into her mouth.

CHAPTER 8

"She actually stole the swimsuit." Savvy waved her hands in the air and recapped the incident at the mall to her roommate, Nicole. The two of them sat on the sofa in their living room.

Nicole wore baggy pants and a t-shirt with 'Fight the Power' on it along with big silver Ankh earrings. Everything in her closet had something to do with fighting causes in the black community. Nicole, often called "Redbone" since she has Tuscan sun colored skin, has strong facial features with full lips, a wide nose, and a broad forehead. She wore her hair in a short box cut, which fit her sense of style.

"No, she didn't." Nicole listened in shock. "I can't believe she did that. She could've gotten both of you arrested."

"I know. She's a thief. I told her I don't want anything else to do with her," Savvy said and shook her head. "I don't have time for people like her in my life."

"Yeah, she sounds like bad news to me," Nicole said.

"She's cool for the most part. There are some things about her I can't seem to understand though."

"Like what?

"Well, in addition to stealing, she seems to be too concerned about how she looks. She doesn't even have any pictures of herself or her family in her apartment. She used to have them on the walls the first few times I visited. Now, they aren't there for some reason."

"That's strange."

"It is. She's insecure about herself despite the fact she looks like a runway fashion model. At least, she used to. She's always comparing herself to lighter-skinned women and seems to think she needs to lose weight."

"You've got to be kidding me. She's already too skinny. If she loses another pound, she'll become a skeleton."

"Right. When we got together today, she ate like crazy. For some reason, she never seems to gain any weight. Her face looks swollen and bloated to me although her body is tiny. I wonder if she has a disease of some kind or something," Savvy said.

"You know, I would say perhaps she's anorexic. However, you said she's eating a lot of food," Nicole said. "You don't hear about black women having eating disorders, though."

"Right. With the amount of food she eats, there's no way she's anorexic. What do they call the eating disorder where people eat a lot of food and throw it up?" Savvy asked.

"I think it's called bulimia. But, that's more of a white girl's disease, right?"

"Black men like black women to keep our curves, which is why I can't imagine Olivia doing that. Not to mention it's gross to throw up."

"Eww. The thought of anyone making themselves throw up is nasty and makes me sick from thinking about it." Nicole scrunched her nose. "Well, if I could be pretty like Olivia, I would have all the men chasing after me. She is freakin' gorgeous."

"Exactly. I don't know what her issue is. It seems to have gotten worse since she started dating Dwain. It's like she doesn't think he's attracted to her and wants her to be perfect. I don't get it."

"Me neither. If she's trying to be a Barbie Doll to impress a man, she's with the wrong guy. Olivia needs to get away from him fast," Nicole said. "I don't care how fine Dwain is; he's not worth it."

"You know, that's the problem with women sometimes. We try to change the way we are for a man and destroy ourselves instead. We need to love the skin we're in and our bodies. It's time to stop trying to be like models in a magazine to feel beautiful," Savvy said.

"You're right. We gotta love ourselves before looking for others to love us. Men love my double D's and my voluptuous booty. I make sure I switch it when I walk by them on campus. They can't resist trying to reach out and grab it." Nicole stood and sashayed her hips seductively.

"Girl, you're too funny," Savvy laughed.

"Shoot, they don't want no skinny girls," Nicole replied.

"Well, if I ever speak to Olivia again, I'm going to have a conversation with her about this before she makes herself sick from losing too much weight. Right now, I have no intention of having anything to do with her for a while. I need some space right now," Savvy explained.

"I understand," Nicole said.

"Hey. On another subject, doesn't Carl Greer work on the same shift you do?" Savvy asked. Carl invaded her dreams almost every night ever since he passed by her at Club Faces. His lean muscular body brushed against hers while gazing at her with his clear, light green eyes. It never failed, right when his succulent lips were about to kiss her lips, she woke in a sweat and out of breath.

"Yes, he does. Do you still have a crush on him?" Nicole had a smirk on her face.

"Well, yeah, kind of," Savvy said and dropped her eyes to the floor. "I don't think he evens notices me when I see him at

FAMU."

"Girl, please. I'm sure he's been checking you out and thinks you're attractive. You know he's had to have seen you on campus," Nicole said.

"Did he tell you that?" Savvy asked with hope in her voice.

"No, he didn't. You know what? I'll tell him all about you when I go to work tonight." Nicole leapt from the sofa and clapped her hands together.

"You're going to tell him? No. You can't let him know I like him. I would die and sink into the ground if he knew how I felt."

"I won't tell him you like him. I'll tell him you're my amazing, beautiful, smart roommate and let him know I would like to introduce him to you."

"Oh, Nicole. I don't know. I'd probably blubber everywhere if he even said hi to me." Savvy chewed her bottom lip and nervously wrung her hands.

"Girl, get over yourself. You got it going on, and he would be a fool not to be interested in you."

"He's the fastest runner on the track team, and he can have any girl he wants. I seriously don't think he would be interested in me. Please don't say anything," Savvy begged.

"Nope. I'm going to say something tonight," Nicole said. "Don't worry. You sound worse than Olivia. You need to know you're gorgeous and guys like you exactly the way you are."

Savvy realized there was no way she could stop Nicole from saying anything to Carl.

"I'll never speak to you again if you say anything to him," Savvy said. She tried to sound angry, but Nicole wasn't buying it.

"Yeah, whatever. You know you want me to. That's why you asked about him," Nicole teased her.

Savvy murmured, "All right fine. Please don't tell him I like him. I'd feel weird if he knew how crazy I am about him."

"Don't worry. I got you, girl. I'll handle getting you an introduction, and you two can go from there. You can thank me later." Nicole chuckled and grabbed her apron from the coat closet to head out the door to work.

"Yeah, okay," Savvy said, telling herself that maybe she needed to be hanging out with Nicole more instead of Olivia.

CHAPTER 9

Dwain held Olivia's hand and escorted her to the porch. He turned her around to face him, and they gazed into each other's eyes. He began kissing her glossy, red lips. She moaned and wrapped her arms around the back of his neck when he put his tongue in her mouth. They pressed their bodies together and leaned on the door.

"You know you were the finest girl in the room tonight, right?" Dwain kissed her neck and shoulders.

"You think I'm prettier than the rest of those women there?" Olivia blushed and leaned her head back when he nibbled on her ear.

"Yeah, baby. The guys on the team couldn't stop staring at you. Even some of the coaches were checking you out," Dwain said proudly.

"No way. I don't want them eyeballin' me," Olivia exclaimed.

"Baby, you've worked hard to get some of that weight off. You deserve to be admired by everyone," Dwain said, kissing her again.

"You're happy with me tonight?"

"You know it, girl. You're sexy in this silver dress. The entire night, I couldn't wait to touch you." Dwain growled and kissed her slowly along the side of her neck and stroked her behind.

"Dwain. You're crazy." Olivia laughed and hit him playfully on his arm.

"I'm for real. I could barely keep my hands off you. If it weren't for me having practice in the morning, I would've been staying the night."

"You're too much." Olivia looked at Dwain with love in her eyes. "I wanted to make sure you'd be happy with my new look. I've worked hard to lose the weight for you."

"Well, I can tell you've dropped a few pounds. Imagine when you get the rest of the weight off, you'll be the bomb-diggity." Dwain studied her closely.

Olivia's smile dropped from her face. "You still want me to lose more weight, Dwain?" She'd already lost sixteen pounds so she couldn't believe what he was saying to her.

"Just a few more pounds, baby. I noticed some fat in your back when you turned around. You know this type of dress shows stuff like that." Dwain pinched the skin on her back.

Olivia did all she could to choke back the tears. She hoped Dwain couldn't see the water welling in her eyes in the dark of the night. The joy she had a moment ago switched immediately to sadness.

"You know what? After you lose the rest of that weight, we'll go on a shopping spree." Dwain didn't notice the change in Olivia's mood. "You can pick out the sexiest clothes and a bikini to wear. We can ride to Miami where I'll show you off on South Beach."

"Dwain, I don't feel well," Olivia stammered and fumbled in her purse for her keys. "I think I need to go in the house now."

"What's wrong, baby? Maybe something you ate? You probably shouldn't have eaten the bread or cake tonight," Dwain said with what sounded like concern in his voice.

"No, I'm fine. I'm worn out right now." Olivia put her key

in the door with a shaky hand. She tried to keep the tears from falling. "I'll call you tomorrow."

"Do you want me to come in?" Dwain asked and started to move through the door behind her.

"No. I mean, that's okay. I'm fine, and I'll call you tomorrow." Olivia gently pushed against his chest to move him back out the door.

"Okay, baby. I'll let you go to bed. Get some rest. I love you." Dwain kissed her on the forehead before strolling away.

"I love you, too," Olivia whispered and closed the door.

She kicked off her high heel shoes to run upstairs to the bathroom. Olivia dropped to her knees in front of the toilet and hung her head above the bowl. She stuck her finger in her throat, which made her gag several times.

Ferociously, vomit traveled from her stomach, through her esophagus, and into the commode. She emptied her stomach of the food she'd eaten at the banquet. Olivia began dry heaving and winced from the pain in her ribcage.

She flushed the toilet and tore off a handful of tissue to wipe her mouth. Anguish wrecked Olivia's body, leading her to cry uncontrollably. She pulled her knees to her chest and shook from overwhelming sadness.

Completely broken hearted with a crushed spirit, she rolled onto her stomach and stretched out her arms and legs. *I want to die right now. Dwain doesn't love me the way I am. I'm fat and ugly. He's going to break up with me. I can't live without him.* She laid her face on the cold bathroom floor and cried herself into a dreamless sleep.

CHAPTER 10

Savvy relaxed in her beanbag chair in the living room. Her favorite show, "A Different World" played in the background.

She studied notes from her Financial Accounting class, which had to be the toughest course ever. Her busy school day wore her out, and she kept dozing off. She dreamt about the show's main character, Dwayne Wayne, wearing his flip-up glasses and kissing her.

A loud commercial jolted her awake, and she realized she would never finish studying if she didn't get a good catnap. She pushed herself out of the beanbag, turned off the lamp and TV, and lay on the sofa for a thirty-minute study break.

The sound of keys jingling in the lock on the front door startled Savvy awake. The door creaked open, and whispers floated through the air. Savvy recognized Nicole's hoarse whisper saying "Shhh," and started to call out to her. She realized the other voice belonged to a guy. They were trying to talk quietly although they were giggling when they entered the apartment.

Savvy sunk into the sofa. Nicole found someone to cuddle with tonight. She didn't want to ruin their mood, so she remained quiet.

Laughter and more talking followed the sound of Nicole's bedroom door closing. The back of the sofa where Savvy laid, pressed against Nicole's wall. The guy had a deep voice and said he would turn on the boombox. The song, "In Between The Sheets" by the Isley Brothers, started playing and she heard them bumping around. The talking changed to moaning and groaning.

Savvy felt her face flush once she realized they were having sex. The pleasurable sounds, grew more intense with a steady beat of the headboard hitting against the wall. She had to get out of the living room away from this private moment.

Savvy gathered her books in her arms and tiptoed to her bedroom. She gently closed her door and thankfully, the sounds of the sexcapades going on in Nicole's room drowned out.

Savvy chuckled to herself, put on her pajamas, and got into bed. She quickly drifted off to sleep to dream about Carl Greer.

CHAPTER 11

"Oh my, gosh." Olivia groaned upon waking to find she had fallen asleep on the floor. She struggled to push herself up. The position she laid in made her legs stiff. She gripped the bathroom counter to attempt to stand.

Olivia patted around on the wall for the switch to turn on the bathroom light. She stared in the mirror, startled by the raccoon's eyes which glared back at her. Mascara streaked her cheeks, and her eyes were red and swollen. She looked like a monster.

Grabbing a cloth from the towel rack, she turned on the cold water to wash her face. Olivia slowly scrubbed off her makeup and examined her puffy eyes in the mirror. She barely recognized herself.

Olivia pushed back the thoughts in her mind about Dwain. She had to get better control of her life.

She removed her elegant dress, which now had puke on the front and dropped it in the hamper. Her stomach lurched from the smell. The dress was probably ruined, which was fine because if it revealed all of her back fat, she never planned to wear it again. Once she slipped on her leopard print silk pajamas, she got into the cool bed.

Pulling the covers to her chin and looking at the ceiling, she whispered, "Dear Lord, please help me to lose the weight that I need to. I want Dwain to be happy. I know I can do it. Please, don't let me lose him. I love him, and I love You. This I ask in the name of Jesus. Amen."

She closed her eyes and fell into a deep sleep. She dreamed about Dwain sailing away in the ocean on a sailboat without her. She paddled in a canoe trying to catch him, yet the strong currents kept pushing her back to shore.

The sound of the doorbell aroused Olivia from her sleep forty minutes later. She glanced at the clock next to her bed. *Who is ringing my doorbell at two in the morning?* She rubbed her eyes and lay back on the pillow, figuring it had to be a dream.

The doorbell rapidly rang three more times again. Olivia groaned and rolled out of bed to put on her robe. Her bare feet padded across the cold floor and down the carpeted stairs. She tiptoed to the front door and peeked through the peephole.

A short, Hispanic girl, stood on the porch with her arms folded. She had her long, curly brown hair pulled into a ponytail. She wore a TSUF sweatshirt and sweatpants with white sneakers.

The girl rang the doorbell again. She kept looking past her shoulder and back at the door. She tapped her foot impatiently and popped her chewing gum.

"Who are you and what do you want?" Olivia said through the door.

"This is Isabella, and I want to talk to you about Dwain," the girl said calmly.

"About Dwain? At two o'clock in the morning? I don't know anyone named Isabella. What could possibly be important enough to wake me in the middle of the night?"

"I know it's late, but I have to say something to you. It can't wait until tomorrow. I'm sorry to bother you," Isabella replied.

Peering through the peephole again, Olivia figured she would open the door and see what Isabella wanted, especially because it didn't look like the girl was leaving. Olivia didn't want her waking the neighbors. The girl couldn't be more than five feet tall, so Olivia didn't think she seemed threatening.

After tightening the belt of her robe around her waist, Olivia slowly opened the door and strode out onto the porch in her bare feet. The girl kept her arms folded as she glared.

"Now, who did you say you are?" Olivia asked, staring downward at the girl.

"I'm Isabella, and I saw you at the banquet earlier tonight with Dwain," she said.

"Yeah, now that I think about it, I remember seeing you there. You kept staring at us," Olivia recalled. "How did you know where I live?"

"I followed Dwain here when he brought you home." Isabella chewed and snapped her gum.

"Excuse me? You were stalking us?" Olivia asked in disbelief.

"Yes. He's my man, and I love him. Do you hear me? I love him, and he loves me. You need to stay away from him." Isabella yelled at her and balled her fists. Her face turned red, and her eyes bugged out like an insane woman.

"You know what? I don't know you and have no clue what you're talking about. Dwain is my boyfriend, and you need to get off my porch and leave right now," Olivia yelled back at her.

"You skinny black tramp," Isabella screamed. Before Olivia could blink an eye, another girl jumped out of the bushes next to her apartment. Olivia recognized her to be one of the cheerleaders at the TSUF basketball games. She had what appeared to be part of a nunchuck in her hand.

Isabella grabbed Olivia by the hair and yanked her from the porch and across the four steps. She slammed her hard on the concrete. Both girls jumped her, pummeling her in the head and body.

Olivia cried out "Help. Help. Help me." The girls kept beating her with their fists and the nunchuck. Intense pain filled Olivia's body each time the stick landed on her head. Blood poured out in her hair and across her face. She tried to protect herself with her hands from the beating, which seemed never to end. "Help. Help."

"Hey. What do you girls think you're doing? Get off of her. I'm calling the police right now," Olivia's neighbor yelled out the door.

The girls ran into the darkness, leaving Olivia on the ground crying. She clutched her blood covered head in agonizing pain. She heard a car start and the sound of it screeching away.

Her neighbor, Ms. Beverly, ran out of her apartment in a pink bathrobe with white slippers and knelt next to Olivia. Carefully lifting her shoulders from the ground, she cradled her in her arms. "It's going to be okay. I called 9-1-1, and they're on the way. Hang in there, Olivia."

Olivia couldn't speak as the pain in her head grew more intense. The noise of sirens wailing in the distance grew closer. Everything spun around her. She mumbled incoherently before blacking out.

CHAPTER 12

Savvy rushed through the door of the Emergency Room at Tallahassee Memorial Healthcare hospital wearing her white cotton pajamas, furry white slippers, and a FAMU jacket. A red satin nightcap remained perched on her head. She had forgotten to remove it when she ran out of her apartment once she got a phone call about Olivia.

She had to borrow Nicole's car to get to the hospital. Thankfully, Nicole had given her a key, and she didn't have to wake her and her mystery guest at three in the morning.

Bolting past the waiting room, she heard people moaning or crying from various injuries. She ran to the receptionist's desk and had to stop to catch her breath. The receptionist patiently sat with a smile on her face until Savvy could talk.

"I...am here...to see Olivia Maxwell. Am I in the right place?" she asked, trying to catch her breath from the adrenalin rush.

"Yes. You're in the right place. You can relax. May I ask what relationship you are with the patient?" the receptionist asked.

"I'm her best friend. She doesn't have any family here."

"No problem." She tapped her fingers on a keyboard and glanced at a computer screen. "Go through this hallway and make a right turn at the second corner. She is in room 113," she directed.

"Thank you." Savvy followed her directions and found 113. She eased the door open, then entered the room, which was illuminated by lights on the medical equipment surrounding Olivia. A lamp above the bed shone on her.

Seeing Olivia with her head wrapped in white bandages made Savvy gasp. Her friend didn't even look like herself. Her face swelled with bruises and cuts. Several scratches streaked her cheeks and forehead.

Olivia's eyes remained closed, and for a moment, Savvy couldn't tell if she was dead or alive. It wasn't until Savvy saw the slow rise of Olivia's chest that she breathed a sigh of relief.

"She is resting right now. Olivia is going to be fine."

Savvy hadn't even noticed the middle-aged, pleasantly plump woman sitting beside the bed holding Olivia's hand with knobby, arthritic fingers. She gazed at her with tired eyes and smiled.

"Are you Savvy? I am her neighbor, Beverly," the woman said with a slow, southern drawl.

"Yes ma'am, I am." Savvy struggled to fight back the tears. "Are you the one who called me?"

"Yes, when the paramedics arrived for Olivia, I ran into her apartment and found her purse and shoes to bring to the hospital. Your name is in her phone book with 'best friend' written next to it. I figured you were the one to call," Beverly said.

"Thank you for calling me," Savvy said. "What happened?"

"Well, she got beaten by a couple of girls. Someone began to ring her doorbell around two a.m. constantly. Our apartment walls are thin, so it woke me up too. Next, I heard a lot of yelling and Olivia crying out for help. At that point, I turned on my porch light and said I would be calling the police," Beverly said.

"My goodness," Savvy exclaimed. "Who would do this to her? This is crazy."

"Yes, it is," Beverly agreed. "One of the girls kept saying something like, 'Dwain is her man and for Olivia to stay away from him.' Is Dwain Olivia's boyfriend?"

"Yes, he is," Savvy confirmed. "Have you called him yet?"

"No. I wasn't sure and thought I would call you. You can handle it from here and contact her friends," Beverly said.

"What have the doctors said about her injuries?" Savvy asked.

"Well, they said she took quite a beating to the head. They wouldn't tell me much since I am not a family member. Hopefully, she doesn't have a concussion. There were some deep cuts on the back of her head, and you can see all the scratches and bruises on her face. They said she'd recover although she will have some pain."

"They beat her up bad for sure," Savvy replied. "I'm going to give Dwain a call and tell him to get here right away."

"Okay. I am going to go home now. I need to get ready for work in a few hours." Beverly stood up, stretched and grabbed her purse from the nightstand. She squeezed past the bed and walked stiffly toward Savvy.

"No problem. Thank you again for being here with her and for calling me. No telling how things would've turned out if you hadn't intervened." Savvy hugged her.

"I thank God for waking me up. I wasn't sleeping well anyway from my arthritis. I heard everything," Beverly said and embraced Savvy tightly. She took out a pen and paper from her purse to write her contact information. She handed the paper to Savvy. "Here is my number to call me later with an update."

"I will keep you updated."

After she left, Savvy sat in the chair next to the bed. She

gazed at Olivia again and mulled over who could've done this to her.

Olivia's purse sat on the nightstand. Savvy grabbed it and reached in to get Olivia's phone book to search for Dwain's number.

Savvy rummaged through the purse and discovered a prescription bottle of pills. She pulled the bottle out and rolled it in her hand to see the label. "Hy-dro-chloro-thia-zide," she sounded out the name of the drug. *Hmmmm. What in the world are these pills for?* She dropped the bottle back into the bag. She would ask her about it later.

Savvy found the tiny address book she knew Olivia always kept with her and thumbed through to find Dwain's number. She picked up the phone handset on the nightstand and pushed the buttons to call him.

The phone rang several times, and Dwain finally answered.

"Hello?" Dwain sounded like he'd been in a seriously deep sleep.

"Dwain, this is Savvy. Sorry to wake you so early in the morning," she said.

"No problem Savvy. Whassup?" Dwain yawned.

"It's Olivia. She's in the hospital. She got beat up a few hours ago."

"What? In the hospital? Beat up?" Dwain sounded fully awake. "Who did this to her?"

"I don't know what happened other than what her neighbor told me. She called, and I got here a moment ago," Savvy said. "Olivia is still sleeping. Evidently, a couple of girls jumped her in front of her apartment."

"Which hospital?"

"Tallahassee Memorial Healthcare in the Emergency area," Savvy said.

"I'm throwing on my clothes now. If she wakes up, tell her I'm on my way."

Savvy put down the phone and studied her dear friend. *I can't believe someone would do this to you. Although I'm furious about the swimsuit incident at the mall, I would never wish anything like this on you.* "I'm here for you, Olivia. No matter what," she whispered. She put her hands on her shoulder and started to pray.

CHAPTER 13

The sound of hushed whispers floated through the air and mingled with a beeping noise. Olivia couldn't make out the voices talking around her. A sharp pain shot through the back of her head, which caused her to let out a loud moan.

"Olivia. Olivia. Are you awake?" That was Savvy's voice.

"Baby, it's me, Dwain. Wake up, baby. Savvy and I are here."

The sound of Dwain's voice made Olivia struggle to open her swollen eyes. When she finally managed to peek out slightly, the bright light forced her to close them quickly. She tried again and slowly began to see the worried faces of Savvy and Dwain. She heard herself answer groggily, "Yes. I'm awake. Where am I?"

"Olivia, you're in the hospital," Savvy answered. "You took quite a beating last night."

"Baby, don't worry about anything right now. Rest and don't try to move too much." Dwain rubbed her arm.

Olivia winced when Dwain's hand touched a bruise. She pulled her arm away. "Ouch. My arm hurts right there."

"Oh. I'm sorry, baby. I didn't mean to hurt you." Dwain drew his hand back.

"My head is killing me." Olivia grimaced from the pain and reached her hand to her head. She noticed all the gauze. "Why am I wrapped like a mummy. Am I dying?"

"No, no, Olivia. You're not dying," Savvy reassured her. "You took some hard hits to the head. The doctor who checked on you wouldn't tell us much. Thankfully, you don't have any broken bones. He said they're going to do a CT scan of your brain to make sure there isn't any bleeding going on."

"Do you know who did this to you?" Dwain asked as he angrily pounded his fist into his hand.

"I don't know. My brain seems foggy right now," Olivia began slowly rubbing her forehead.

"Don't' worry about it right now," Savvy suggested.

"Wait. I vaguely remember something. A Hispanic girl. Yeah. She was at the banquet. She kept staring at me throughout the whole dinner."

"Okay. Don't strain yourself but what else can you remember?" Savvy questioned.

"In the middle of the night, I heard my doorbell ringing. I got out of bed to see who it was. This girl said she needed to talk to me about something. When I checked her out, I didn't feel threatened since I'm much taller."

Olivia's eyes darted back and forth to gather her thoughts. "I stepped out on the porch to find out what she wanted. Before I knew it, another girl jumped out of the bushes, and they started beating on me."

"Oh, Olivia. That's awful," Savvy exclaimed.

Olivia's eyes began to water. "I recognized the other girl from the TSUF cheerleader squad. I remember seeing her at a game before. She stood out to me since she's the only black cheerleader."

Savvy noticed Dwain's face change from concern to surprise. He leaned back from the bed and dropped his eyes to the floor. The muscles in his jaw began to tense up, and he started bouncing his leg nervously.

Olivia groaned and touched her head again. She continued, "She said her name is Isabella and something crazy about being in love with Dwain." Olivia paused and gazed at him. "She said she loved you and you love her. What's she talking about Dwain?"

"Baby, don't worry about that right now. I don't know anyone named Isabella. She's probably a football groupie or something. You know, a lot of girls become obsessed with me. You need to rest. I don't want you making yourself feel worse worrying about this craziness." Dwain's left eye began twitching.

"I need to find out who they are. They stalked me," Olivia exclaimed. "They beat me in the head with a stick and were trying to kill me. What if they come back for me?" Olivia asked, frantically looking back and forth at Dwain and Savvy with her eyes wide in fear.

"Calm down, baby," Dwain said. "We'll focus on that later. Hold up; I need to call my coach to let him know I'll be late for practice. I'll be right back." Dwain exited the room.

Savvy raised her eyebrows and seemed surprised.

"You know, Olivia, I think what you need to do right now is rest. Breathe in and out deeply." Savvy demonstrated and encouraged her to do the same. She imitated her and began to relax. "Much better. You're going to be fine. When you recover, we're going to call the cops and file a police report against these tricks," Savvy stated firmly.

"Ok, thank you, Savvy. I don't know why they would do this to me." The weight of recalling everything had exhausted Olivia, and she sank into the pillow and drifted back to sleep.

Savvy sighed and pulled Olivia's covers to her neck. She eased out of the room and went into the hallway. Dwain was on a pay phone, his back toward her. She headed in his direction hoping they could discuss what happened to Olivia. Dwain's angry voice caught her attention when she got closer.

"Isabella. I told you not to do anything stupid," Dwain hissed. "If you waited like I told you to, you wouldn't be in this trouble right now."

Savvy couldn't believe her ears.

"Look. I love you, too. You've got to stop trippin' on Olivia. She and I've been out only a few times," Dwain pleaded on the phone. He listened to the response and huffed in frustration.

"I know, I know, we were together at the banquet since you told me you had to work. I told you I had to bring someone with me," Dwain said. "She doesn't mean anything to me. I love you, baby."

Savvy had enough. She quickly marched in front of Dwain and stared at him with her arms folded until he noticed her. He almost dropped the phone when he realized she heard his conversation. He started to stutter and told the girl he would call her back.

"Savvy, I didn't see you standing there," Dwain tried to explain as Isabella's angry voice bellowed through the handset.

"Obviously. You didn't think I heard your conversation with your so-called coach? Is that what you're trying to say?"

"Yeah, uh, yeah. That's right. I had to call my coach to let him know I would be late."

"Stop right there, Dwain," Savvy snapped and stuck her index finger in front of his face. "Don't you stand there and lie to me. I heard everything you said to Isabella and what you said about Olivia. Not only that, I know you don't have football practice on a Sunday."

"It's not what you think it is," Dwain said.

"What do you think I think it is?" Savvy rolled her neck like her head was on a swivel. "Look, it doesn't' matter what I think. What matters is what Olivia will think when I tell her what I heard you say on the phone. That's what you need to be worried about."

Dwain grabbed Savvy's arm and tried to plead with her. "Savvy, please don't say anything to Olivia. Isabella doesn't mean a thing to me. She's obsessed with me and is jealous of any woman I'm around. Olivia doesn't need to be worried about this stuff. You know how much I love her."

Savvy yanked her arm from Dwain. "Don't you dare put your hand on me and lie to me again. I heard everything. Do you hear me? Everything. Olivia loves you and will do anything to please you. This is what you do to her? She's in the hospital right now because of your cheating on her."

"Savvy, please listen to me," Dwain begged.

Savvy backed away from Dwain and pointed her finger as if placing a curse on him. She squinted her eyes viciously, which made Dwain stop in his tracks and notice she wasn't playing.

She stomped into Olivia's room with her heart pounding in her ears. *What am I going to tell her? How will she deal with finding out her man has been lying and is a cheater? This is too much for anyone to handle.*

CHAPTER 14

Savvy peered at Olivia. She seemed to be resting well. Once the doctor discharged her from the hospital, she would have to find a way to tell her about Dwain.

A nurse wearing blue scrubs and Big Bird clogs entered the room to check Olivia's vitals. She had tired eyes and a friendly smile. "Your friend is going to be fine. I know she appreciates you being here."

"Did anyone contact her parents? I can get their number to give them a call."

"Olivia has requested for us not to reach out to them. She was adamant she did not want them informed about this situation," the nurse said.

"Oh. Okay." Savvy wondered why Olivia didn't want her parents to know she was in the hospital. "Do you have any idea about when she'll be released to go home?" Savvy asked, frowning when she noticed Dwain entering the room.

"When the doctor makes his rounds, he will determine when she can go home. We won't know anything for a while," the nurse responded. "Why don't you go and get some sleep. She needs rest to help her recover."

Dwain spoke up, "Yeah Savvy, why don't you go ahead and leave and I'll stay with her for now."

He really needs to shut up right about now before I hurt him. Savvy narrowed her eyes at Dwain and decided to restrain herself from saying something to him.

"I guess I'll run home for a minute and come back to check on her later," Savvy said to the nurse.

"Don't worry. She's in good hands. My name is Annette, and I will be here until seven. The nurse on the next shift will help you when you return," she replied and walked out of the room.

Savvy gazed at Olivia and shook her head. She took her bruised hand and gently patted it. She whispered, "I'll be back later on today, Olivia. Don't worry about a thing. I'll get you out of here once the doctor says it's okay. I love you, my friend."

She grabbed her purse and headed toward the door where Dwain stood.

"I'll keep watch on Olivia and let her know you'll be back later," Dwain mumbled without making eye contact with her.

"Yeah, sure." Savvy glared at him and brushed by to leave the room. She didn't have much to say to Dwain right now. *His dealings in the dark would soon come to light. Very soon.*

Savvy walked out of the hospital to Nicole's car. She gritted her teeth thinking about scandalous Dwain and what happened to Olivia. Somehow, she would have to help her work through all this craziness.

Savvy got in the car and glanced at herself in the rearview mirror. She laughed loudly when she realized the hair bonnet remained on her head.

When Savvy pulled into her apartment parking lot, she noticed a car with a FAMU sticker on the bumper parked in front. Since she hurried to get to the hospital, she hadn't paid any attention to it when she left. *Oh. This must belong to Nicole's mystery guest. Who's she kicking it with from FAMU?*

Savvy quietly let herself into the apartment and tiptoed into her bedroom. She took her coat off from over her pajamas and hung it in the closet. She climbed into bed and snuggled into the covers, which were warm from her electric blanket.

"Ahh. This feels so good." She sighed and closed her eyes while taking several deep breaths until she drifted to sleep. The creaking sound of Nicole's bedroom door opening woke her. She heard Nicole and her guest whispering when they passed her room.

The front door opened and closed quietly. *I have got to see who this guy is.* Savvy rolled out of the bed and tiptoed to her window which faced the front of their apartment. She spread the blinds apart with her fingers to peek outside. The two of them stood in front of the door kissing like newlyweds.

Savvy couldn't see his face since his back faced her. "Dayum. He is fine," Savvy mumbled. His jeans fit his booty perfectly, and his muscles rippled through his FAMU sweatshirt.

Nicole stood on her tiptoes to wrap her arms around his neck. Savvy squinted to see his face and still, could only see the back of his head. The bright moonlight cast shadows on the two of them, which made it where she could only see the outline of their bodies.

Nicole and the mystery man reluctantly broke away from their embrace. He jogged downstairs to the parking lot. When he walked toward the car with the FAMU bumper sticker, the street light illuminated his face.

Savvy choked when she recognized his angular jaw. She blinked her eyes several times before checking again to make sure she didn't imagine what she thought she saw. She put her hand to her mouth in disbelief and her stomach hurt from disappointment when she recognized Nicole's lover.

Carl. It's Carl. Carl Greer.

CHAPTER 15

Savvy plopped down onto her bed, hurt from what she witnessed. She couldn't believe her roommate betrayed her. *How could Nicole do this to me? We've been such good friends so why would she lie to me? She's never expressed any interest in Carl.*

Savvy replayed in her mind seeing Carl and Nicole kissing on the front porch. She closed her eyes tightly to get the scene out of her head.

Nicole played with her heart by offering to fix her up with Carl. *What kind of friend, let alone a roommate, does this to someone? This is crazy.*

Savvy heard Nicole come back into the apartment and the sound of running water in the kitchen sink. *Now, how am I supposed to handle this situation? Of course, Carl isn't my boyfriend, however, Nicole knows how much I like him. This is just a game to her. Nicole is basically laughing in my face each time I fantasize about Carl. Unbelievable. There's no way I can continue to live here because I can't trust this trick with anything now.*

Savvy decided that she needed to confront Nicole. No way would she be able to walk around faking. She jumped off the bed, opened her door, and walked slowly to the kitchen. Nicole stood barefoot in her fluffy yellow bathrobe. She was washing dishes in a sink full of soap bubbles and humming to herself.

Nicole smiled at Savvy when she sensed her presence.

"Good morning, Sunshine. I wasn't expecting you to be

awake this early."

I can't believe she's acting fake with me like nothing happened last night.

Nicole continued smiling at her. "Well, since you're awake, how about I make breakfast for you? I'm clearing the sink to find a skillet to use. I think I'll scramble eggs with bacon and make pancakes. Sound good?"

"No, I'm not hungry right now," Savvy said through clenched teeth.

Nicole's smile faded, and she crinkled her eyebrows in concern. "Are you okay? You never turn away my great cooking. You got cramps?"

"I'm fine, just tired. I had a lot of studying to do last night," Savvy replied. "By the way, I fell asleep studying in the living room. I awakened when I heard you come in."

"Oh. I'm sorry I disturbed you. I thought you were in your room. If I had known you were studying in there, I would've stopped in to wake you to go to bed," Nicole laughed.

"Yeah, right. Did you have company last night?"

"Company?" Nicole asked.

"Yes, I heard you talking to someone when you arrived."

"Oh, yeah. Right. I needed help with my Statistics class, and I asked Gary from work if he could tutor me. I know it sounds crazy to study after being on the late shift. It's the only time Gary could be available. He's extremely smart and helped me out a lot."

Liar. "You were getting tutored by Gary last night in your bedroom? Nicole, why are you making that up?" Savvy folded her arms and tried to keep her cool.

"Yes, I figured we could work at the desk in my bedroom. I didn't want to disturb you. Why are you questioning me like I'm on a witness stand?" Nicole focused on washing the dishes.

"Well, perhaps you have your classes mixed up. I think you must have been studying Anatomy instead of Statistics." Savvy glared at the side of her face.

"Girl. You're trippin'. Why would you say such a thing?" Nicole stopped washing the dishes, put a soapy hand on her hip and gave Savvy an exasperated look.

"I heard you in your bedroom. You weren't in there studying. I heard you having sex. I guess you don't realize how thin the walls are in this apartment. So, were you and Gary having sex?" Savvy asked. Gary had big warts on his hands and face and was not an attractive guy in any way, shape, or form.

"Well, okay, Savvy, aren't you the Private Investigator? You figured it all out," Nicole said and clapped her soapy hands together, causing a poof of bubbles to float into the air. "Yes. I had sex with Gary. This is embarrassing. I had no idea you could hear us. I felt sorry for him. He's such a sweet guy. He has a hard time getting anyone to go out with him. You know, with warts and all."

Liar. "You mean to tell me; you had sympathy sex with Gary?"

"Yes. Sympathy sex. That's what happened. I know, it's crazy. I admit I did it." Nicole proceeded to wash the dishes.

"Interesting story." Savvy scowled at Nicole. "Considering I saw Carl Greer leaving out this morning and you kissing him on the front porch. I'm trying to figure out if Gary is still in your bedroom or did he leave before Carl?"

Nicole stuttered, "Carl? Wuh? Wha? What do you mean?"

Savvy wasn't about to play this game. "Look, Nicole, I thought I could trust you since we're friends. Now, I see you're not the person I thought you were. You stood here and told lie after lie to me. I know you had sex with Carl."

"Savvy…let me explain," Nicole began.

Savvy cut her off. "I never would've thought you would fake like you were going to set us up. I can't believe you slept with him yourself. I realize it takes a special kind of liar to do something like this to her friend and roommate. I don't know anyone conniving like you. I hope it's worth you losing a friend who loved you like the sister you never had."

Nicole's face turned bright red from shock and embarrassment. She dropped the glass she'd been washing. It shattered into pieces when it hit the kitchen floor. She covered her face with her soapy hands and began to cry.

Savvy shook her head in disgust and turned around to leave the kitchen. She stomped back into her bedroom and slammed the door. She heard Nicole's sobs. *She can cry her way to hell if she wants to. I don't care about her anymore.*

CHAPTER 16

The hospital released Olivia two days later. Thankfully, she didn't have a concussion, and there weren't any fractures or internal bleeding. She still had pain when she touched the back of her head. Black and blue bruises covered her face and body. Her body felt like it had been in the boxing ring with Muhammad Ali.

Savvy, Dwain, Lil' Bud, and Andrea visited with her in the hospital. They lifted her spirits with their laughter and stories. Their presence prevented her from getting bored or focusing on what those girls did to her.

Olivia couldn't wait to leave the ugly, unfashionable hospital gown behind and finally have access to her clothes, makeup, and hair products. She hated the fact Dwain had to see her like this.

Olivia couldn't help noticing how Savvy quickly left the room every time Dwain visited. She chalked it up to her imagination and exhaustion from everything.

Since Dwain and Savvy were in class at the time of her discharge, Olivia caught a taxicab back to her apartment. She didn't want them to skip class to bring her home. She knew they wouldn't be happy with her for not calling them.

As she shuffled slowly from the taxi to her apartment, she noticed a red stain on the sidewalk where the girls beat her up. Her eyes grew teary when she recalled how they attacked her.

Dwain evaded her questions about Isabella when he visited

with her at the hospital. He kept saying she was a girl who has a big crush on him. But Olivia couldn't dismiss the sinking feeling that he wasn't telling her everything.

Her house phone rang right when she opened her apartment door. Still, in pain, she headed slowly to the phone in the kitchen and breathlessly said, "Hello" on the last ring.

"Olivia. What are you doing home?" Savvy asked. "I called the hospital, and they said you were discharged. I planned to borrow Andrea's car to pick you up. How did you get there? Did Dwain come and get you?"

"Hey, Savvy. No, I called a cab. I didn't want to disturb anyone," Olivia explained.

"Girl, please. You know you shouldn't have taken a taxi ride home by yourself," Savvy exclaimed.

"I'm okay. Don't worry about me. I'm fine."

Savvy shook her head. "Look, I'm glad you are home. Are you still going to file a police report?"

"Yes, I figured I'd give them a call after I get settled in."

"Okay. Make sure you tell them everything that happened to you," Savvy demanded. "Also, there are a couple of things we have got to discuss. I didn't want to talk about it until you left the hospital. You won't believe what Nicole did to me. Anyway, I'll fill you in on everything when I see you. I can catch the bus to your place in about an hour. Is that okay with you?"

"Yes. That'll be fine. I'll see you soon. Oh, and Savvy, thank you for being there for me. I know you were mad at me the other day at the mall. I appreciate all you've done for me," Olivia said.

"Girl, no matter how crazy you are, I still had to be there for you," Savvy laughed. "We'll talk later when I get there. See you soon."

CHAPTER 17

Savvy rang the doorbell, and Olivia peeked out. "Open up. It's me."

Olivia opened the door and let out a huge sigh of relief when she saw Savvy's face. Savvy was careful to hug Olivia gently to keep from hurting her.

"How are you doing my friend?" Savvy questioned and inspected Olivia with her eyes from head to toe. Despite her injuries, she was still amazingly gorgeous, even though she was skinnier than ever.

"I'm making it. Thank you for coming over," Olivia said, leading Savvy to the kitchen table.

"I still can't believe those girls beat you up. This whole situation is crazy," Savvy said and sat in a chair at the table. "Is that red stain on the sidewalk your blood?"

Olivia cringed. "Yes, Beverly left me a message to let me know she tried to clean it up, but the stain is still there. It makes me sick to my stomach."

"There are some insane people in this world," Savvy said.

Olivia lamented. "It creeps me out to know someone followed me home and had the nerve to ring my doorbell and jump me."

"I know, it doesn't make any sense," Savvy agreed. "What has Dwain said about what happened to you? Has he been here yet?"

"No, he hasn't. He had classes and practice. He'll probably come by later this evening," Olivia said.

Savvy rolled her eyes. She contemplated if she should jump in and tell her about Dwain and ultimately decided to tell her about Nicole first.

"Well, you know I mentioned I had something to tell you. You won't believe what Nicole did to me," Savvy exclaimed.

"What did she do?" Olivia asked.

"Girl, you know how much I like Carl Greer, the track star at FAMU, right?"

"Of course. You made it clear you have a crush on him. He's your future baby's daddy."

"Exactly. He works with Nicole. She told me she would put in a good word for me with him to see if he would ask me out. Instead of hooking me up, this heffa put in a whole lot more words for herself." Savvy clinched her fists in anger.

"What do you mean? What did she do?" Olivia asked.

"She brought him home with her the night you landed in the hospital. They were having sex in her bedroom. She didn't know I happened to be in the living room, napping. I overheard everything. I thought she had some new guy she started seeing or something," Savvy explained. "But when I got back to the apartment after visiting you, I peeked out the window, and Carl kissed Nicole before he left. Can you believe that?"

"No way. No, she didn't. She wouldn't do that to you. She's like a big sister to you," Olivia said in shock.

"Yeah, she did do it. I never thought in a million years she could be conniving and dirty," Savvy said and shook her head. "I mean, I know Carl wasn't my man or anything. Why did she pretend to plan to introduce me to him? She could've told me she was interested in him herself. On top of that, she even lied and told me Gary from her job, was the person she had sex with."

"You mean that guy with the warts? That's nasty," Olivia said in disbelief.

"Yes. Obviously, a lie."

"That's messed up. What are you going to do now?" Olivia asked.

"I don't know. I'm thinking since I leave for my internship this summer, I'll find someplace for when I return in the fall. I may get my own apartment and not have to deal with crazy roommate mess like this," Savvy said.

"Well, you know we can be roommates like we said we would before," Olivia suggested.

"I thought about that too, but, I'm still mad at you for what you did at the mall. I don't know if we'll make good roommates." Savvy wagged her finger at Olivia.

"Oh yeah, that," Olivia smirked. "Well, think about it in case you change your mind. In the meantime, I wouldn't trust Nicole with anything else."

"You can best believe the trust is completely gone," Savvy agreed. "You know, I can't ever forget what she did to me. I don't have much to say to her. It's like I don't believe a word coming out of her lying mouth anymore."

Olivia nodded. "I completely understand how you feel. That's hard to forgive. She's a backstabber."

"By the way, I'm being insensitive. I'm laying all of this on you right after you got out of the hospital," Savvy apologized. "I should've waited until you're better. Do you have a lot of pain right now?"

"It's like I've been hit by a truck. Thankfully, the pain pills are helping a lot." Olivia rubbed the back of her head. "Believe me; it helps to hear about something else to get my mind off this craziness."

"By the way, have you called your parents to let them know about your attack?" Savvy questioned. "I asked the nurse at the hospital, and she said you didn't want them informed. My parents would be furious if someone jumped me."

"Girl, no. I would never tell them about anything like this. They'd accuse me of doing something wrong to deserve it," Olivia said, shaking her head.

"They wouldn't believe what happened?" Savvy was surprised at Olivia's response.

"Nope. They always think I must have provoked someone, and it had to be my fault. I don't have the patience to deal with any of them right now," Olivia said. "They'll never know this attack happened."

"I understand." Savvy stood and scrounged around in the cabinets. "What do you have to eat anyway? I can make us some Ramen noodles and sandwiches."

"Yuck. Ramen noodles. Those are the nastiest noodles ever. They're loaded with sodium. I'm not trying to get bloated from all of that salt," Olivia said.

"Just drink a ton of water after eating them to flush the salt out of your body," Savvy laughed. "By the way, when you mentioned taking pain pills, it reminded me that I have a question for you."

"Ask away," Olivia said.

"Well, I wasn't snooping or anything, however, when you were in the hospital, I had to go into your purse to get your phone book to for Dwain's number," Savvy said and sat back at the table.

"Oh, you know that's no problem. I don't mind you going in my purse. I trust you," Olivia replied.

"Well, I came across a prescription for something I've never heard of before called hydrochlorath-something. Do you have a serious disease or problem?" Savvy asked.

"A serious disease? Girl, no. Those are only water pills," Olivia laughed.

"Water pills? For what?" Savvy asked.

"For situations like eating those nasty Ramen noodles." Olivia laughed again. "You have to get excess water off you to keep from getting bloated and gaining weight."

"You're using them for weight loss?"

"Well, it helps. Do you want to use some? I found this doctor who can hook you up." Olivia said.

"No, I'm not interested in using any. I'm concerned about you," Savvy continued. "I know I mentioned how it seemed like you've lost a lot of weight when we tried on the swimsuits. You're not healthy anymore. What's going on?"

"Savvy, I don't know why you're getting all concerned about me losing a few pounds. I'm good, okay?" Olivia responded.

"No, it's not simply a tiny amount of weight. You were already skinny when we met, and now your skin is starting to hang off you. I know you eat since I see you stuff yourself whenever we go to a restaurant. Are you binging and purging?" Savvy asked.

"What? Eat and throw up? Are you serious?" Olivia scoffed. "Why would you ask me that crazy question?"

"Well, how else can you explain what is going on with you? Your face looks bloated, and yet, your body is skinny. I don't know all the signs of an eating disorder; however, after discovering you're taking water pills, I know something is not quite right. Also, I noticed you keep complaining about your gums and your mouth hurting. I read when people vomit a lot; their gums may bleed and erode. It can affect your heart, too. I hope you're not bulimic."

"Savvy, you're trippin'. I only increased my exercise time to work out twice a day. I'm trying to get ready for the Black Beach party." Olivia stood to fill two glasses of water from the faucet.

"Working out twice a day? For what? Why do you feel the need to work out to the extreme? You were looking great, and now you're too thin, Olivia." Savvy began to get frustrated.

"That's your opinion. Look, I need for you to back off the weight issue. Nothing is going on, and you need to leave this alone," Olivia snapped.

"Is it Dwain? Is he the reason you're losing all of this weight?" Savvy pressed on.

"Savvy, I told you to leave this alone. I'm doing this for me, and it has nothing to do with Dwain," Olivia lied.

"Okay, fine. I'll leave it alone for now. I'm glad you aren't doing this for Dwain anyway. He doesn't deserve you." Savvy leaned back in her chair and folded her arms.

"Excuse me? What are you saying?" Olivia asked and returned to the table with the glasses of water.

"Well, I didn't want to tell you this now, but, you need to know the truth about Mr. Wonderful," Savvy said.

"Oh, first you attack me about my weight, and now you're going to start lying about my boyfriend," Olivia said, frowning.

"You need to hear me out, Olivia. I'm not lying," Savvy pleaded.

"What? What could you possibly say is wrong about Dwain?"

"Olivia, when you were in the hospital, Dwain said he had to call his coach about missing practice. I left your room when you were sleeping and headed to where Dwain went to use the payphone," Savvy said. "He didn't know I stood right behind him and heard his conversation."

"What? You overheard everything he said to his coach?

What are you trying to say?" Olivia began to sound impatient.

"Not to his coach. To Isabella." Savvy paused and stared at Olivia. "Dwain called the girl who beat you up."

"Isabella? What are you talking about? He doesn't even know her," Olivia exclaimed. She slammed her bruised hand on the table in front of Savvy, causing her to jump in her chair.

"No, Olivia. He does know her. He's dating Isabella, and I heard him say he loves her. He got mad with her for coming to your house and jumping you. He knows her extremely well. He's been lying and cheating on you," Savvy said softly.

"Dwain wouldn't do that to me. He loves me, and I know he wouldn't cheat on me. You didn't hear him right. You need to stop saying those awful things about my boyfriend," Olivia yelled.

"Look, I know this is upsetting, and you don't believe me right now. I wouldn't lie to you about something like this. I even told Dwain I planned to tell you. He begged me not to," Savvy explained. "You're my friend, and I care about you too much to not tell you. You can do whatever you want with this information. It's the truth, whether you accept it or not."

"Savvy, this is too much. You're making my head hurt. I think it would be best if you leave now." Olivia stomped toward the front door.

"Don't be mad at me for being real with you," Savvy said and followed Olivia. "That's what real friends do. We tell each other the truth even when it's painful. I'll go. Know I'm here for you. You don't have to go through this alone."

"Leave, Savvy." Olivia opened the door.

Savvy walked outside and turned back to Olivia with sadness in her eyes. "Goodbye, Olivia." Olivia slammed the door in her face.

CHAPTER 18

Olivia paced around the living room trying to process what Savvy told her. How dare she say something crazy like that about Dwain. *She must be jealous of our relationship since she doesn't have a man. That must be it. She hates the fact that Dwain loves me and treats me like a queen.*

Olivia sat on the sofa and shook her head in disbelief, thinking about how wrong Savvy was to accuse Dwain of this nonsense. *All this time, I thought Savvy was my best friend. Instead, she's clearly jealous. I'm better off without friends like her.*

She walked to the phone and called Dwain. His phone rang four times before his answering machine picked up. The sound of Keith Sweat's song, "How Deep Is Your Love," played before his deep sexy voice said, "Hey, this is Dwain. You know what to do when you hear the beep."

"Hey, babe, this is Olivia. I don't know if you got my message earlier. I'm home now. Call me soon. I miss you." Olivia hung up the phone disappointed he hadn't tried to reach her since she left the hospital. She figured he was still at practice.

In the meantime, she decided to call the police department and request for them to send an officer so she could file a report.

Shortly after her call, the doorbell rang. She peered through the peephole, and a big burly man with curly, dark brown hair in a police uniform stood on her porch. She opened the door, and he smiled. He began talking in a heavy, southern drawl. "Hello, I'm Officer Oberlton. We received a call that someone wanted to file a report on an incident."

Olivia nervously nodded. "Yes, Officer Oberlton, I'm the one who called."

"Do you mind if I come in?" the officer asked.

"Please do, come on in," Olivia responded and led him into her apartment.

"Did this incident occur in the Tallahassee city limits?" Officer Oberlton inquired.

Olivia nodded and began to tell him what happened. He listened patiently and followed her out to the blood-stained sidewalk. He reached into his ink-stained shirt pocket to remove a notepad and pen.

"What you experienced is a crime of aggravated assault and battery. The Violent Crimes Unit will handle the investigation of this crime against you," he explained. "Do you know the girls that assaulted you?"

"I know one of them is named Isabella. She's Hispanic and petite. She had on a The State University of Florida sweatshirt. The other girl is Black. She's also petite and light-skinned. I've seen her cheering on the TSUF cheerleading squad. That's all I know about them," Olivia said.

"Were there any witnesses?" Officer Oberlton asked.

"Yes, my next-door neighbor, Beverly, heard everything. I think she's still at work."

"Okay. Please ask her to contact us to provide a statement as soon as possible. Here's your case number, and someone from the Violent Crimes Unit will contact you. You can call the number on this card to get an update on the case or to provide additional information." He handed a business card to her. "Do you have any questions?"

"No. I don't have any questions." Olivia took the card. "Thank you, Officer Oberlton."

The officer sauntered out to his police car and drove off. Olivia closed the door to her apartment and leaned against it, mulling about how to handle this situation.

Olivia really needed Dwain. Reflecting on her attack was just too much to handle alone. She grabbed her purse and keys and headed out the door to drive by his apartment.

When she pulled into his lot, Dwain's Saab caught her eye. He lived in an apartment facing the parking lot on the first floor. Olivia figured he must've just arrived at home since he hadn't answered her calls. She couldn't wait to tell him about this craziness with Savvy and for him to comfort her.

She started to back in and noticed a girl coming out of Dwain's apartment. He stepped onto the patio without a shirt or shoes. They hugged and kissed before she headed toward the parking lot. Olivia gasped when she recognized Isabella.

Olivia's blood began to boil. Her skin became hot, and she stewed inside. Her head throbbed in pain when Isabella crossed through the parking lot. She clenched her hands onto her steering wheel, leaving nail prints in the leather, and contemplated several scenarios in her mind.

I can't believe this ho is kissing my man. I'm 'bout to jump out of this car and stomp her into the ground. Her hand grabbed the door handle, and pain shot through the back of her head. She caught her breath with the realization of the fact she was still sore from her bruises and had a head injury. She had to come up with a different plan. *I should run her over with my car.* No, she told herself. The last thing she wanted was to go to prison for killing someone. Isabella would end up with Dwain while she was locked up.

Olivia pounded her steering wheel with frustration as she

tried to figure out her next move.

Isabella got into a maroon-colored Toyota Camry with a TSUF sticker on the bumper. Olivia decided to follow her wherever she headed, hoping to figure out a plan while she trailed her.

Olivia maneuvered through the Tallahassee traffic, close behind Isabella's car. They drove across town toward FAMU and headed on to a two-lane highway past a golf course. She turned into a neighborhood with several quadruplexes on both sides of the street.

Olivia slowed behind Isabella, who turned into one of the parking lots. She made a mental note of the address and made a U-turn on the street to head out of the neighborhood.

Her heart pounded in her chest, and her breath became shallow. She thought about what she'd witnessed. Savvy had been telling the truth.

Olivia drove back to her apartment with tears blinding her eyes. She didn't even remember making her way through town. She sunk into a daze thinking about everything happening to her. *How could Dwain do this to me?* Olivia swiped away her tears. *After everything I did to please him and to be perfect, why did he have to cheat on me? Am I still too fat? It's because she's light-skinned.*

She stared at herself in the rearview mirror and screamed, "I'm a fat, black pig. My fat face is what drove him into the arms of Isabella. Dwain tried to let me know I needed to lose more weight, and I failed. I failed."

Defeated, she stopped looking in the mirror, slowly got out of the car, and dragged herself toward her apartment.

Weak with despair with her head pounding, she entered the door. She headed straight to the answering machine in the living room, and there weren't any messages. Dwain hadn't even called to check on her.

Olivia sat on the sofa in a numb daze, massaging her throbbing temples with her thumbs. *They're going to pay for hurting me like this. How dare he cheat on me. This isn't over. I'll find a way to get them both back some way, somehow.*

CHAPTER 19

Savvy sat at the kitchen table writing a paper for her English class. The phone rang, and the caller ID box showed Olivia's name. It had been two weeks since Olivia kicked her out of her apartment. Reluctantly, after three more rings, Savvy took a deep breath and answered.

"Hello?" Savvy said into the phone.

"Savvy? It's me, Olivia." Olivia's voice was timid.

"I know. Your name showed on caller ID," Savvy said dryly.

"Look, I know we haven't spoken in a while, and I wanted to call you to say I'm sorry," Olivia said quickly.

"What are you sorry for this time?"

"Savvy, I miss you. I'm sorry I yelled at you and kicked you out. I didn't believe what you said about Dwain." Olivia spoke so fast; Savvy could hardly understand her. "You were right Savvy. You were right."

"About what?" Savvy asked.

"About Dwain. He's a liar. I know he's cheating on me with Isabella. They were together at his apartment. I'm sorry I didn't believe you. I can't believe my stupidity in thinking you made the story up," Olivia said apologetically.

"So, now you believe me, and you're calling me why?" Savvy asked.

"I'm calling you to ask for your forgiveness. I never should've treated you the way I did, and I'm sorry," Olivia cried into the phone. "I've been a mess and trying to figure out what to do. I should've called you sooner. I'm embarrassed about how I treated you and didn't think you'd want to hear from me."

"Okay, okay. Against my better judgment, I forgive you," Savvy said. "I know you've been through a lot. I'm not going to hold this against you. It sounds like you've punished yourself enough for how you treated me."

"You don't know how hard this has been for me. I haven't been going to work, and thankfully, our manager has been supportive after what happened. My face has finally healed from the scratches and bruises. I still get headaches from time to time though," Olivia explained.

"I've been wondering why I haven't seen you on the job. I thought about calling to check on you. However, you made it crystal clear you didn't want to have anything to do with me. You might need to get those headaches checked out to make sure your head is okay," Savvy said.

"I know, I know. I'm wrong for how I treated you. Can we start again with our friendship? Please?" Olivia begged.

"Yeah, yeah, yeah. We can start over," Savvy agreed. "Now slow your roll, and tell me what's going on."

"Well, I filed the police report just like we talked about. Can you believe they still haven't arrested Isabella or the other girl for trying to kill me? I thought they would've done something by now," Olivia exclaimed.

"I'm surprised it's taking this long. Have you called the police department to get an update?" Savvy asked.

"I've called almost every day. Each time, the investigator only tells me he's working on it and for me to be patient," Olivia complained.

"Okay, perhaps he hasn't been able to find out anything. Try to trust the process, and believe they'll make a move soon."

Savvy tried to comfort Olivia.

"I'm trying hard to wait on them. If they don't do something soon, I'm going to have to do something myself," Olivia exclaimed.

"Like what?" Savvy questioned. "Don't do anything stupid, Olivia."

"Don't worry; I've talked myself out of many ideas."

"Well, have you thought about going to the TSUF campus police? Perhaps they can do something in the meantime. Why don't you give them a call?" Savvy advised.

"You know, I hadn't thought about that. I'll call them now, and see if they can do something," Olivia agreed. "Savvy, I'm thankful for you, and I appreciate you for being my friend. Can we get together this Friday to hang out? I miss seeing you."

"Sure, let's plan for Friday to start a new chapter. Let's talk later this week. Maybe we can go see that Spike Lee Movie, "Do the Right Thing." I heard it's good." Savvy suggested. "Now call TSUF, and see if they can help you out."

"Will do. Thanks, Savvy," Olivia said.

"Bye." She sighed with relief and hung up the phone. She was glad to have her friend back again. However, she had a nagging feeling Olivia was keeping something from her.

CHAPTER 20

Friday night in Tallahassee bustled with college students hitting the various nightclubs and bars for stress relief.

Olivia picked Savvy up from her apartment to go to The Moon, seeing as it had been a while since either of them had been to the club. They both thought it would be a good idea to go dancing and check out the guys instead of seeing the movie.

Savvy had on a short emerald green dress with high heel gold sandals with a matching purse and gold jewelry. She had on precisely enough perfume to give a man a faint whiff of it when passing by.

Savvy opened the car door and noticed Olivia had on baggy blue jeans with an old gray t-shirt. She had her hair pulled into a messy ponytail and didn't have on makeup. Surprisingly, her face healed completely except for a scar on her forehead.

"Hey, girl. What's with the jeans, and why didn't you do your hair or makeup?" Savvy questioned Olivia and fastened her seatbelt.

"I couldn't figure out what to wear, and this humidity destroyed my hairstyle. I hate the weather here in Tallahassee where it rains long enough to make everyone run for cover. It's crazy how you can see steam coming from the ground when it stops. Doesn't make for good hair days," Olivia explained and began driving out of the neighborhood.

"Girl. You got that right. I feel the same way. But, do you think they'll let you into The Moon wearing jeans and that t-shirt?" Savvy asked.

"They should. If they don't, I'll run back home and change. No big deal." Olivia turned into a bank parking lot. "By the way, I need to get some cash from the Buck machine. I'll be right back." Olivia parked the car and jumped out to run to the ATM.

Savvy noticed Olivia also wore sneakers which was highly unusual for her.

When Olivia returned to the car, she stumbled around to the passenger side where Savvy sat. "Hey, do you mind driving for a minute? My head is hurting. I want to pop a couple of aspirins to get some pain relief before we get to the club."

"Sure, no problem." Savvy opened the door to get out of the car. Once she got into the driver's seat, she said, "By the way, you know you can't get into the club wearing those shoes. Where are your dressier ones? You have a closet full of cute sandals."

Olivia stared at her feet like she suddenly realized she had on sneakers. "Oh yeah, I forgot to mention I need to stop by a friend's house to borrow her shoes. She has some cute ones I want to wear tonight. She lives off Darryl Drive, which isn't too far from The Moon. We can head there right now. I'll tell you where to go."

"Okay, that's good. Which way?" Savvy asked and fastened her seatbelt before backing out of the parking space and veering onto the road.

"Just turn right at this corner and left on the next street," Olivia directed.

They drove past FAMU's campus and headed onto a two-lane highway leading out to the country.

"I think it's right past the golf course. Slow down," Olivia said in a strange way, which made Savvy glance at her. She noticed her eyes appeared dull and empty. "Yeah. This is it.

Make a left here."

Savvy turned onto the street Olivia pointed out. They passed several apartment buildings. "These are nice quadruplexes. Maybe I'll come back out and see about getting one for me here," Savvy said.

"Yeah, they're nice." Olivia's voice was hollow which made Savvy glance at her again. Her face reminded her of when she stole the swimsuit at the mall.

"Are you okay?" Savvy asked.

"Yeah, I'm fine. Go further." Olivia pointed to the side of the street. "See that maroon Toyota Camry sitting in the parking lot on the left? Go into that one, and back into the spot next to it."

It started to get dark, and Savvy could barely make out the color of the car. She noticed a TSUF sticker on the bumper. When she backed into the parking space and put the car into park, Olivia quickly jumped out.

Olivia opened the back door to her car and pulled out a huge brick. Before Savvy realized it, she bolted to the maroon car, lifted the brick above the windshield, and threw it with all the force she could. It hit the window and slightly cracked it before it bounced off and fell to the ground.

Savvy yelled, "Olivia. What are you doing? Have you lost your mind?"

Olivia ignored Savvy and grabbed the brick again. This time, Savvy could see her raging eyes and spittle on her twisted lips. She repeated the same motion and threw it on the windshield with even more force. It shattered the window, bounced off the car, and hit a red Geo Prizm parked on the other side of it causing its alarm to go off.

Olivia jumped back into the car. "Floor it, Savvy. Get us out of here," she yelled at the top of her lungs. She searched around with wild eyes to see if anyone had seen them.

Savvy pushed the gas pedal to the floor as she screeched out of the parking lot. She almost hit another car from racing out onto the dark street.

"Come on. Drive faster before we get caught," Olivia barked.

"I can't go any faster. Why did you do that?" Savvy yelled back and maneuvered the Honda onto the road.

"I'll tell you after we get away from here," Olivia said. Savvy turned out of the neighborhood on two wheels.

They drove back toward FAMU, and Olivia had Savvy pull into a gas station. Savvy parked, jumped out and ran around to Olivia's side of the car. She yanked the door open, grabbed Olivia's t-shirt, and pulled her out of her seat. Despite the fact Olivia towered over Savvy, Savvy had greater strength. Since Olivia's body has wasted away, grabbing her was like handling a skeleton.

Savvy slammed Olivia's back against the car and yelled in her face. "What is wrong with you? You had me drive you to someone's place for you throw a brick at their car and expect me to be your get-a-way driver? Have you lost your frickin' mind?"

Olivia leaned back on the side of the car and appeared dazed. She glanced at Savvy. "I can understand why you're upset with me."

"*You can understand why I'm upset with you?*" Savvy glared at Olivia with disgust and shook her. "That has to be the stupidest thing you could ever say."

"I know you don't understand. It's something I had to do," Olivia said, still looking dazed.

Savvy shook her head and released Olivia's shirt. "You better believe I don't understand. Why did you have to involve me? Huh? If you choose to live this kind of drama-filled life, why do you have to bring me into it and risk me getting in trouble?"

"I knew we wouldn't get caught," Olivia tried to explain.

"Oh, shut up," Savvy yelled and did her best to shoot arrows through her glare at Olivia. "The more you open your mouth, the more I want to smack you."

"I get that. I don't blame you if you did. I needed you there with me." Olivia was now eerily calm.

"Who owns the car? Why did you decide to put a brick through that window?"

"The car belongs to Isabella." Olivia shrugged. "You know, the slut who beat me up."

Savvy's eyes got wide. "Isabella's car? How did you know what kind of car she drives and where she lives?"

"I saw her coming out of Dwain's apartment with my own two eyes. They kissed on his front porch," Olivia fumed. "When she left, I followed her to this apartment complex. I've gone by her place a million times, and Dwain's car has been there almost every night. It's not fair that she and the other girl who jumped me are living their lives without pain. I'm the one who's suffering to no end. She took my boyfriend and needs to pay for what they did. You know I'm mad about the fact they got away with trying to kill me, and the police never did anything."

"But the TSUF campus police arrested her and the other girl out of their class this week. I also heard they may get kicked off the cheerleading squad," Savvy reminded her.

"Yeah, they were arrested. I found out all they got is a scolding with only having to do 200 hours of community service. That's all they got after almost ending my life," Olivia said with tears welling in her eyes. "Two criminals are roaming free on the streets, and I have to deal with that every single day. I'm scared to be outside by myself not knowing if they're going to do it again. I can't sleep at night, and when I do, I have nightmares about them hitting me in the head and seeing my blood everywhere."

"That's all? Community service?" Savvy asked in shock. "That can't be right."

"Yes, that's all. I had to manage things my own way since I couldn't depend on law enforcement or the university to do anything. Savvy, you don't know all the things I could've done to her. You have no idea what it's like to be attacked the way I was. To make things worse, seeing her with Dwain put a dagger in my heart. It hurts me to deal with this," Olivia cried out clutching her stomach and bending in agony.

Savvy couldn't think of anything else to say. Olivia became overwhelmed with grief and wailed uncontrollably so Savvy tried to hug her. When she reached out to her, she noticed red paint on Olivia's jeans, which she didn't see earlier. "How did you get paint on your jeans?" Savvy asked.

Olivia glanced at her jeans and sniffled. "Well, Dwain is going to find a nice surprise when he leaves the club tonight," she explained.

"What do you mean by a nice surprise?" Savvy asked, studying her friend.

"Well, you know, I decided after everything he did, it's time to let him know he can't cheat and expect me to look like a fool to everyone. He took a piece of me I can never get back." Olivia quickly swiped away tears with the back of her hand. "I called him a million times after I found out about him being with Isabella, and he's never returned my calls and ignores me. It's like I don't even exist in his mind anymore. After all, I did to make him happy; this is how he treats me."

"What did you do Olivia?" Savvy dreaded the answer.

"Since he loves his black Saab, I decided I would help to decorate it." Olivia suddenly had a sly smile on her face, and her tears mysteriously disappeared.

"Decorate it? How?" Savvy asked nervously.

"His favorite color is red. He wants to become a member of Kappa Alpha Psi Fraternity like crazy. He even wears their colors like he already pledged. I figured, he should have a car to match," Olivia explained. "I happened to have a can of red paint on hand."

"Go on," Savvy prodded.

"I followed him to Club Faces and waited for him to go inside. Once he walked in, I strolled past the Saab with the can and pretended to trip on a rock in the parking lot. When I fell, I threw the paint all across the front of his car." Olivia laughed in a sinister way that scared Savvy.

"No, you didn't," Savvy exclaimed and put her hand to her mouth. "Who goes around with a can of paint in a club parking lot? Please tell me you didn't do that."

"Yup. I sure did, and he can't prove I did it. He's hurt a ton of women. It could be any one of them he scorned like me," Olivia said and pranced around in the parking lot like she'd won the lottery.

"You know what? You need help," Savvy said and stared at Olivia in disbelief. Her friend's drastic swings in mood were frightening. "You need some serious counseling."

"Counseling? For what?" Olivia asked. "I did what any other woman who's been cheated on would do. Dwain and Isabella are lucky I didn't do what I thought about doing."

"I don't even want to know what you've thought about doing," Savvy said. "I think with all of the things you've been dealing with, it wouldn't hurt for you to find someone to help you get through this. You know, the same way you want to be a psychologist one day, you can get help from one."

"You're kidding me, right?" Olivia asked astonished and stopped moving to stare at Savvy.

"No, I'm not. I don't want you hurting anyone, and I don't want you to get hurt," Savvy explained.

"So, you think I'm crazy? You think I'm cuckoo for Cocoa Puffs or something; even though, I'm the one who's the victim?" Olivia glared at Savvy and stood in front of her with her arms folded. "You know what? I'm going to drive you home now cause you think I've lost my mind. You're supposed to be my friend." Olivia jumped into the car, and Savvy reluctantly got in on the passenger side.

"But you're doing it all wrong, Olivia," Savvy said. "Do you realize how much trouble you can get into for vandalizing their cars? What if there were security cameras at Club Faces? They will know you poured the paint on Dwain's car."

"I'm taking care of what the police can't seem to. Nothing happened to them for what they did to me. Nothing. There's no way they can say anything to me," Olivia cried out and sped down the street, weaving in and out between cars.

"Okay, okay. You're driving too fast, Olivia," Savvy exclaimed. "Don't get us killed right now. Slow down."

Olivia gave a wicked laugh when she realized she'd frightened Savvy. "Girl, I'm good. I didn't mean to scare you."

She drove into Savvy's lot, and Savvy frantically got out when she parked, afraid of what Olivia might do next.

"Olivia, I want you to get counseling. In the meantime, we need a long break from each other. I can't handle this emotional roller coaster with you right now. I need to focus on getting my education without landing in jail or dead. You have to make some changes in your life. I pray you'll listen to me, and go see a psychologist to help you before you do something you'll regret one day," Savvy said sadly to Olivia and closed the car door.

Olivia glared at Savvy and sped off into the darkness.

PART 3

LOVE THE WAY YOU LIE

CHAPTER 21

1999

"Dr. Maxwell," Malia, the receptionist, poked her head into Olivia's office. "I wanted to inform you the last patient on the schedule called in to cancel."

"Oh, thanks for letting me know. I am tired after seeing Miss Ortega. She wore me out." Olivia sat at her desk and fanned herself. Sweat poured from her pores despite the cool room.

"Are you okay, Dr. Maxwell?" Malia scrunched her brow with concern. "You don't look well."

"I don't feel well either. I wonder if there's a bug going around or something." Olivia stood with shaky legs. "My heart is racing like crazy. It's like I just finished running a marathon."

"Well, sit and let me get you a glass of water," Malia instructed and turned around to exit the room.

Olivia felt as though the room was spinning in a dizzy twirl. Her ears started to ring. She clutched her chest with one hand and used the other to try and steady herself on the desk. Everything appeared fuzzy and in slow motion. Her lungs seemed slow to fill, and she began taking quick, shallow breaths.

"Dr. Maxwell," Malia screamed and ran to Olivia. She felt Malia's hands under her arms right before she slumped to the ground and blacked out.

Olivia awakened to the sound of a siren and sensed movement. Something sat on her face, and she became aware of cool air going in and out of her nose. She groaned and opened her eyes only to see two men, which startled her.

"It's okay Dr. Maxwell. You're in an ambulance right now. I'm Roberto, and this guy is Dino." He pointed at the other man.

"An ambulance?" She realized she had an oxygen mask on her face and lifted it to talk. "What's going on? Why am I here?"

"Ma'am, your receptionist called us because you passed out. She told us you complained of your heart beating extremely fast right before you fell. We're monitoring it, and sure enough, you have quite a race going on in your chest," Dino replied.

"Where are you taking me?" Olivia asked still holding the mask and beginning to panic.

"We're taking you to one of San Antonio's finest hospitals. Right now, I'm going to have you put this thing back into place. It's there to help you breathe. Relax. Dino and I will handle everything to get you safely to the emergency room." Roberto lowered the oxygen mask to her face.

"Okay, we're going to give you something to help you feel more comfortable. Is that all right with you?" Dino questioned.

Olivia nodded her head. A prick from a needle going into her arm made her flinch. The next thing she knew, the sound of the ambulance siren faded out, and the paramedic's faces begin to appear fuzzy. She struggled to keep her eyes open and couldn't.

She woke in a hospital room with an IV tube attached to the inside of her elbow with a white bandage holding it in place. Lights flashed on various pieces of medical equipment, and the heart monitor beeped next to her bed.

She groaned and groped in the dark to find the bed remote to ring for a nurse. After pushing a button to raise the top part of her bed to a sitting position, she pressed the red alert key. Immediately the door opened, and a woman with blue scrubs entered the room.

"Hello, Dr. Maxwell. I see you are finally awake. My name is Avryl, and I'm your nurse until 7 am. How can I help you, Sweetie?" She walked to the bed to straighten out the blanket on Olivia and adjust her pillow.

"I didn't realize I had fallen asleep. The last thing I remember is riding in the ambulance," Olivia croaked. "Can I get a glass of water. My throat is dry."

"Sure. No problem." Avryl poured ice water into a cup from a pink pitcher on a metal tray and placed a straw in it before handing to Olivia.

"What time is it?" Olivia cleared her throat and coughed after sipping on the water.

"It's four in the morning."

"Four? Oh, my goodness. I have been here a long time. What all happened to me?" Olivia asked.

"Well, you had quite a night. You came in with a rapid heart rate. That is what we call tachycardia. It is a condition which raised it to more than 120 beats per minute at rest," Avryl explained. "To convert it back into a normal rhythm, the emergency team had to use a defibrillator on you."

"No way. You have got to be kidding me," Olivia exclaimed. "How in the world did that happen?"

"I don't know. The hospitalist will come in later and can explain more to you about what is going on. In the meantime, you should simply rest. Is there anything else I can get for you?" Avryl asked.

"No. Nothing, I can think of. Thank you." Olivia heard the

door closing behind Avryl and dozed off.

She heard a familiar voice gently saying her name, which aroused her from her sleep. "Olivia? Olivia? Can you hear me?"

She slowly opened her eyes and squinted at the light. Her father's face, wrinkled in concern, startled her. "Daddy," she cried, overwhelmed from the shock of seeing him.

"Olivia, yes it's Daddy," he responded with tears in his eyes.

"Daddy. I'm terribly sorry. I know you're disappointed in me. I failed you, Daddy. I failed you, and I'm sorry," she wailed uncontrollably.

"Olivia, don't cry. It's okay, honey." He leaned toward her and hugged her tightly. "I love you, and it's going to be okay. You haven't failed me. Not at all. You're sick, and it's okay."

Hearing him say he loved her caused Olivia to cry even louder. He rocked her and stroked her hair while she clung to him.

"You love me, Daddy?" Olivia blubbered.

"Yes, I do," he whispered and pulled back from their embrace to gaze into her eyes. "I love you, and I am glad to see you are okay."

"Daddy, you don't know what it means to me to hear you say that you love me. You and Mom have never said that to me. I didn't think you cared anything about me," Olivia sobbed.

"I know, and I'm sorry. I apologize for not being there for you. Ever. I should've been there. When I got the call from Malia about you being in the hospital, I caught the first flight here. I thought we almost lost you," he said.

"Thank you, Daddy." Olivia sniffled and scanned around the room. "Where's Mother?"

"She uh, she uh, she couldn't come," her Dad stuttered and dropped his eyes to the floor.

"Do you mean she *wouldn't* come?" Olivia felt anger creeping into her body.

"Honey, you know she doesn't like to fly. She's nervous enough from knowing you are in the hospital," he tried to explain.

"Dad. Stop. Don't try to cover for her. We both know she wouldn't be able to stand seeing her less than perfect daughter laying in the hospital being even more unperfect. She would've jumped on a plane in a heartbeat if Sheree lay here in my place. You know it, and I know it. Please, don't try to make excuses for her." Olivia's heart monitor showed her rate increasing.

"Please don't get yourself stressed out right now. It's not good for your heart. You're right, I shouldn't cover for your Mom, and I'm sorry she isn't here," her father apologized.

"Why did I have to be on my deathbed for you to come and see me? What happened to my graduation from undergrad and my Master and Doctorate degrees in psychology? None of you cared enough to be there. That's why I haven't bothered to go home to see any of you. Now you think I'm dying, and you want to lay your eyes on me?" Olivia became agitated. Her heart beat rapidly, and her blood pressure kept rising.

"I understand you're angry with me and all of us. Again, I'm sorry for not being there for you, and I wish I could change that."

Years of pent-up frustration started boiling over. Olivia ignored the increasing beeping of the heart rate machine and continued lighting into her father.

"Why did you always let Mother treat me bad? How could you let her be cruel to me just because I'm dark skinned? I can't help the skin I'm in. She put those bleaching creams on me, which burned me. She thinks I'm black and ugly. Why does she hate me the way she does when I am her child? Please tell me why?" Olivia pleaded.

"She doesn't hate you. She kind of associates you with her father since you resemble him. He used to be a tall, dark-skinned man."

"But what does his skin color have to do with me?" Olivia questioned.

"I don't know if you remember the story about how he tried to kill his whole family in a house fire. They all got out except for him. Your mother never got over what happened."

"And?" Olivia prodded impatiently.

"She looks at you and sees him. You are the spitting image of her father. Your mother feels the same way about all dark-skinned people. It jogs this bad memory for her."

"Do you know how ridiculous this is? A hatred for me and all dark-skinned people because of her suicidal father? I have nothing to do with him. How can she blame me for his sins?" Olivia stared at him in disbelief and began to feel weak from too much exertion of emotion.

"I know, it wasn't right. Throughout the years; I've tried to get that out of her head. I can't control her actions, Olivia. I'm sorry I haven't been a strong enough man to handle the way she treats you." He hung his head in guilt.

Olivia sighed and noticed the sorrow on his face. She didn't mean to take all her anger out on him. She took a deep breath and softened her voice. "Daddy, I didn't mean to mention that and blame it on you right now. I'm glad you're here."

"Baby, you are beautiful no matter what color your skin is. I love you no less than I love your sister. I know I haven't seen you in a long time. I can tell you aren't healthy. What is going on with you?" He sat on the edge of the bed and gazed at Olivia with love. She choked with tears again and hung onto him.

They heard a knock at the door, and a short man entered the room wearing a white lab coat and a stethoscope around his neck. He shook Olivia's and her father's hand. "Hello, I'm Dr. Rodriguez, the hospitalist on duty."

"Hello, I'm Olivia's father, Oliver Maxwell."

"It's nice to meet you, Mr. Maxwell." Dr. Rodriguez turned to Olivia. "I would like to share your test results with you."

"Yes?" Olivia said anxiously.

"You are fortunate to be here right now. There has been a lot of damage done to your body and to your heart. I need to ask you a few questions to help me understand your condition." He glanced at Olivia's father. "I have sensitive information to review with your daughter."

"I can leave the room so you two can talk." Mr. Maxwell began to stand from his chair.

"Please stay Dad." Olivia grabbed his hand. She looked at the doctor and nodded. "It's okay for him to hear whatever you have to tell me."

Dr. Rodriguez pulled up a chair. "Have you ever been told that you have an eating disorder?" He studied Olivia squarely in the eyes.

"No, well, n-not exactly," Olivia stuttered. "I mean, a friend in college asked me more than ten years ago. Of course, she had me all wrong."

"Okay, let me say this a different way. Here is what I see from the results of our examination of you and the testing we did. What brought you here to the hospital is you passed out due to an irregular heartbeat. Your heart rate measured at 120 beats per minute, which is what we call tachycardia. If prolonged, this can lead to heart failure."

The doctor paused and continued. "On top of that, you're dehydrated, which can lead to kidney failure. Fortunately, your kidneys are fine. We are giving you fluids now in this bag that is hanging behind you. For someone your height, a weight of 105 pounds is dangerously low. Also, you have an inflamed esophagus, raw gums, and swollen glands along your jawline," the doctor continued. "Olivia, from what I am seeing, you have an eating disorder called bulimia nervosa."

"I, um, I don't think I have an eating disorder." Olivia shook her head in denial.

"Often, we see this type of self-inflicted disease from cycles of binge eating, purging, using diuretics and laxatives, and exercising excessively for many years. This can cause your heart to go out of control and beat too rapidly," he explained. "Let me cut to the chase. How long have you been eating and regurgitating your food?"

Olivia appeared embarrassed and dropped her eyes to her lap, realizing she couldn't fool this doctor. She let out a deep breath and confessed. "I initially tried it in high school for only a few weeks. My mother called me fat and insisted I had to lose weight to go to my Senior Prom." She glanced at her father, and shock spread across his face like he had had no idea.

"I started again in college, and it has lasted on and off until now. I guess it's been about ten years. I always hid it from everyone in school and at work. I didn't realize how hooked I had become or that I was messing my body up. I wanted to look perfect. Now, you're saying I've damaged myself instead?"

"Eating disorders are dreadfully serious. Some people do not get a do-over. You're fortunate to have a chance to get control with this condition. We are going to hold you here a few days to monitor your heart and make sure everything is functioning properly. I am also going to have the nurse talk with you about programs which can help you with your disorder. I strongly suggest you do something now to prevent any more damage from taking place in your body." He stood to leave.

"Okay, I would like that information from her. Thank you, Dr. Rodriguez," she responded sheepishly.

Dr. Rodriguez exited the room, leaving Olivia and her father alone to soak in all he shared with them.

"Olivia, I can't believe you've been throwing up for more than ten years, and no one knew. Why? You've never been fat. What made you do something like that?" her father questioned in disbelief.

"I wanted my body to be perfect. In high school, I did it to please Mother. In college, my boyfriend wanted me to lose weight. I never thought I would've done this for all these years. It became a way of life for me," Olivia said, her voice filled with regret.

"I know you can beat this. I think you should go into a program for help. You're a strong woman, and you'll be much better," her father reassured her.

"Thank you for believing in me, Daddy. I didn't realize I was hurting myself. I mean, my heart and my kidneys might be damaged. I had no idea." Olivia sighed and laid her head back on the pillow. *I can't believe I've done more harm than good. On top of that, I'm still fat.*

"At least now, you can stop this cycle and get on the road to good health."

"I'm sorry about what I said earlier. I'm glad you're here with me. I can't imagine going through this alone." Despite her anger toward her family, she found comfort in having her father with her to help get through this ordeal.

Once discharged from the hospital, Olivia reviewed the information the nurse provided to her about the National Eating Disorders Association.

An inpatient treatment center for eating disorders in

Colorado seemed promising with an exquisite view of the Rocky Mountains. The six-week program would be away from everyone and everything she knew. Perhaps it would be the best way to gain control finally and conquer this demon.

She headed to Colorado three days after leaving the hospital.

CHAPTER 22

Checking into the treatment center had to be the hardest thing Olivia ever had to do. If it weren't for Malia talking her into doing this for her health, she wouldn't have gotten on the plane.

"Welcome to the Mountain River Resort, Dr. Maxwell." A pleasant middle-aged woman with a clipboard greeted her. The limousine driver handed Olivia's two suitcases to the bellman and thanked her for the generous tip.

Olivia breathed in deeply and smelled the fresh, cool air. She gazed around at the colorful flowers surrounding the property emitting a blend of sweet fragrances into her nostrils. Birds singing songs to heaven brought about peace and serenity.

"My name is Joyce, and I'm your Resident Counselor. Did you have a good flight?"

"Yes, I did. I enjoyed seeing the snow-capped mountains when we flew in. I couldn't take my eyes away from the window. Such a change from the hot weather in San Antonio," Olivia exclaimed. The beautiful scenery had brightened her mood.

"I am sure you will enjoy cooling off here." Joyce smiled. "Please follow me inside, and we will get you settled into your room. We will go on a tour and get you to the café for lunch. Afterward, we'll begin your first counseling session."

The check-in lounge overwhelmed Olivia upon entering.

Carefully done decorations created a calm and serene environment.

A picture window displayed the majestic mountain peaks and valleys. Olivia inhaled sharply and digested the beauty of nature. The pictures in the brochure did not give this place justice.

Women of all sizes and shapes sat on plush sofas and chairs in a common area. They read or engaged in lively conversations. Several glanced at Olivia and gave her warm smiles and gentle hellos. She took in all she could before following Joyce who patiently waited for her.

The bedroom suite décor amazed Olivia more than the rest of the property. The smell of eucalyptus filled her nose when Joyce opened the door. "Oh, my goodness. This room is gorgeous," she exclaimed.

Olivia envisioned herself sleeping in the king-sized bed, surrounded by the multitude of oversized sage green and white pillows. The spacious bathroom had a marble shower and separate jacuzzi tub along with plush white towels hanging on the racks. The living room contained a cream-colored sofa with a green blanket folded on it. A desk and chair were on the opposite wall. White sheer curtains covered the sliding door, which led to a balcony overlooking a pool.

"Wow." Olivia was at a loss for words.

"Are you pleased?" Joyce asked.

"Yes, I love it." Olivia beamed.

"Great. Let's head out to walk around the rest of the center."

Joyce proceeded to show Olivia the maze of meeting rooms, fitness center, activity room, counseling stations, staff quarters and offices. They concluded the tour at the dining café where Joyce reviewed her schedule and ground rules over lunch.

"Olivia, you have taken the most important step in your journey to recovery from bulimia. It is a serious and complex disorder which can affect you physically, emotionally, and socially," Joyce explained.

"Right. I still can't believe I've been trying to be perfect for so long. My body has taken a beating. I wish I realized it sooner."

"Well, at least you responded to your episode in a way to get the help available. We have a dedicated team of experienced professionals who are here for you. You will meet with the clinician and dietary staff later today. We will work to develop a customized care plan to fit your nutritional, spiritual, psychological, medical, and relational needs," Joyce said before asking, "How does that sound to you?"

"It sounds good. When I researched your facility, I was impressed to see the fact you are dually licensed as an eating disorder and mental health treatment center," Olivia answered.

"Also, our therapy sessions are evidence-based. We include exercise, yoga, art therapy, cooking classes, and equine therapy as a comprehensive treatment approach. The plan is to eliminate the behaviors which contribute to your bulimia. You will develop a healthier relationship with exercise and food. Our goal is to give you a set of new skills to cope with stressful situations in life. Once you finish your six weeks here, you will leave with an individualized discharge plan. We recognize the hardest recovery may take place after you leave," Joyce continued.

While they talked, Olivia glanced around the café. She noticed women and several teenage girls eating together. She caught a glimpse of a woman with an afro and one with braids coming through the door, who were both extremely thin.

"What's going through your mind right now?" Joyce asked when she realized Olivia seemed distracted.

"Oh. I'm sorry. I'm observing the variety of ladies here. I'm shocked." Olivia paused.

"What surprises you?" Joyce questioned.

"Well, there are black women here," Olivia said.

Joyce chuckled. "Yes, there are women of all races in our program."

"Sorry if I sound ignorant. I'm a psychologist and am familiar with various eating disorders. However, in seeing very thin black women, I am curious about whether or not they are here because of bulimia or even anorexia?" Olivia was perplexed. "I mean, I'm not trying to be in their business, but if that is the case, I personally never heard of black women, other than myself, being bulimic," Olivia explained.

"Good observation," Joyce responded.

"Maybe, I need to go back to grad school. I can't believe I've been ignorant about the impact of this disorder in the African-American community. From my experience to this point, this is mainly a white woman's disease." Olivia felt her skin grow warm from embarrassment.

"Your thoughts are not unusual. Many people have the same mindset you do about bulimia not being an issue for black women. It's not a cultural norm, and folks often won't talk about it with anyone. However, it does occur more often than most think," Joyce confirmed.

"I have to admit; there's no way I would've ever admitted to anyone the fact that I have this disorder. I wonder if it's the shame of not representing the strong black woman image. You know, most usually take pride in having meat on our bones," Olivia pondered.

"You are certainly right, and it's good to hear you say that before you have even had your first session. Most women in our program experienced isolation when dealing with this disorder.

They never think it's something they can discuss since they are embarrassed. It's more common than people realize because it's not your usual topic of conversation," Joyce said.

Olivia released a sigh of relief. She no longer had to suffer alone as she had been for ten years.

"Now, let's head to the counseling station and get you started." Joyce stood and placed their food trays on a conveyer belt. Olivia followed her to begin her process of healing.

Okay. Here we go. Time to peel back the layers of my brain, and figure out what is going on. Olivia sighed.

"Over in the corner is a changing room. Please go in there to remove your clothes and shoes and leave on your bra and panties. You will find a robe hanging on a hook for you to put on. We need to get a baseline weight for you," Joyce instructed.

"No way. You can't weigh me right after I ate. That's not fair," Olivia whined.

"Don't worry. We'll weigh you again in the morning," Joyce replied.

"Ugh. Wait. I need to go to the bathroom first," Olivia protested.

"Now, Olivia, let's not pretend I don't know your intention of going to the restroom. Starting today, you will not regurgitate any more of the food you eat. It is not going to be easy. But, I know you can do it. I have been exactly where you are. So, we are here to make you well. Is that understood?" Joyce stared Olivia squarely in the eyes.

Olivia realized Joyce is the first person to ever call her out in the moment of her plan to purge. She dropped her eyes from Joyce in humiliation. "Yes, I understand. I'll go change my clothes." She slunk into the changing area. When she returned, she couldn't help but feel exposed in the thin robe and nervously tightened the belt around her waist.

She balanced herself on the scale and refused to look. "Okay, Olivia. You weigh 105 pounds. You can get off the scale now." Joyce jotted the number on her clipboard.

"105," Olivia repeated.

"Are you pleased with this weight?" Joyce asked.

"I didn't realize I could be this weight and still be fat," Olivia sighed.

Joyce flashed a gentle smile, then took Olivia's hand. "Believe me when I tell you, we're going to help you during the time you are here. I have something I want to show you."

Joyce handed Olivia a red marker and placed an oversized piece of paper on the floor. "What I would like for you to do is to draw a life-sized outline of how you see body shape. You don't have to be a skilled artist. Do the best you can."

Olivia huffed but took the marker, and knelt on the paper to begin drawing. She didn't understand this stupid exercise.

"Very good," Joyce said once Olivia completed the task. "Now, I need for you to lie on this second piece of paper. I'm going to draw your actual outline. Are you comfortable with this?

"No, I'm not," Olivia said without hesitation. "However, I paid a lot of money to be here. I'll do it even though I don't like it," Olivia agreed reluctantly.

Joyce took a black marker, and once Olivia laid on the paper, she outlined her.

"See. That wasn't bad." Joyce helped Olivia from the floor. "You can put your clothes back on. Once you come out, we will sit and chat."

Olivia put her warm-up suit and shoes back on before returning to Joyce. They sat in chairs in front of the two drawings.

"Now, I want you to examine each of these pictures. Tell me

what you see," Joyce instructed.

Olivia scanned back and forth between the two outlines. She shook her head slowly before responding. "Joyce. I don't know what to say right now."

"What are you thinking?"

"You made a mistake on your outline of me. Your picture has me looking extremely skinny. No way is that my shape." Olivia pointed at the paper drawn with the black marker.

"It is not a mistake. This shows your actual shape."

"Now you know, I'm a lot bigger than that. Do you see how tiny you made my stomach and thighs?"

"Nope. Olivia, your perception of your body, is much bigger than what you are. In your picture, you drew round hips, a large stomach, and huge arms. You can see, your true body shape is quite the opposite."

Olivia couldn't believe Joyce's words, and her neck prickled with heated anger. "I'm not sure how you came to this conclusion. It is completely wrong."

"I know this is a lot to absorb right now. It's okay. We have a reason for doing this exercise upon arrival. It brings about a reality check and allows us to know how you feel. We're done for today. You did considerably well. Now you can go back to your room to relax or roam around the resort until time for dinner. But before you go, do you have any questions for me?" Joyce asked.

Olivia sighed. "I don't have any questions. I'm in a state of shock. Bear with me. I need to adjust to all of this."

"I understand. We will see you this evening at dinner. Tomorrow, we'll meet at 8:00 am. Okay?" Joyce stood and walked Olivia to the door.

"Okay. Thank you, Joyce. Goodbye." Olivia walked to her room with her head hung low.

I should pack my bags and go home. Why did I come here for this nonsense? I can counsel myself instead of letting these people humiliate me. She sat on the sofa and read the materials Joyce had given her covering the ground rules.

To develop a healthy image of their bodies, the staff did not allow magazines on site or watching television. This rule applied to keep them from obsessively comparing themselves to celebrity women. *I know they don't think I can be here for six-weeks without reading any magazines? I need to get a ride to the store to get a couple to sneak in. There is no way I am giving those up.*

Before the program, Olivia had a habit of buying stacks of fashion and gossip magazines from the grocery store. She would spend time throughout the day flipping from the front cover to the back. She became obsessed with how beautiful and skinny the models and movie stars were.

The residents all had to eat regularly scheduled balanced meals. They couldn't remove food from the café or store snacks in their rooms to avoid the temptation to binge. *Yeah, right. Watch me find a way to get my food in here.*

To use the bathrooms in the common areas, they had to notify a staff member whenever they needed to have the restroom unlocked. The counselor would stand outside the door to see if they were throwing up versus using the toilet. They could not go to their rooms right after meals. Strategically scheduled group sessions occurred immediately after eating to keep them from purging.

Olivia sighed and placed the book on the coffee table. She wrapped the blanket around her and stepped through the sliding doors onto the patio. The cool air hit her face and refreshed her. The majestic view made her pause and say a prayer. *Lord, you have given me a chance to get healed. I don't want to disappoint you or myself any more than I already have. Help me to make the choice today to stop destroying my body. I know it won't be easy, but you brought me here for a reason. I'm ready, and I can do this. Amen.*

***

The next day, Olivia met a few of the residents at breakfast after she weighed in.

"Hi, I'm Beth, and this is Connie. Welcome to paradise." The ladies laughed and invited Olivia to join them at their table. Beth had short, red hair and Connie's was long and brown and pulled into a ponytail. They appeared to be in their thirties and wore workout clothes.

"Thank you. I love the resort. It's hard to believe I'm not on vacation," Olivia nervously chuckled and set her food tray on the table.

"Well, you are in some ways. This place is incredible. I checked in four weeks ago and wish I didn't have to leave in two weeks. But I must get back to my husband and kids. Have you had a chance to get out and enjoy some of the classes available?" Connie asked with a strong southern accent.

"No, not yet. Today is my first full day. I'm looking forward to working out this morning. Perhaps I'll try horseback riding later," Olivia responded.

"You won't be disappointed," Beth replied. "Don't be nervous about being here. You probably are a bit overwhelmed after hearing about all the rules. It's a lot, but, it will help you eventually."

"I sure hope I can follow them," Olivia confessed.

"One warning to you though, there are cameras, and some residents are spies. Watch out for them because they will turn you in. I thought I could get away with sneaking food into my room. Would you believe my neighbor reported me as if I was a bad kid?" Connie whispered.

"Wow. That is crazy," Olivia responded.

"Just remember why you are here." Beth cut her eyes at Connie. "It's not easy to have an eating disorder, and it's not easy to get the help. At least you made the first step by showing up. You'll see the benefits soon. You must trust the process."

"I will do my best," Olivia said.

"Hey. We better get going. We have an archery class in fifteen minutes. We'll see you around. Welcome again," Connie said. They gathered their dirty dishes and left the cafeteria.

Olivia sighed and picked at her meal. *If I hurry and eat this, maybe I can make it to my room and throw it up before my 8 o'clock session. One more time and I'll be good.*

Just as she finished eating, the two black ladies she saw the day before approached her.

"Hi, I'm Wynetta." The woman with the braids extended her hand to Olivia to shake.

"Hi. Nice to meet you Wynetta," Olivia responded with a smile.

The other lady with the perfectly shaped afro smiled and shook her hand. "I'm Vera. We saw you checking in yesterday and wanted to introduce ourselves."

"I saw the two of you also. I was shocked to know I'm not the only African-American woman here. I had no idea, so many of us are dealing with eating disorders," Olivia shared.

"Girl, please. We exist, but none of us ever talk about it. You'll be surprised at the fact that most of us are here for bulimia or anorexia," Vera replied.

"Right. People tend to focus on black women who deal with issues by eating too much and gaining a lot of weight from comfort food. You don't find too many of us who are the opposite," Wynetta chimed in. "Sorry for any assumptions, but from the looks of things, my guess is you're dealing with bulimia?"

"Good guess. How can you tell?" Olivia questioned.

"The fact you're eating gives you away," Wynetta responded.

"Oh yeah, right," Olivia said.

"Don't be embarrassed. We all have been where you are. Just know, you're not alone, sister girl. We can get through this together and live a healthy life," Vera encouraged Olivia.

"Thank you. You don't know how much your words mean to me," Olivia replied.

"We'll catch up with you later. You'll do fine," Wynetta said as they walked away.

In spite of their words, Olivia headed to the bathroom after dinner and ended up being caught trying to sneak to regurgitate. Another resident told on her. She looked completely foolish and apologized to the staff.

After attending the morning group session, Olivia finally had the opportunity to work out. She struggled with the limitations of exercising vigorously for only one hour a day. Many of the residents had exercise addiction like she did.

Since they were in the Rocky Mountains, they could go on short hikes and bike rides. Gorgeous trees and flowers surrounded the winding trails. However, even the outdoor options lasted only an hour.

Thankfully, she could indulge in archery, meditation, poetry writing, cooking, horse-back riding, dancing, and drumming classes to fill in the day.

Olivia finally decided to stop resisting and completely immersed herself into following the rules.

***

Time flew by quickly. The six weeks helped to turn her life around, and Olivia realized how much abuse her body had taken throughout the years. The counseling sessions brought out how many of the issues she had with herself were a result of trying to be perfect for her mother and men. The program, although tough, saved her life the same way it did for many others.

By the time graduation from the program took place, she and several of the women had become close friends. They promised to keep in touch with each other for support.

Olivia finally achieved wellness spiritually, emotionally, mentally, and physically. She was proud of her accomplishments and vowed to help other women with eating disorders as soon as she returned to San Antonio.

CHAPTER 23

Beads of sweat poured from Olivia's pores. Her sneakered feet pounded on the treadmill for forty-five minutes. She tapped on the button to slow to a walking pace and lowered the elevation to zero percent. She reached for her towel to wipe her face before taking a big swig from her water bottle.

Bobbing her head to the music playing in her Walkman headphones, she started singing the song, 1999, along with the musical genius, Prince. This cassette tape had to be her favorite, and she listened to it every chance she could. She planned to buy concert tickets to see him perform on New Year's Eve to celebrate going from the year 1999 to 2000.

Everyone got overly anxious about what might happen with Y2K. Rumors of havoc in computer systems around the world had people in a frenzy. Olivia knew she wanted to party her way into the New Year no matter what occurred.

Olivia brought the treadmill to a complete stop. She pressed the cassette button to turn the Walkman off. After taking the headphones from her ears and putting them around her neck, she got off the machine and wiped her sweat from the equipment with her towel.

Her body welcomed being back in the gym after missing her usual rigorous workout for ten weeks. Olivia never thought she could survive without getting her exercise in twice a day. After finishing the month and a half at Mountain River Resort for her issues with bulimia, she realized she didn't have to work out multiple times daily. Her goal of sticking with a reasonable exercise program was a serious process, and she planned to succeed.

The sound of weights clanging filled the gym with people making efforts to stay or get into shape. She walked away from the treadmill and recovered from running by stretching her muscles.

Olivia moseyed to the free weights area to do strength training since she realized she had fifteen additional minutes to exercise. She stood in front of the mirror and started doing bicep curls with twenty-pound weights in each hand. She glanced behind her and became aware of a guy sitting on a weight bench watching her. He quickly shifted his eyes away when he realized she'd spotted him checking her out.

Olivia chuckled to herself and considered how the extra pounds she put on during her weeks away from the gym, seemed good on her. Her butt was now shapely and round instead of flat. She didn't mind having some cushion back there now. Her purple and white workout pants and matching sports bra showed off her new curves. Certainly, this guy must have noticed.

After she finished with her set, Olivia decided to flirt since this man couldn't seem to stop sneaking peeks at her. She strutted toward him with her newly found confidence. He prepared to lift what appeared to be an impossible amount of weight on the bench press. "Do you need a spotter?" she asked, leaning above him with a big smile.

He sat up on the bench with a flirtatious smirk. He raked his fingers through his wavy, red hair to move back a few curls, which fell over his left eye. Gorgeous, clear green eyes sparkled when they locked with hers.

The faint smell of a musky cologne mixed in with his sweat pleased her nostrils. *Now how can someone smell this good while working out?* Moisture glistened on his massive chest. The San Antonio Spurs, Tim Duncan jersey, could barely contain his muscles.

Her eyes zoomed in on his powerfully rippled thighs covered with well fitted, black shorts. She swooned at the thought of them intertwined with hers.

"I think I'll be okay without a spotter today. Thank you for asking." He smiled and laid back on the bench.

"Okay, let me know if you need some help lifting it off your chest when you can't do it on your own," Olivia chuckled and headed back to her weights. She made sure to switch her hips when she walked away in case he watched.

Sure enough, she glanced in the mirror and noticed him lift his head to see her behind. She turned around and winked at him. He smiled and puffed his chest before raising the weights effortlessly to do ten reps of bench presses with what had to be over 300 pounds.

He dropped the weights back into position on the rest, raised himself on the seat with a red face, and caught his breath. Olivia admired his strength and noticed how his muscles bulged even more with veins popping out underneath his skin.

Olivia grabbed her dumbbells to complete another set. The reflection in the mirror of the redhead guy coming her way made her pause. She began curling the weights one arm at a time, purposefully ignoring him.

"I thought I would offer you the same help. Need a spotter?" He flashed his ten-million-dollar smile, from his finely chiseled face, with a twinkle in his eyes.

"Nope. I got this. Thanks," Olivia replied and slowly

continued with her set.

Olivia placed the weights on a rack and noticed he did not go back to his bench. He stood close enough for her to smell his cologne again. Smiling, she turned around and smoothed away a wisp of hair from her forehead.

He extended his gloved hand to her. "I'm Ross O'Neill. I hope you don't mind giving me your name. I figured I could at least introduce myself to you since you offered to help me if I needed it."

Olivia laughed and shook his hand. "Well, Ross, my name is Olivia, and it's nice to meet you. You probably don't use a spotter much. I thought I'd get a good laugh if you said yes. You seem to be impressively strong lifting those weights."

Ross blushed. "I guess you can say I like to challenge myself. Seeing a pretty woman energizes me. Thank you for checking on me." Ross's focus on Olivia made her heart skip a beat. A look of pure mischief crossed his face.

"Oh, there's a pretty woman somewhere?" Olivia joked and looked around her to see who he could be referring to.

"Standing right here in front of me. You're absolutely gorgeous." Ross studied her from top to bottom, which made her cheeks hot.

"Me? After working out? You're full of it," Olivia said in disbelief.

"No. I mean it. I know you must hear that all the time," Ross said.

"No, I don't, but, thank you, I guess," Olivia said and batted her eyelashes.

"Olivia, I'd like to get to know you better. Would you mind joining me at the smoothie shop next door? I apologize if I sound too forward." Ross smiled.

His invitation caught Olivia by surprise especially with her hair sweated out.

"Well, sure. A smoothie sounds quite refreshing. Let me shower in the locker room, and I'll meet you next door in about thirty minutes. Does that work for you?"

His face beamed with a smile and his dimples showed again. "Perfect. I'll meet you in the lobby, and we'll walk there together. See you in a few." Olivia peeked at his muscular butt strutting away to the men's locker room, which caused her to let out a loud sigh.

She headed to the shower. She'd never been attracted to white guys, but this man had her body doing all kinds of strange things. She smiled at her attraction to him. Perhaps Ross was the answer to her prayers for a husband who would give her light-skinned babies.

CHAPTER 24

Savvy nervously pressed the buttons for the phone number listed in the newspaper article. She wasn't sure how this call would turn out. She had to see what might happen.

After two rings, a receptionist answered the phone, "Dr. Olivia Maxwell's office. This is Malia. How may I help you?"

"Hello, Malia. May I please speak to Dr. Maxwell? I am an old college friend of hers and would like to surprise her if she is available," Savvy said. She paced the floor, nervous about what the receptionist would say.

"Sure, no problem. I will patch you through to her phone line. You called at a good time. She has seen her last patient for the day. Please hold."

Savvy took a deep breath. *I wonder if she will even remember me after all of this time.* A familiar voice said, "Hello, this is Dr. Maxwell."

"Yes, hello Dr. Maxwell," Savvy said formally. "My name is Savannah. Is this a good time to speak with you?" She held her breath waiting for a response.

"Savannah?" Olivia paused. "Do you mean Savannah like Savvy? Savvy Menefee?

"Yes, Olivia. It's me, Savvy," Savvy exhaled and replied.

Olivia screamed in joy, which made Savvy pull her ear from the phone.

"Oh Savvy. It's good to hear your voice. Where have you been? I missed you. Can you believe it's been more than ten years? Where are you? What are you doing now?" The words spilled out of her mouth into the phone in a flurry of excitement.

"Olivia, slow down, slow down. I can barely catch what you're saying," Savvy laughed. "I'm glad I found you."

"You don't know how much it means to me to hear from you. I thought you'd never have anything to do with me again. I've been too ashamed to call you even after all of these years," Olivia said. "How did you find me?"

"Yeah, it's crazy how time passed us by. I happened to read an article you wrote in the newspaper about eating disorders. I called the phone number listed and found you," Savvy explained. "I see you're Dr. Olivia C. Maxwell now."

"Yes. Can you believe it? I finally did what I always wanted to do in my life and became a psychologist. I relocated to San Antonio after I finished my residency program. What about you? Where are you now?" Olivia asked.

"You won't believe this, but I transferred to San Antonio two months ago," Savvy said. "I didn't even know you were living here until I read the article."

"No way," Olivia responded in glee. "We landed in the same city. We must get together right away because we have a lot to talk about. I want you to tell me all about your life. Are you married yet? Kids? I still can't believe I'm hearing your voice and you live right here in San Antonio."

"Girl, please. Not married and no kids. What about you?"

"Absolutely not. I don't know who would even want to marry someone like me," Olivia said, the excitement leaving her voice.

"Whatever. Our dating life is obviously a topic we need to

have over drinks. Let's meet tonight. Do you want to go to Happy Hour somewhere?" Savvy asked.

"Yes. Have you been to Swampyfood Café yet? They have this drink called a Swampy Cane, delicious crawfish and a cheese fondue that is hands-down, the best in town. This restaurant is the spot to go if you like seafood," Olivia suggested. "I just looked over the calendar, and my schedule is clear. Let's meet there at 4:30. Sound good?"

"Perfect. I've been wanting to go there," Savvy responded with joy. "I can't wait to see you, Olivia."

"You completely made my day, Savvy. I'll see you in a few."

Savvy hung up the phone with a smile.

Around 4:15, Savvy pulled her red BMW into the restaurant parking lot. When she parked her car, she noticed someone backing a beautiful, white Mercedes Benz SL class convertible into the space next to her. The car had a license tag with "DR OCM" on it.

The door opened, and Savvy gasped to see Olivia stride out in purple, 3-inch heeled, pumps, an elegant purple Chanel suit, and carrying a purple Louis Vuitton Monogram Vernis bag. Her neat bun at the top of her head gave her a sophisticated, supermodel appearance. She wore an elegant pair of Tiffany sunglasses which set the whole outfit off. She seemed much healthier than their college years. Savvy hurried to turn off the ignition and hop out of the car.

"Olivia," she squealed and ran to her.

"Savvy," Olivia shouted. They embraced each other in tight hugs with tears spilling from their eyes.

Savvy pulled back and examined her friend. "Oh, my goodness, Olivia. You're still gorgeous and absolutely amazing."

"You can't be old enough to go to Happy Hour. I swear, I can't tell you've aged any since college. Halle Berry must be your twin with your haircut. You're wearing that spunky short style even better than she does." Olivia admired. "Come on, let's go inside and get a seat."

Many young urban professionals packed in the restaurant to start their weekend with drinks. The festive New Orleans décor and lively zydeco music filling the air set the atmosphere for a good time.

Olivia and Savvy pressed their way through the crowded bar and grabbed a table outside in the courtyard where they enjoyed their beverages and shared appetizers.

"You have to tell me, how's the dating scene here?" Savvy questioned and took a big dip of the gooey cheese fondue with her piece of bread. She had to stretch it high to get it out of the dish.

"Well," Olivia said before slurping the last part of her Swampy Cane drink. She waved for the server to bring two more to the table. "It hasn't been all that great for me since I've been busy with work. But, I did start dating this guy I met a few weeks ago at the gym."

"Oh, do tell. Give me details. Details," Savvy exclaimed.

"Well, his name is Ross. He has amazing wavy, long red hair, green eyes, dimples, and is built like the Incredible Hulk." Olivia's face beamed from thinking about him.

"No way. Wait a minute. Red hair? Are you telling me he's white?" Savvy asked.

"Yup. He's an Irish man. I never would've thought I would date anyone other than a black man," Olivia laughed. "But, here in San Antonio, a lot of them completely ignore me. I realized I had to open my mind to other dating opportunities. I'm glad I did. Ross is amazing. Not to mention the fact that if I marry him, I will have good-looking, light-skinned babies instead of them being dark like me."

"Excuse me? I know you didn't say that. I don't understand why you still have such a complex with being dark-skinned. You're gorgeous. You need to stop thinking you're unattractive since you're not lighter. Why do you continue to feel this way after all of these years?" Savvy questioned.

"As you know, it's one of those things my mother scarred me with since I'm the only one who is not light-skinned in my family. Remember when I told you I wondered if she had an affair with a dark-skinned man who could be my biological father? I still think I must have been adopted. Humph, wouldn't that be something?" Olivia pondered and mixed the drink with her straw.

"It's too bad your mom made you feel that way. Please stop letting your skin color make you feel unworthy of love," Savvy pleaded.

"I know. I need to get over it," Olivia agreed.

"Well, I'm glad you've found someone, regardless of his color. The main thing is for him to treat you like the queen you are," Savvy said.

"That's right," Olivia chimed in.

"I hope I find someone soon. I'm more than ready to get married. We're not getting any younger you know. Not to mention I want someone I can at least go out with on dates. I'm even thinking about freezing my eggs. I heard it's the best way to make sure I can have a baby later if I don't get married in time."

"I hear ya. A lot of white women have been freezing their eggs for years, and black women are now figuring this whole idea out. That's not for me though. To tell the truth, I don't even know if I want to have kids. They stretch your body out and make it sag where it shouldn't." Olivia munched on a piece of fried crawfish.

"At least there's an option for women who genuinely want to be a mom," Savvy responded and took a sip of her drink.

"Well, instead of going that route, maybe Ross has a few of his friends he can introduce to you. They're all bodybuilders if it's okay with you."

"Uh, yeah. Fine, muscular bodies? Yeah. Hook me up," Savvy exclaimed. "What kind of work does Ross do?"

"He's a professional bodybuilder and owns the smoothie shop that's attached to the gym," Olivia said. "That's actually where he suggested we go after we met. We got to know each other and hit it off right away. I had no idea the place belonged to him."

"A bodybuilder? Wow. I know he must be completely healthy with that kind of background." Savvy took another bite of bread dipped in the fondue.

"The only downside is he has to travel a lot," Olivia whined. "He goes to other cities for bodybuilding competitions and to train some guys. There are weeks when he's gone four to five days. I want to go with him sometimes. He said it's crazy busy when he goes on these trips, and he'll find time for me to join him eventually. On top of that, I can't be away from my job right now with all of the new clients I've picked up."

"I hope to meet him one of these days when he's in town. It sounds like he loves his work," Savvy said. "By the way, are you modeling now? If not, you should be. You look amazing and healthy."

"Thank you, Savvy. I feel great now. Did you notice I have a booty?" Olivia stood to pose and stick her butt out to the side before sitting down.

"I see it. Girl, you're too funny," Savvy laughed.

"I do need to tell you, though, I checked myself into a facility for people with eating disorders," Olivia confided in her.

"It's the best thing I could've done for myself. You were right about me being bulimic when you asked me about my weight loss all those years ago. I experimented with laxatives, enemas, bingeing, purging, and exercise addiction on and off for ten years. I denied the existence of my problem, and you saw right through me."

"Oh, Olivia. I'm glad you finally got help and are much better now. You scared me with the way you lost weight to the extreme," Savvy said.

"Yeah, I had no idea how bad it had gotten until I landed in the hospital. I can't believe I started abusing my body entirely to be perfect for Dwain. Stupid."

"Whatever happened to him anyway?"

"He got that girl Isabella pregnant and dumped her. I heard he injured his knee playing football. Remember all the talk about the possibility of him winning the Heisman Trophy award? Well, he didn't get it. You know that news made me happy." Olivia laughed and clapped her hands together.

"Good. That's what they both get for doing you wrong."

"Right, let's toast to that." They raised their drinks and clinked them together to celebrate.

"I know your parents must be proud of you for becoming *Dr.* Olivia C. Maxwell," Savvy said, her voice filled with pride.

"You would never know it since they didn't even come to any of my graduations," Olivia said, her mood turning sour as she set the glass back on the table.

"Uh-uh. They didn't come to celebrate your Doctorate degree?" Savvy couldn't believe her ears.

"Not my undergraduate, Master, or Doctorate degrees. My mom said she couldn't leave her six cats behind and doesn't trust anyone else with them," Olivia said bitterly. "Yet, they attended my sister's graduation from cosmetology school. I've been talking to Dad more only since he thought I would die in the hospital. Isn't that something?"

"Wow. Well, let's perk ourselves up with another drink and move on to another topic," Savvy suggested. "Have you found a good church here? I need to get connected soon instead of hopping all around the city."

"Girl, come with me to Redeemed Saints Baptist Church, and you will love it. It's a Bible teaching church, which focuses on ministry, magnification, maturity, missions, and membership. Everyone is friendly, and they welcome you with open arms. The pastor is an excellent preacher and gives an awesome message."

"You sound like a commercial. I can tell you love it there. That's what I need. I'll go with you this Sunday. I can't wait to visit. I think I heard your Pastor on the radio and he's a great teacher. I enjoyed his sense of humor, and he can sing, too."

"Well good. You can meet me there at 8 am for Sunday School, and we will attend the service at 9:30. You're going to love it."

"All right, in addition, I need your list for doctors, hairdresser, dentist, etcetera. You know how it is when you move somewhere and have to get these things lined up."

"You have to go see my girl KareKare at Irie 6. She'll make your hair absolutely gorgeous. Also, Dr. J.B. is the best dentist in town. He has an art gallery attached to his office on the east side of San Antonio. You'll love him. If you need an attorney, I'll give you his wife's information too. I'll email you with my list of everything."

"Thank you. I need to get my hair done sooner than later." Savvy patted the side of her head.

"Girl, please. It looks like you recently left the hair shop," Olivia exclaimed.

"You're too kind. I have to keep pressing my new growth with my flat iron to make it lie smoothly." Savvy ran her hand along the edges. "Hey, back to talking about school stuff. I still can't believe it's been ten years since we've talked. I'm glad we are able to reconnect and start over." Savvy said.

"I can't blame you for never accepting my calls. I stopped trying when you hung up on me. Man, you were mad. Girl, you can hold a grudge," Olivia exclaimed.

"Well, we can let bygones be bygones. We have grown up quite a bit since then."

"Yes, we most definitely have. I would like to beg for your forgiveness in person right now." Olivia pleaded with her eyes. "Savvy, please forgive me for pulling you into my mess. I have missed our friendship dearly. I pray we can put all of that behind us."

"Of course, I forgive you. Remember, I'm the one who called you." Savvy laughed. "We're good and can move on now."

"Thank you. It feels good to have that wall torn down between us." Olivia said.

"Okay, since you brought up those crazy days, did you ever get in any trouble for what you did to Dwain and Isabella's car?"

"Girl, naw. Even if they suspected me, they never even approached me with that nonsense," Olivia laughed. "As it turned out, I got in trouble for something stupid that probably saved me from getting arrested at some point."

"What did you do?"

"Well, you know I had sticky fingers, like when I stole that swimsuit. By the way, I'm still sorry I did that to you, and I can understand why you were mad at me. I started stealing stuff in elementary school to get affection from my mother. She would always give me praise when I gave her the things I took." Olivia shook her head.

"What a shame to have a child steal for attention," Savvy exclaimed.

"Anyway, I had a paper due and went to the library to find an article I needed for my report. I had to rush and didn't have any money on me to make a copy on the Xerox machine. I figured I could tear the page out of the magazine, stick it in my bag, and finish working on it at home. Girl, you won't believe what happened. The metal detector alarm buzzed when I walked through the library door. Evidently, the section I ripped out had a sensor attached."

"You have got to be kidding me. What happened?"

"Can you believe they sent the campus security and I had to go before a court of my peers? They sentenced me to two hundred hours of community service. I had to clean up trash on the side of the highway, and other students would drive by me and laugh. Hence, the reason I've never stolen anything ever again," Olivia confessed.

"That's what you get. I wish I could've seen you out there cleaning the streets. I would've driven by honking my horn and laughing too." Savvy giggled until her side hurt. "What a funny story and a great payback for stressing me out when you stole that swimsuit."

"Yes, I had to straighten up and fly right," Olivia chuckled. "Enough about me. What about you? What have you been doing since college?"

"One of the companies I interned with, hired me on to work in their Marketing department in Des Moines, Iowa. I know you're probably wondering if there are black people in Iowa. There are more than most people realize. I finally pledged in the Des Moines Alumnae Chapter of Delta Sigma Theta Sorority.

My life-long dream." Savvy exclaimed.

"I'm jealous. I never did pledge, and I don't know when I will ever have the time. The Deltas are very active in San Antonio. I can introduce you to some of the ladies I know." Olivia offered. "So how did you end up in the Alamo City?"

"I transferred for warmer weather, a more diverse culture, and a promotion I couldn't refuse. I received a nice bump in my salary and a great position within the company."

"How awesome. You deserve it Savvy. Cheers to you," Olivia said, clinking her glass against Savvy's to toast. "I'm blessed to have you in the same city. We're going to have a ton of fun together here. You'll love it. I've got to introduce you to Da Crew."

"Who is Da Crew?" Savvy asked.

"Girl, they are the coolest people in San Antonio. Until I met Ross, I think we partied almost every night. I don't know how we made it to work each day since we were kickin' it hard," Olivia laughed. "It's a group of ladies and guys who love to have a good time. We're like brothers and sisters without any drama. We party, travel, laugh, cry, celebrate, you name it. I can't wait for you to meet everyone."

Savvy laughed. "They sound like what I'm looking for. Good people to get together with for fun."

"Let me make a few phone calls and see what's going on this weekend. Maybe we can all meet for drinks tomorrow night. I'm waiting to hear back from Ross about getting together tonight."

"Sounds good to me," Savvy exclaimed and clapped her hands in joy.

Olivia's phone buzzed, and she fished it out of her purse. "Hey, babe. Let me call you back in a few minutes. I met with a dear college friend of mine for drinks, and we're finishing now," Olivia said and smiled at Savvy. "Okay, talk to you in a few.

Bye."

"Sounds like you talked your man up," Savvy teased and finished her drink. "Olivia, seeing you has made my day. I missed our friendship. We had the best fun in college despite the crazy times together. You had a way of making me live my life to the fullest. I'm glad I found you."

"Me too. I'm happier than a kid on Christmas morning. I promise you, I'm in a much better place in my life, and I won't pull you into any shenanigans anymore. Girl Scout Promise." Olivia held three fingers of her right hand in the air with her thumb holding the pinky.

"You better not." Savvy wagged her finger at Olivia with a stern look.

Olivia laughed and signaled the server for their bill. "I'll call you tomorrow and let you know what the plan is with Da Crew. Come on, let's head out and I can go see my man."

Olivia insisted on paying for everything to treat Savvy. They strolled out of the restaurant to the parking lot to hug goodbye. "Have a good time with Ross, but not too much fun, if you know what I mean." They giggled and got into their cars.

Savvy blew a kiss at Olivia and drove away, savoring their wonderful reunion.

CHAPTER 25

Olivia parked in her garage and ran into the house to turn on the oven. She couldn't wait to see her man. She changed out of her suit into daisy duke shorts and a white t-shirt before calling Ross.

"Hey, baby, it's me. Sorry I couldn't call you back immediately. One of my friends from college lives in San Antonio now. We met at Swampyfood Café for drinks. We haven't seen each other in forever."

"Hey, that's great babe," Ross purred into the phone. "I've been thinking about you all day."

Olivia giggled. "And I've been thinking about you too. I can't wait to see you tonight."

"Yeah, hey, about that," Ross said.

"Dinner is going to be tasty. I'm making your favorite dishes. I also picked out a wine rated a score of 94 out of 100 by the wine critics, so you know it will be good. The meat has been marinating all night, potatoes are chopped, and we will have a medley of scrumptious vegetables. I only need to pop all of it in the oven. What time are you coming over?"

"Babe, um, unfortunately, my plans have changed," Ross said hesitantly.

"Changed? What happened?"

"Well, you know I have to go to Corpus Christi tomorrow to help out with the bodybuilding competition. One of the guys

I've been training is struggling with a major category he'll be competing in. He needs me to come tonight to help him out with his prep. I'm already on the road heading south on I-37 to get there," Ross explained.

"You've got to be kidding me, right?" Olivia exclaimed. "I thought we were going to have some time together. You promised you would be here which is why I worked hard to plan this dinner for you."

"I know, I know. I'm sorry I don't have any other choice. This guy will lose this competition if I don't help him."

Olivia groaned loudly and walked downstairs from her bedroom to the kitchen to cut the oven off.

"I know you're disappointed and I promise, I'll make this right for you," Ross pleaded.

"Yeah, whatever," Olivia said dryly. "When are you coming back?"

"On Tuesday or Wednesday. I figured I would stay there and work with some of the other guys to get them ready for the next one in the Valley. Afterward, I'm all yours," Ross said.

"That's almost a whole week. You know we're supposed to go to a show at the Carver Cultural Theater on Sunday night. I already bought the tickets," Olivia said, not bothering to hide her anger.

"This Sunday? Oh, babe. I'm sorry I totally forgot. I thought the show wasn't until next week. Again, I'll make all of this up to you. I promise."

Same old sorry excuse. "You say that all the time Ross. I can't ever plan anything for us to do since you always cancel on me. What's going on with you for real?"

"Did you just ask me that?" Ross asked, anger rising in his voice. "I'm out here trying to do my job is what's going on. What are you accusing me of Olivia?"

"Ross, I'm trying to figure out why it is you always cancel our plans. In some cases, you've stood me up and left me sitting in restaurants or at home by myself," Olivia said, her voice shaking now.

He seemed to calm down. "I know, and I'm sorry, babe. Stuff happens. I get a little caught up in helping everyone else sometimes. I admit I don't manage my time well. Be patient with me, and I promise you, things will change for the better."

"Fine, Ross. Call me when you get to Corpus to let me know you made it there safely."

"I will, babe. I'll call you once I get there. I love you."

"Yeah, okay. Love you, too." Olivia snapped her cell phone closed.

She clenched her fists until her nails hurt her palms. She didn't want to be a possessive girlfriend, but something didn't feel right. Olivia breathed in deeply and slowly exhaled out of frustration. She scanned the kitchen and considered calling Savvy to invite her to come by to eat, so all this food didn't go to waste. After stewing in anger, she decided she didn't want any company.

I need to get out of this house before I lose my mind.

Olivia slipped on her sneakers, stuffed her cell phone into her pocket, grabbed her keys and wallet, and headed outside. Her house was in a beautiful, historic part of downtown San Antonio. It was an easy walk to the famous Riverwalk. Maybe she could clear her head with some exercise and people watching.

The night air felt warm, yet comfortable for walking the short distance. She reflected on her relationship with Ross. It had really changed. He used to be attentive when they first met and could barely stay away from her. He spent almost every night at her house. Now she barely saw him.

Recently, he started traveling more. At first, he left for a day or two, which increased to three or four. Now, there were times where Ross had to be gone for an entire week.

When she reached the Riverwalk, the sights and sounds refreshed her. Colorful awnings and lights attracted people to the area along with the many shops and eating establishments.

Surprised to hear her stomach growl, she began looking at menus posted in front of restaurants along the way. The smell of a blend of seasonings filled her nostrils and made her mouth water. Upon seeing one of the many Mexican eateries, she decided to stop in to get a bite to eat. Olivia grabbed a seat at the dimly lit, crowded u-shaped bar, which faced the dining side.

"Hola. What can I get for you, *Señorita?*" the bartender asked, placing a cocktail napkin on the bar. He slid a basket of tortilla chips with salsa in front of her.

"Hola, mi amigo. I'll have a top shelf margarita on the rocks without salt on the rim. Can you also bring me a menu? I'd like to order dinner." The bartender nodded and began to make her drink.

The freshly made warm tortilla chips were delicious with the chunky salsa. She munched on one after another, watching the bartender artfully make her drink. After shaking the stainless-steel shaker in one hand above his head, he placed a beautiful, painted margarita glass on the bar in front of her and filled it to the rim. She smiled in approval and carefully raised the glass to her lips for a refreshing sip. *Ahh. Just what I need to forget about Ross for now.*

Her eyes focused on a guy sitting at a table with a woman, a kid, and a baby. Olivia did a double take and stared after realizing he had long red hair like Ross. He also had the same body build, which was too much of a coincidence. She squinted, trying to see his face, yet could only see the back of his head.

Wondering if this man was Ross made her stomach queasy. The way he shook his head when he laughed even reminded her of him. The boy at the table had red hair like Ross. The dim lighting in the room kept Olivia from being able to make out the face of the woman.

"Of course, it can't be Ross. He's on his way to Corpus Christi. Quit letting your mind play games on you," Olivia mumbled and slowly placed her drink on the bar. The person next to her gave her a strange look. "Oh, sorry. I'm talking to myself," she apologized.

The guy with the family reached into his back pocket to pull out his wallet and pay for their meal. Olivia held her breath in anticipation of when he stood up. *Turn around so I can see your face.* The woman gathered their leftover containers and held the boy by the hand. The man put the baby in a stroller. Olivia stared at them until they left the restaurant.

She exhaled, realizing she stopped breathing and became dizzy.

"It can't be Ross. He definitely doesn't have kids. I'm sure of it," she said aloud before noticing the stare from the person next to her again. "What? You know you talk to yourself, too."

The knots in her stomach eased, and Olivia laughed at herself. *How can I possibly think Ross could've been sitting with a family in a restaurant when he's on the road to Corpus Christi? That's crazy. I have to learn to trust my man better than this.*

Olivia realized she'd never ordered her dinner and no longer had an appetite to eat anymore. She paid for her drink, tipped the bartender, and started walking back to her house.

She flipped open her cell phone to see if she'd missed any calls from Ross. It had been about three hours since they had spoken, and he should be in Corpus Christi by now.

When Olivia got home, she checked the volume on her

phone to ensure it was at the highest level possible. She walked upstairs to her bedroom, disappointed.

"I'm being silly," she mumbled and removed her orange nightgown out of the dresser drawer. She grabbed the remote from the nightstand to turn on the TV and found a marathon of old episodes of "Good Times" to watch. The soft sheets and comforter welcomed her when she slid in and pulled them to her chin. Before she knew it, she woke to sunlight streaming through her window.

"Ugh. I can't believe it's morning already," she moaned and rolled out of bed, smoothing her tousled hair from her face. She checked her cell phone to see what time Ross called last night.

No call.

She checked her landline answering machine.

No messages.

Olivia punched in Ross's number and got his voicemail. She ended the call and carefully punched in the number a second time.

"Hey. This is Ross. After the beep, you know what to do. Chao." Olivia frowned upon hearing his message. "Ross, this is Olivia. Baby, where are you? You have me worried. I thought I would hear from you when you got to Corpus Christi last night. Call me right away please."

What if he's been in a car accident? She turned on the TV and watched the news with dread waiting to see if anything was reported.

"Maybe I need to call a few police stations. No. I'm being silly," she reassured herself and paced the room. "I'm sure he's fine and probably forgot to plug in his cell phone last night. I will hear from him. Okay, pull yourself together Olivia, and get to cycling class."

Olivia dug through her dresser drawer to find her black

cycling shorts, lime green sports bra, and socks to wear. She pulled her hair back into a ponytail, slipped on her shoes, and put on her baseball cap. She grabbed her gym bag before leaving the house.

Her stomach growled, reminding her she never ate dinner last night. Thankfully, she had a granola bar in her bag to munch on during her drive to the gym.

There were two bikes left in the packed cycling class. Another woman entered in at the same time, and they rushed to the bikes to make sure no one else beat them. Olivia pulled her hand towel and water bottle from her bag and placed them on the handles to secure it.

"Whew. I'm relieved I made it here in time," the lady said to her.

"Me too. I didn't think there would be any bikes left," Olivia responded and raised the seat for her height.

"I don't know why my kids had to pick this morning to act out. My husband had already left for work, and I had to get the kids together to bring them to the gym. I need this workout to get my nerves back in order," the lady laughed and adjusted her bike.

"Well, this class will definitely do it. I love this instructor," Olivia said. "By the way, my name is Olivia."

The woman stuck her hand out to shake her hand. "I'm Dahlia. Nice to meet you."

Olivia noticed how attractive and fit Dahlia appeared to be. She had smooth ginger brown skin, long black hair, and expressive ebony eyes. *Why does she look vaguely familiar? Probably because she looks exotic like the singer from Prince's group, Vanity 6.*

"I haven't tried this class out yet. I got off maternity leave a few weeks ago and am recently getting back into the gym."

"You've got to be kidding me. You had a baby? I can't

believe that. You don't have an ounce of fat on you," Olivia exclaimed and switched into her biking shoes.

"All I can say is I have good genes," Dahlia laughed. "I often exercised during my pregnancy until time to deliver the baby. I even ran a half marathon in my fifth month."

"No way. Well, I sure hope when I get married and start having children that my body bounces back like yours," Olivia said, watching the instructor come in and turn on C+C Music Factory's song, "Gonna Make You Sweat," to get the class ready for the strenuous workout.

"Are you planning to have a baby anytime soon?" Dahlia asked.

"Girl, no. I have a new boyfriend I started dating a few months ago. We've been thinking about getting married. I doubt it will be anytime soon," Olivia said.

"Well, you never know. He may ask you sooner than you think. My husband and I celebrated our fifth-anniversary last month. I became pregnant on our honeymoon. We met here at the gym when I traveled to town for a conference and decided to sneak in a quick workout. The chemistry felt strong right from the beginning. He proposed within six months after we met."

"What a great love story. I met my boyfriend here at the gym, too. Maybe that's a telltale sign."

"I hope it happens for you. You'll have to keep me posted. The kids and I come here every other week to visit my husband. We have a beach home in Port Aransas, which is about three hours south of here. We have another house in San Antonio so he has a place to live for his job. We rotate weekends for him to come home and for me to bring the kids to visit."

"It sounds like you two have a good system in place. It's important to spend time together." Olivia's mind drifted to

Ross. *Umm. It would be nice if Ross and I had time with each other again.*

"I agree. We arrived in town yesterday and had a nice night out on the Riverwalk. Unfortunately, I have to leave tomorrow with the kids since my son has karate lessons in Port Aransas. It's not convenient. However, we make it work," Dahlia said.

The instructor got on her bike and started speaking into a head mic to start the class. "Well, here we go with this monster workout. It's nice to meet you. We should exchange numbers to keep in touch and get together sometime," Dahlia suggested.

"Good idea. Let's do that after class," Olivia said and tilted forward on her bike to begin to ride. At least the class would get her mind off Ross for an hour. Surely, there would be a missed call from him when the class ended.

CHAPTER 26

"I wonder what my girl is up to tonight?" Savvy asked herself and grabbed the phone to dial Olivia's number.

Olivia answered on the first ring sounding anxious. "Hello?"

"Hey, girl. Why do you sound stressed?" Savvy asked.

"Oh, hey, Savvy," Olivia sighed.

"Well, that's no way to greet your best friend," Savvy teased.

"I'm sorry. I thought I would get a call from Ross," Olivia apologized. "I haven't heard from him since he got on the road going to Corpus Christi. I'm worried about him."

"When did he leave? Didn't the two of you get together last night after we met for Happy Hour?" Savvy asked.

"No, girl," Olivia brooded. "He called and said he had to go to Corpus instead to help some guy who he's been training. Evidently, he needed his help to get ready for this big competition today. He does this all the time. Not to mention he won't be back until Tuesday or Wednesday. I bought tickets for us to attend a show at the Carver Cultural Theater tomorrow."

"Oh no, Olivia," Savvy exclaimed. "I'm sorry you're having to deal with this craziness. I'm sure he has a good excuse for not calling. Maybe he got super busy with helping the bodybuilder. Perhaps he had to focus on the competition today. You'll probably hear from him soon."

"I sure hope so. You know the crazy thing is, I walked on the Riverwalk last night to clear my head, and I spotted a guy who resembled Ross with a woman and two kids. Now you know my mind is playing tricks on me," Olivia snickered.

"You've got to be kidding me," Savvy laughed. "Too many Swampy Canes from Happy Hour had your brain swimming."

"Right. I said the same thing. I've got to stop worrying about him like this. He makes it hard not to when he doesn't call me or changes plans at the last minute."

"Wait a minute. Are you saying he's done this before?" Savvy questioned.

"Yeah, he has. It's weird with the timing. It always seems to happen on the weekends. He spends several days with me during the week and poof, he disappears," Olivia responded.

"Oooh, Olivia, this doesn't sound too good. Have you gone to his house to check out if his car is there? In case he didn't get on the road, he might be home."

"No, I didn't want to turn into a stalker girlfriend. Plus, I'm embarrassed to admit, I've never been to his house. I don't even know where he lives," Olivia said reluctantly.

"What? How could you not know where he lives after dating him for this long?" Savvy scolded.

"I know, it sounds strange. He told me he's ashamed of his bachelor pad. Evidently, it's tiny, and he's the worst when it comes to cleaning. Ross claims he has this massive collection of comic books, workout stuff, and dirty laundry everywhere and it's no place for us to hang out. I even offered to help him clean up. I guess he's afraid I might accidentally trample his treasured comic book collection or something," Olivia explained.

"That has to be the biggest crock of lies I've ever heard," Savvy exclaimed. "He doesn't want you to come over? So, he always has to go to your place? Olivia, it sounds like he has something to hide."

"You think so?" Olivia asked, trying not to sound pissed off. "I don't know why he would need to lie to me. We have such a great relationship, other than his disappearing acts. I mean, when we're together, the chemistry is strong. It's like we can't keep our hands off each other. He treats me like a queen, and we have a lot of fun together."

Savvy breathed in deeply and tried to find a delicate way to say what she had to without pushing her friend away. "Olivia, a queen would never have to worry about where her man is. I don't know Ross yet, however, from what you told me, I don't think he's being on the up and up with you. I used to date a guy who pulled disappearing acts on me. I found out he lived with another woman. I want you to do some investigation to find out if something is going on."

Olivia's voice cracked with emotion. "I hear what you're saying. For my own sanity, I have to believe he wouldn't do anything crazy. But, I'll check it out if I don't hear from him tonight."

Savvy sighed. "Okay, my friend. You know I only want the best for you. Keep me posted on what you find out. In the meantime, speaking of tonight, are we getting together with Da Crew?"

"I'm sorry, Savvy. I've been worried about Ross and totally forgot to reach out to them to find out whassup for tonight. After dealing with this stuff, I don't want to go out."

"No problem. Do you want me to come by and keep you company? I have a great bottle of wine I can bring over. We can chat some more or watch a movie," Savvy offered.

"Naw. I wouldn't be much fun right now."

"Well, how about we meet at your church tomorrow and have brunch afterward? I'll even go to Sunday school with you. We can have a girly day out with mimosas. If you haven't heard from Ross, I'll be your date for the show at the Carver Cultural Theater," Savvy suggested.

"That sounds like a good idea. I'm glad you're coming to visit my church this Sunday. Don't forget, Sunday School starts at 8 am and church at 9:30. We'll have plenty of time to eat." Olivia sounded back to normal. "There's a fabulous brunch at this hotel called La Castle on the Riverwalk. I'll call and make reservations for us there."

"All right. Well, let me know if you have a change of heart and want to get together. Don't sit and sulk all night by yourself waiting on Ross to call you. Promise?"

"Promise. I love you for being such a good friend to me Savvy. You always know exactly what to say."

"I love you too, Olivia. I'll see you in the morning. Good night, my friend. Please get some rest," Savvy said and ended the call.

Savvy shook her head. *Ross is definitely hiding something from Olivia.*

CHAPTER 27

Olivia sighed and looked at the time on the clock. 7:13 pm and she still hadn't heard from Ross. She filled his voice mailbox until it wouldn't receive any new messages.

She decided to get a smoothie at his shop to find out if his employees heard from him.

The setting sun turned the sky violet and orange as she drove into the parking lot. Her headlights shined on someone who looked like Dahlia leaving out of the gym and heading toward the smoothie shop. She carried a baby in one arm and held another child by the hand.

Olivia honked her horn and stuck her hand out the window to wave. Dahlia didn't notice so Olivia decided she'd just talk to her inside the shop.

Olivia found a spot to park a few cars down from the shop. She opened her door and stopped in her tracks when she noticed a red Corvette like Ross's in the back of the lot. It sat in his usual spot.

She tip-toed to the window and peered in. "Why in the world am I acting like a detective?" She mumbled.

The shop's bright lights illuminated Dahlia standing at the counter. She chatted with one of the employees. He began making smoothies for her and her son. The little boy's curly, red hair, flopped around on his head as he jumped up and down in anticipation of his drink. Dahlia laughed over his excitement and hugged him while balancing the baby on her hip.

Oh, how sweet. She looks like a wonderful mom. I know I'm crazy standing out here staring in this window. Let me take my butt inside and stop trippin'. Right before she stepped toward the door to go inside, someone else came from the back of the shop and headed to the counter.

He walked to Dahlia, who smiled and closed her eyes before he planted a big kiss on her lips. He took the baby from her arms and rubbed the red-haired boy on his head.

Olivia squinted to see better. Her eyes widened in shock when she realized it was Ross.

If Olivia didn't know better, she would think she had an out of body experience. She clutched her chest, thinking her rapidly beating heart would jump out. *Oh my, God. This can't be happening.* She breathed in deep gulps of air to keep from passing out.

The palms of her hands became sweaty and shook uncontrollably to the point where her keys almost slipped from her fingers. She stumbled away from the store window and ran frantically to her car. Her body trembled excessively. She almost could not open the door to get in and weakly fall into the seat.

Choppy thoughts flooded Olivia's mind when she put everything together. *Ross. And Dahlia. Dahlia said she's married. She's visiting her husband from Port Aransas. Her husband has a house in San Antonio. Dahlia met her husband at the gym. They have kids. A new baby. This is the family I saw at the restaurant. Dahlia said she went to the Riverwalk last night with her family. He's the guy with red hair along with his red-haired kid. It's Ross. It's definitely Ross. He's not in Corpus Christi. He's right here. In San Antonio. With his wife and kids.*

The air didn't fill her lungs fast enough with each breath Olivia tried to breathe. Her head spun wildly. She didn't want to believe what her eyes witnessed.

She gripped the steering wheel until her hands hurt. Nothing could erase the vision of his family.

She closed her eyes to pray it is all a dream fervently. *This has got to be a dreadfully bad nightmare. Wake me up now, God. I know this isn't real.*

She opened her eyes in hopes she imagined everything. She immediately noticed Ross standing in the entryway, bouncing the baby up and down in his massive arms. He used his body to hold the smoothie shop door open for Dahlia and their son to exit. He escorted them to her vehicle and placed the baby in the car seat. After he helped the boy buckle up in the booster seat, he hugged and kissed Dahlia in what seemed like an endless embrace.

Olivia ducked lower in her car to make sure no one could see her. She heard the roar of Dahlia's engine when she started her blue Jaguar before driving away.

What am I going to do? Should I run him over and drive my car through his smoothie shop? Or maybe I should chase her down and tell her about us?

She decided to call him. After dialing his number, she peeked through her window toward Ross. The street light above him helped her see him pull his phone out. He nonchalantly glanced at the screen and slipped it back into his pocket before heading back into the smoothie shop.

Olivia sat in her car in disbelief and anger taking in everything that happened. "What am I supposed to do?" she screamed and pounded the steering wheel with her fists.

How dare he do this to me. I'm going in there to cuss him out. She grabbed the door handle and paused. No. She was not going to act a fool in public. The last thing she needed was for one of her patients to see her going off on Ross like an insane woman.

Olivia turned the ignition and drove to the back of the

parking lot. She backed into a dark space several spots from Ross's car where she had a good view of the shop.

She sat and waited. And waited. And waited. His betrayal left her isolated and alone.

Finally. The employee exited the store, followed by Ross who locked the door. They chatted for a minute and walked separate ways to their cars.

Olivia stared at Ross getting into the Corvette. When he drove out of his parking space, she waited for a second and followed him at a distance. He jumped on Highway 281 and headed north.

Ross exited the highway. Her stomach lurched when she thought he spotted her in his rear-view mirror at one point. She slowed to put more distance in between them and hunched lower in her seat. She could barely see over the steering wheel.

He turned right and drove through town until he reached a well-landscaped subdivision. She followed until he pulled into the driveway of a magnificent two-story brick home. Her stomach turned flips when she saw the blue Jaguar in the driveway.

Queasiness filled Olivia's stomach from seeing Ross pull into the garage. The door seemed to close in slow motion.

She drove around the corner from his house and parked her car. Her nerves made her hands shake, and her breathing became shallow. "I can't believe this," she shouted.

Olivia called Ross's number again. This time, a woman answered. "Hello? Hello?" she paused. "Hello? Is anyone there?"

Olivia almost dropped the phone. She wasn't expecting anyone to answer. Immediately, she recognized Dahlia's voice. "Uh, hello? Who is this?"

Dahlia laughed in a friendly way. "Well, I think you should

tell me who you're looking for since you called this number. Who is this?"

"I'm l-looking for Ross," Olivia stuttered.

"Ross is in the shower. Who should I tell him is calling?" the woman asked.

"I'm a friend of his. I didn't realize he had company in town. Are you his sister?"

"His sister? No, this is his wife. Wait, who did you say you are? Your name only says OM on his phone," Dahlia questioned and began to sound suspicious.

"I'm a friend. I'll call him back. Sorry to disturb you. Bye." Olivia ended the call.

She slumped weakly in her seat and gazed at her phone. The conversation replayed in her head. *How am I supposed to handle this madness? I'm about to lose my mind.*

CHAPTER 28

Savvy picked up the remote and turned the TV to the BET channel to listen to the "Bobby Jones Gospel Show" before getting ready for church. She loved having her praise and worship in the morning to get her mind right for the day.

After putting on her cream-colored, two-inch sandals, she checked herself in the mirror to make sure she appeared suitable for church. The A-line, sleeveless, knee length, peach-colored dress, had a custom-made fit.

She smiled at her reflection and unwrapped the silk scarf from around her head. She carefully fixed each section of her spiky pixie haircut with her fingers. *Watch out Halle Berry, here I come. She ain't the only one looking cute with this hairstyle.*

She grabbed her Bible, Coach purse, and keys, and headed out the door.

The drive to the church was an easy ride north on Interstate 35 to Schertz. She turned into the church parking lot and noticed it appeared to be nearly full for Sunday School. Thankfully, they had spots reserved for first-time visitors. *What a nice touch.*

She walked into the church where a greeter gave her a warm hug and held the door open. "Welcome to Redeemed Saints Baptist Church. We're glad you came to worship with us today."

"Thank you. I'm glad to be here."

176

She scanned around the foyer for Olivia and didn't see her.

Savvy pulled her cell phone from her purse to call Olivia right before spotting her hurrying along the sidewalk. She waved to make sure she could see her when she entered the church.

Olivia appeared disheveled although she dressed impeccably in a sleeveless, fitted, navy blue, St. John's dress with pearl earrings, a matching necklace, and three-inch heeled pumps. She carried a Prada clutch under her arm and removed her sunglasses once she spotted Savvy.

"I'm glad you made it," Olivia exclaimed and embraced her.

"Me, too. I'm looking forward to the service today," Savvy replied and focused on Olivia. "Hey. Are you okay? Fix the front of your hair. A few strands are out of place."

Olivia nonchalantly ran her fingers through her hair and sighed. "Girl, no. I'm not okay. It's a long story. I don't want to interfere with my blessing here in church thinking about it right now. I'll spare you the details until we go to brunch where we can have mimosas and probably something stronger." Olivia shook her head. "Come on, let's go get a seat in Sunday School before it gets too packed. The Deacon who teaches this class is passionate about the Bible, so it fills up fast."

"Yes, sounds like we must discuss this later. Let's go get a Word from the Lord."

Savvy enjoyed Sunday School and the church service to the extent she decided to become a member immediately. Their focus on being a Bible teaching ministry along with the mission to build God's kingdom reassured her to look no further.

After meeting with the Pastor, they headed to the parking lot.

"Why don't we leave your car here, and you can ride with me to the restaurant?" Olivia suggested.

"Sounds good to me," Savvy agreed.

Olivia lowered the convertible top and put on Jill Scott's song, "Golden."

"This is my jam," Savvy exclaimed and began singing along.

"Girl, mine too. Anything Jill Scott puts out is good music. This whole CD is the bomb."

Olivia handed Savvy a bright red scarf to tie on her head to hold her hair in place. She brought out a pink leopard print one to tie on hers.

"How cute," Savvy squealed.

They laughed, and Olivia sped off to head south on Interstate 35 toward downtown.

After valet parking in front of La Castle Hotel, they walked into the restaurant. The amazing spread of food on the buffet delighted Savvy. Her stomach growled with joy from the smell of bacon and freshly baked bread.

The maître d recognized Olivia immediately, and they greeted each other with a kiss on the cheek.

"Hello, Dr. Maxwell. Welcome back to La Castle." He held her hand and smiled.

"Thank you, Javier. This is my dear friend, Savvy, and this is her first visit to the brunch."

"Wonderful, and welcome Miss Savvy. I am sure this will not be your last time dining with us." Javier kissed her cheek. "Shall I escort the two of you to your preferred table?"

"Yes, that would be wonderful," Olivia agreed.

Javier seated them on the patio overlooking the Riverwalk. The morning temperature wasn't too hot for the time being, considering it would be a scorcher by early afternoon. Thankfully, the clouds along with a table umbrella kept them cooler in the San Antonio sun.

"Wow. This place is beautiful. We have the best spot in the restaurant. I love it," Savvy exclaimed.

"Wait until you taste the food. It will melt in your mouth," Olivia said with a smile.

When the waiter served them their first round of mimosas, Olivia asked, "Would you please leave the bottle of bubbly here at the table?"

The waiter laughed. "No problem Dr. Maxwell. Let me get an ice bucket for you. You can wave at me whenever you need a refill."

"Thank you and believe me; you will be pouring a lot," Olivia said. Savvy giggled and took a sip of the cold mimosa made with freshly squeezed orange juice.

"Let's hit the buffet. Once we get our food, you have got to tell me what's been going on." Savvy stood from the table.

"I hope you're ready to get an earful," Olivia said and led the way to the buffet stations.

They didn't waste any time loading their plates with bacon, sausage, grits, fruit, and made-to-order omelets and waffles, before heading back to the table to bless the food.

"Well, I won't keep you waiting any longer. Ross is married," Olivia said flatly and nonchalantly blew on the steaming piece of omelet on her fork.

"No. What? Please say you're kidding Olivia," Savvy exclaimed. "How did you find out?"

Olivia chewed slowly and spoke in between swallows, which appeared to be hard to take. "It's crazy how I found out. I met his wife, Dahlia, at the gym in a cycling class. She's cool, and we even exchanged numbers. She's absolutely striking and had a baby recently. She said they have a home in Port Aransas, and she comes here every other week with her kids to visit her husband. I had no idea her husband would be Ross. I saw them with my own two eyes, at the smoothie shop together with their children. He kissed her," Olivia said sadly.

"Unh-unh. That son of a…that explains why he disappears. This fool is living a double life." Savvy did her best to keep from cursing.

"Yup. And, my mind wasn't playing tricks on me at that restaurant on the Riverwalk. The guy I saw turned out to be Ross, Dahlia, and their kids after all."

"Wow. I can't believe he did this to you and his wife."

"I know. It doesn't seem real. I realize it all makes sense now. Me not being able to go to his house. He lied about traveling to train other bodybuilders and going to competitions. Those were times when he probably visited them in Port Aransas, or they were here in San Antonio," Olivia put her fork on her plate and peered at Savvy with her eyes filling to the brim with tears.

"Oh, Olivia. Please don't cry. I know it hurts bad right now. You're going to be okay." Savvy grabbed her napkin and reached to dab tears from Olivia's cheeks.

"I've been trying to figure out what to do. Should I cuss him out or stomp him in the street? I followed him to his house last night and finally found out where he lives. Dahlia's car sat in front of the house. I even called his cell phone. She answered." Olivia's voice cracked, and the tears began streaking black mascara on her trembling cheeks.

"Hey now, we don't have to discuss it any more right now. This is terrible," Savvy said and reached in her purse for a packet of tissues to hand to Olivia. "Let's get more champagne. Mimosa's ain't gonna cut it at this moment." She motioned for the waiter to come to their table and fill their glasses.

"I'm sorry I'm sitting here blubbering about myself. We're supposed to be enjoying a nice brunch," Olivia said, wiping her face and blowing her nose.

"Girl, don't even apologize. After everything you

experienced, I'm mad you didn't call me last night. I would've come by right away. You wouldn't have had to deal with this by yourself."

"I know, I know. I needed some time to myself to get my head together. I almost didn't make it to church. I'm glad I did since Pastor preached the sermon I needed to hear today."

"Me, too. Well, what are you going to do about Ross now?"

"I don't know. I'm thinking I'll wait and see when he actually calls me. When he does, I'll know that his wife has left town. This will allow me to figure out his pattern. I'm trying to figure out a strategy to slam him with the fact I know what he's doing. Also, I have his wife's phone number. She gave it to me at the gym. I think she deserves a phone call," Olivia said and took a big swig of her champagne.

"You would call her?" Savvy questioned and considered this idea. "You know, sometimes, we women need to stop hiding the truth from each other. Letting her know may be a good idea. She deserves to be made aware of Ross's games. She will at least have the information needed to make her own decisions about what to do with her cheating husband."

"Right. I should call them on three-way and bust him out with her on the line," Olivia exclaimed and clapped her hands.

"Cheers to messing with his game." They raised their glasses in the air, clinked them together, and took another sip.

"Well, enough about this craziness. I'm starving, and my omelet is cold. I'm going back to the chef to get another one. Let's eat up," Olivia said and headed back to the buffet line.

"Sounds good to me." Savvy joined her.

They finished their brunch and decided to walk on the Riverwalk to digest their food. They hung out until time for the matinee show at the Carver.

After the awesome performance, Olivia dropped Savvy off

at her car in the church parking lot. They hugged tightly before letting go. Savvy stared her in the eyes with her hands gripping both of Olivia's shoulders.

"Please, I beg you, don't do anything crazy, Olivia. If you are thinking about revenge, I need you to promise to call me. I will talk you out of doing anything you may regret later. Promise?"

Olivia innocently blinked her eyes several times. "I promise. Don't worry. I won't jump off any ledges. I'm not the same person I used to be in college. I've grown up since then. I love you, Savvy. Thank you for listening to me and being with me today. We'll talk later." Olivia hugged her tightly again, and they parted ways.

CHAPTER 29

Olivia's phone rang on Sunday night at 10:39 pm. The ringing broke her out of her thoughts of plotting revenge against Ross. She snatched it from the table. When she saw his name, she took a deep breath to prepare mentally for his lies.

"Yes," Olivia said without any expression in her voice.

"Hey, baby. I got back to town sooner than I thought. I missed you. I can't wait to get my lips on yours," Ross purred into the phone.

"Why didn't you return my calls?" Olivia asked angrily.

"What? Oh, I dropped my phone, and it malfunctioned all weekend. Also, I got busy with the competition. I had no idea it wasn't working right until a minute before I called you. I didn't mean to make you worry. I'm sorry, baby," Ross explained desperately.

"Are you serious? For three days? You expect me to believe that story?" Olivia cringed.

"Why wouldn't you believe me? You know, you've been trippin' lately. Well, tell you what, let me make it up to you. I'm thinking I can come by tonight to see you."

"Just like that? You think you can disappear all weekend long? Do you really expect me to let you come over? You must think I'm stupid or something," Olivia exclaimed. "Ross, be honest with me. Why didn't you call me this weekend?" She didn't expect him to tell the truth, but a part of her desperately hoped he would.

"I told you what happened to my phone," Ross answered, sounding agitated. "What? You don't believe me? This is no way to treat your man after being apart from each other. Come on, let me see you and I promise, you'll feel better when we're together."

An idea snapped into Olivia's mind. "You know what? I actually have a surprise for you. Let me call you back in about thirty minutes. Okay, baby?" Olivia slathered on a romantic voice for Ross.

"Now, that's what I'm talking about. My girl. Don't make me wait." Ross sounded excited like a kid on Christmas morning.

"Don't worry; I won't make you wait at all. Keep your phone on you," Olivia said in the sexiest voice she could muster and hung up.

Olivia ran from the living room to the kitchen pantry to pull out a garbage bag. She stomped to her bedroom closet and yanked out Ross's favorite San Antonio Spurs jersey, autographed by Tim Duncan. He paid top dollar for it in an auction. She found his expensive, never worn, Jimmy Choo Belgravia leather high top sneakers, and Ferragamo dress shoes and threw them all into the bag. Two of his Tag Heuer watches, along with a bottle of Tom Ford cologne, and his Oakley sunglasses were tossed in. He always took great pride in how he dressed and had expensive taste in everything he put on.

After changing into a black warm-up suit, baseball cap, leather gloves, and tennis shoes, she loaded everything into the trunk of her Mercedes. She found an old wood baseball bat in the garage, which she put into a gym bag and placed it on the back seat. She slid behind the steering wheel, took a deep breath and headed to his house.

Ross just didn't know. He had messed with the wrong woman.

Olivia called Ross once she made the thirty-minute drive into his neighborhood and parked around the corner from his house. She had a view of his driveway even in the dark. "Hey, baby," she cooed into the phone.

"Hey, my love. I'm wondering how much longer you're going to make me wait," Ross said back to her.

"Well, you don't have to wait any longer. I'm ready for you except, I need for you to stop at the wine store to get a bottle of Chandon for us to toast with. You know the Brut Classic I love? Get that one, and hurry to my place for your surprise."

"I'll stop at the store on my way. I can't wait to see you. Girl, I have plans for you," Ross said excitedly.

"Okay, see you soon." Olivia closed her flip phone.

She scooted lower in her Mercedes to spy on Ross's house. She held her breath when he backed his Corvette from the driveway and sped out of the neighborhood. He didn't notice her car parked on the corner.

Olivia turned around in her seat to get the gym bag. She pushed the button on her keychain to pop open the trunk. Her heart jumped around in her chest like it bounced on a trampoline. Contemplating what she planned to do made her hands shake nervously.

Stepping out of the car, her legs were weak like putty, causing her to almost fall. She steadied herself and slung the gym bag on her shoulder. She grabbed the garbage bag with his belongings, from the trunk. She gently closed it to keep from drawing attention to herself.

Olivia glanced around the empty streets of the neighborhood. A light drizzle began to fall, which made the grass sparkle in the dark. The sound of crickets and a barking dog was all she could hear despite the rapid thumps of her heart in the quiet night. She lowered the hat on her head and carried the bags toward Ross's house.

Once she got in front of his home, she put the bags on the ground and trembled as her anger built. Olivia burned inside from Ross's betrayal and lies. Her fury grew from the pain he caused her and the time she wasted on him. The way he used her, left her heart beat up.

He used me to betray his wife and kids. What about all those days and nights we shared together? He did nothing but lie to me about being his beautiful, Black African Queen. I guess it was all an act to make me think he loved my dark skin.

I fell for it all. Ross knew exactly what to say, even down to telling me I tasted like Belgium chocolates. He made a fool of me. Beautiful Dahlia is now the wife of a cheating husband.

These thoughts hit Olivia like a ton of bricks, almost bringing her to her knees.

The drizzle turned into a steady rain and began to pelt her covered head and body. Olivia grabbed the bags and slowly glided to the side of his house. She tried to stay hidden in the shadows. She crept to his back fence, lifted the latch, and pushed against the wet gate, hoping it would open. It creaked and swung inward to let her in. She waited for a second to make sure the neighbors didn't hear anything. Her heart pounded in her chest, and each breath sounded labored from anxiety.

Hearing nothing except for dogs barking in the distance, Olivia ran through the gate and almost slipped on the wet grass. "Whoa," she cried before glancing around to make sure no one heard her. After balancing herself, she laid the two bags on the patio.

The backyard appeared to be well manicured and had several, enormous Live Oak trees, which stretched high to the sky. She squinted in the darkness and could make out a swing set and a slide. "Humph," she said shaking her head at the thought of Ross and his children playing out here.

She tried the doorknob on the back door. Surprisingly, it opened. *Stupid. Some people always leave their homes unlocked. I bet he thinks he can whip anyone trespassing since he's a bodybuilder.*

Olivia picked up the bags and slowly tipped into the house, closing the door behind her. After wiping the rain from her face, she paused, allowing her eyes to adjust to the darkness. She dropped the bags on the floor and stood, dripping wet, in the kitchen, which led to the living room.

The moonlight illuminated the immaculate living room through the front window. The light highlighted pictures of Dahlia, Ross, and their kids on the walls. Tears rolled from Olivia's eyes. *That's supposed to be me in those pictures. Not Dahlia.* A wave of nausea became overwhelming at the thought of what Ross stole from her. She swallowed the lump in her throat to keep from vomiting.

Seeing the family photos snapped Olivia back into the moment at hand, and she realized she needed to act quickly.

Red lights flashed before her eyes when she reached into the gym bag and pulled out the baseball bat. Before she had time to register what she should do, she started swinging the bat wildly and smashed every lamp in the room, one by one. A scream hurled from her mouth, which she did not recognize to be her voice. Glass popped her in the face each time the piece of wood landed on everything in her path.

The crash of glass startled her when the bat landed hard on a coffee table. She repeated the motion and knocked statues off the end tables. The next swing shattered the screen of the television causing sparks to fly. She jumped back in surprise, yet continued, knocking electronic equipment off the shelves attached to the walls.

Broken glass crackled beneath her shoes when she ran to the back of the house into a room, which appeared to be filled with awards and trophies from his competitions. She paused, taking in what had to be some of his most prized possessions.

Raising the bat high above her head and screeching until her lungs hurt, she lowered it hard, smashing every trophy. "How dare you do this to me," she yelled with each swing. "I hate you, Ross. I hate you."

She stopped to catch her breath after wearing herself out from beating them to smithereens. She threw the wooden weapon on the ground and began to grab awards, lift them high in the air and slam them to the ground until they broke apart.

Exhausted and shaken from her emotion, Olivia found the bat where she threw it, and drug it to what appeared to be the master bedroom. She got another surge of energy when she noticed the king-sized bed with a picture of Ross and Dahlia embraced above it. Filled with fury, she let out a tribal yell. She swung like Hank Aaron to shatter the picture frame and knock it off the wall.

A tube of Dahlia's lipstick lay on a dresser. She pulled the cap off and wrote on the mirror, "Ross. Rot in hell," in bright red letters. She didn't recognize her face in the mirror with puffy eyes and specks of blood on her cheeks and forehead from the broken glass.

Olivia turned away from the mirror and stuck the lipstick in her pocket. She ran back to the kitchen where she grabbed the garbage bag. She opened it and removed his Tim Duncan Spurs basketball jersey.

She quickly scanned the room and found a lighter next to a candle on the countertop. She pulled off her gloves, put the lighter in her hand, and flicked it on. She became mesmerized by the flame. Olivia stared at the orange fire dancing before her eyes, and the light hypnotized her until the heat started to burn her thumbnail.

Dangling the shirt in the air, Olivia began to flick the lighter again. Immediately, the shirt started to burn with the flame working its way through the number 21. She could feel the heat on her face, and she heard her evil chuckle. "Burn, baby burn."

Suddenly, she got scared about how fast the fire spread and threw the jersey into the sink. She frantically turned on the faucet to smother the flames, causing white smoke to fill the air. Olivia turned the water off and dried her hands on her pants.

She glanced at the clock. She'd been here thirty minutes. It was time to go.

Olivia's hands trembled when she placed the splintered baseball bat into the gym bag, gathered the garbage bag, and ran out the front door into the rain. The storm matched the dreariness of her heart.

She removed both pairs of his shoes from the garbage bag and hurled them one by one on top of the house. One shoe tumbled off and landed in a thick, thorny, rose bush on the side. The other one stayed on the roof.

Angry tears blended in with the rain, which did not stop her. Olivia pulled out his two watches and slung them on the concrete ground several times until the faces shattered to tiny pieces. She threw the pieces onto the front porch.

She took out his bottle of cologne and screamed when she flung it at the front door. It smashed, and the rain washed away the cologne, which covered the door. She no longer cared if any of his neighbors heard her. At this point, nothing mattered anymore.

She removed the sunglasses from the bag and placed them on the ground. Stomping on them until they were unrecognizable gave her great satisfaction. She tossed them on his porch. The expensive price tags on all his favorite things didn't compare to the priceless love she had given to him.

Olivia dug into her pocket for the red lipstick. She ran to the big picture window on the front of the house and wrote "PLEASE GIVE DAHLIA, YOUR WIFE, MY REGARDS," in big bold letters. She threw the lipstick in the sopping wet grass.

The rain stopped. Her wet clothes felt heavy like her emotions. Her phone vibrated in her jacket. After gathering her soggy gym bag, she dug her phone out, and Ross's name showed on the screen. She returned it to her pocket and sauntered to her car to drive out of the neighborhood.

Her phone rang multiple times, and she ignored each of the calls. She finally listened to her voicemail messages.

"Olivia. Where are you? I'm standing on your porch ringing the doorbell. Come open the door, baby. I can't wait to taste your lips."

Next message. "Olivia, baby, when are you going to let me in? Did you leave to go somewhere? Call me back."

Next message. "Okay, Olivia. I'm not sure why you aren't answering my calls. I'm sitting in my car in the rain waiting for you to come open the door. You know I need to get my hands on you, girl."

Next message. "Olivia, okay, that's it. I don't know why you aren't opening the door. I guess you're playing games with me. I'm going back home. Call me back."

After hearing the last message, Olivia drove to a gas station and removed a piece of paper from her purse with a number scrawled on it. She nervously tapped the buttons on her phone to make the call. Someone answered after two rings.

"Hello?" the voice said sleepily.

"Hello, Dahlia?"

"Yes, this is Dahlia."

"Dahlia, this is Olivia. We met at the gym." *Should I really go through with this?*

"Olivia. Yes. How are you? It is good to hear your voice." Dahlia said joyfully into the phone. "You're calling awfully late. Is everything okay?"

Olivia's eyes welled with tears. *I can't believe that the words I'm about to say will change her life forever.*

"Dahlia, there's no easy way to have this discussion with you. I apologize for waking you up. I need to tell you something. Woman to woman."

"Okay. You're making me nervous. What's going on?" Dahlia questioned.

"I want to discuss something with you about my boyfriend. The one I mentioned to you."

"Yes, yes, I remember you mentioning the two of you are thinking about marriage, which is wonderful."

"Well, I found out that my Mr. Wonderful boyfriend has been unfaithful."

"Oh no, Olivia. That's awful. I am sorry about this horrible news. It's terrible this is happening to you. How cruel of him to cheat on you."

"Yes, I found out he's married and has kids."

"You've got to be kidding me. Oh, Olivia. Finding out he cheated, must be devastating for you," Dahlia exclaimed.

"Yes, it is. My question I have for you is, do you think I should tell his wife?" Olivia asked and held her breath waiting for the answer.

"Well, of course. His darkness needs to be brought to light. Don't let him get away with this, Olivia. His wife needs to know.

I wouldn't hold back on telling her. She deserves to be aware if her husband is a stinkin' liar and cheater. So, yes, tell her," Dahlia said passionately and angrily.

"Okay. Well, Dahlia, there's no easy way to tell you this, and I'm sorry I just found out. My heart is broken about sharing my misery with you of what my boyfriend has done. I didn't know he's married. I'm angry and sick from what he's done to his family and me," Olivia said hesitantly. "Dahlia, my boyfriend's name is Ross."

Silence.

"Dahlia. Did you hear what I said?" Olivia asked nervously.

"Yes. I heard you. I find it strange your boyfriend and my husband have the same name. Ross is my husband's name," Dahlia said quietly. "What are you saying, Olivia?"

"Dahlia, Ross O'Neill, your husband, is the same man I've been dating. He and I have been seeing each other for several months now. He never told me about your marriage. I'm sorry he did this to both of us. I would never have dated him if I had known. I'm extremely angry right now," Olivia cried into the phone.

"Are you sure it's the same person, Olivia?"

"The bodybuilder with long, red hair. I found out yesterday when the two of you kissed in front of his smoothie shop. It's the same, Ross."

"Did the two of you sleep together? Have you ever been in his house?" Dahlia asked angrily.

"Yes, we have slept together. He comes to my house and never told me where he lived. He always had an excuse for not having me over. Dahlia, you have to believe me. I didn't know," Olivia exclaimed.

Dahlia seemed extremely calm. "I believe you, Olivia. I'm

not mad at you. I appreciate you telling me for me to know the truth. This is not the first time, and you're not the only one. I needed proof, and you gave it to me. All I can say to you is, thank you."

Olivia couldn't believe her ears. "Not the first and not the only? You mean to tell me he's cheated on you before?"

"I always knew in my heart he's been lying to me about his trips to different competitions. When I became pregnant, he started staying away from our house in Port Aransas a lot. It had to be right around the time my doctor put me on bed rest. I couldn't have sex anymore. I couldn't figure it out. Now, thanks to you, I have the answers I need," Dahlia said calmly. "Now, I'm going to bed. I must figure out what I'm going to do for the kids and me. Thank you, Olivia, and goodnight."

The call ended.

Olivia sat in her car staring at her phone. Everything looked hazy, making her think she had fallen into a dream world. Unfortunately, she is wide-awake.

Her phone rang causing her to jump out of her trance. Ross's name appeared on the screen, and she answered it. "Olivia, why did you destroy my house?" he yelled.

"Lose. My. Number. Act like you never knew me. Die and rot in hell, Ross. I hate you," Olivia screamed into the phone and hung up.

She hugged the steering wheel and cried for her soul.

CHAPTER 30

"I can't keep living like this anymore."

"Heather, tell me exactly what do you mean?"

Heather, one of Olivia's patients, clopped her oversized black rubber clogs across the floor in a nervous pace. Stopping suddenly, she plopped onto the red Italian leather sofa in Olivia's office. She breathed heavily in deep rasps and attempted to catch her breath.

She ran her hands through her stringy, greasy, black hair three times. It fell back against her pimple peppered forehead, which she unconsciously picked.

Her five-feet-two inches frame carried 292 pounds, with a body shape favoring a round baked potato with legs and arms sticking out. Although she was only nineteen years old, she made herself appear matronly by wearing baggy, black clothing, which covered her from neck to ankles. The only skin showing was her face, which she never attempted to refresh with makeup.

"Dr. Maxwell, I'm sick and tired of doing everything for these spoiled brats. No one ever does anything for me. Sometimes, I want to disappear and run away from everyone. It seems like when I go two steps forward; I fall back three." She stood and clomped across the floor again. She rapidly shook her head back and forth to get rid of her frustration.

"Heather, I know it hasn't been easy for you, and this has

been a struggle for a while. You've made a lot of progress. Let's review some of the ideas you put into place to feel appreciated. Come sit. I want you to breathe in and out slowly a few times to relax. Tell me how you're working on your plan."

Olivia coaxed Heather to return to her seat and walked around her desk to pull a chair next to the sofa to be closer to her. Heather stopped pacing, took several deep breaths, and plopped back onto the sofa. Olivia scrunched her nose when Heather's stench hit her. She tried to breathe through her mouth to keep from smelling her and gagging.

Olivia could see Heather was at her wit's end. She was dealing with an anxiety disorder and childhood post-traumatic stress disorder after her stepfather's brother, Uncle Ernie, raped her. She was twelve at the time, and the abuse continued for four years.

Overeating became her saving grace, but it led her to become morbidly obese. Being overweight gave her the hope of keeping men from looking at her. She stopped bathing regularly and developed a nauseating odor to repulse her uncle from wanting to be close to her. Unfortunately, by the time the abuse ended, she discovered she carried twins by him.

Heather succeeded in hiding her pregnancy from her family for seven months due to her normal belly fat and big clothes. Once her mother found out, and Heather told her that Uncle Ernie raped her, she kicked her out of the house and accused her of lying. With nowhere else to go, she landed in a homeless shelter at age 17 and gave birth to the twins shortly after that.

Short on money, Heather landed in a juvenile detention center after her arrest for stealing diapers and formula at the grocery store. She met Olivia in a required community-based rehabilitative program after her release. Olivia was her voice of reason and helped with visualizing the positive things to focus on in her life.

Heather talked non-stop, and Olivia's mind drifted to the craziness she experienced with Ross after she found out about him and Dahlia. The last year had been depressing for her, and she wondered how she ever got through it.

She never spoke to Ross again, although he filled her voicemail with calls daily for weeks. He dropped by her house uninvited and knocked on her windows in the middle of the night, begging her to speak to him.

On more than one occasion, Olivia caught Ross sitting in his car in front of her clinic for hours. Her co-workers insisted on walking out with her for protection. He followed her through the parking lot, crying for her to give him a chance to explain.

Some of the days, he appeared angry and threatening to her. He told her she would regret ruining his marriage. He transformed back to whining and crying almost in an instant. That strange behavior had never surfaced when they dated.

Nightmares of Ross harassing her stole her sleep. She feared what he might do out of desperation. She often asked Savvy and other friends to spend the night to keep her company. Olivia contacted the police to report him stalking her and requested a restraining order. They sent a unit out to do periodic welfare checks which provided a sense of safety.

Suddenly, she didn't see or hear from him anymore. She heard through the grapevine; he got busted for the sale and use of anabolic steroids. Criminal activity had been taking place in the smoothie shop. He and the guys he trained were doping for a while. He received a two-year jail sentence for his crime.

His smoothie shop next to the gym closed permanently. An athletic maternity clothing store called Dahling's Closet now filled the space in the building. She wondered if Dahlia could be responsible for what happened to Ross. If so, she had achieved her sweet revenge on him.

Thankfully, Olivia had her work to dive into, and she focused on the stressful lives of her clients. Her patients had many crazy things going on, which allowed her to get outside of her world.

Olivia tuned back into Heather's situation. She spent the next hour talking and listening to her until she calmed down. She wrote out her treatment plan and embraced her in a hug, despite the odor. After reassuring her she would be fine, she sent her on her way.

Olivia sighed from brain exhaustion and decided to call Savvy about meeting with Da Crew later that evening. "Hey, girl. Whatchu been up to lately? We need to get together. I could use a drink right about now."

"Hey, Olivia. Work has been crazy busy. I think they want me to live on a plane. Also, I transferred my membership for Delta to the San Antonio Alumnae Chapter. The life of a public servant is never done. I've met amazing sorority sisters who you have to meet. Some of them mentioned they know you. On top of that, I joined three ministries at church. Whew. I'm wearing myself out just thinking about it." Savvy laughed.

"You haven't changed a bit. I'm glad you've adjusted so well to living here." Olivia said. "I was calling to see if you want to hang with Da Crew tonight."

"Oh man. I would love to but, I'm finishing a few things here at work. I'm about to head out of town to visit my folks," Savvy responded. "I can't wait to get home to Mama's cooking."

"Oh, I totally forgot you're leaving tonight. I guess we'll have to wait until you get back."

"Let's definitely plan to get together when I return. Sorry to rush off the phone. I need to talk to my boss before I leave to go home. I still need to get my clothes together for the trip. I hate when I wait until the last minute to pack," Savvy laughed.

"Girl, one of these days, you'll learn to pack ahead of time. Have a great trip, and call me when you get back," Olivia chuckled.

She ended the call and started packing her briefcase. The more she thought about it, the more she felt like a quiet night at home was just what she needed. Heather wore her out, so Olivia decided just to pick up something to cook.

Maneuvering through the crowded store parking lot seemed to be difficult due to the after-work shoppers. After parking in a spot right near the door, she grabbed a grocery cart in the store and started making her way through the aisles.

She decided on wild salmon fillets from the seafood deli. After selecting ingredients for a salad in the produce section, she headed to the wine aisles for a bottle of Pinot Noir.

While taking her time to peruse the bottles of wine, her skin prickled like someone had their eyes on her. She glanced upward and became mesmerized by a handsome man with golden skin and wavy, ebony hair. He had eyes like Tupac and was wearing a Philadelphia Eagles t-shirt with jeans fitting his body perfectly. His lips parted into an ivory smile, and Olivia dropped her gaze.

She nonchalantly continued to search for the wine. The last thing she needed to do was get involved with another man.

"Excuse me; I must apologize for staring at you. I'm hoping you could help me pick out a bottle of wine," he said and approached her.

"You should ask someone who works here to help you," Olivia snapped and side-stepped further away from him. She quickly diverted her eyes back to the racks.

"Whoa. I wasn't trying to be disrespectful, my sister. I haven't seen anyone in this section available to help. You appear to know what to search for. I didn't mean to offend you at all."

He held his hands in front of him in surrender.

Olivia raised her head and glanced at him. He seemed sincere. *I guess I did sound a little bit rude.* "I didn't mean to snap at you. I thought you were using a pick-up line to try to hit on me or something."

She couldn't help notice his long, thick eyelashes. His eyes were hypnotizing to the point she had to make herself look away again.

"I can't say I didn't notice how attractive you are before I asked the question. I'm sincere in wanting a suggestion on a wine. My apologies."

"No, no. It's okay. I had a rough day. It doesn't excuse me for talking to you impolitely. I'm ready to finish shopping in here, so I can get home and relax," Olivia said and faked a smile to try and be friendly. "Do you want red wine or white? Sweet or dry?"

"I'd like to try dry, white wine. Something different from a Chardonnay," he replied. "I'm trying to expand my horizons when it comes to wine. It hasn't been long since I stopped drinking White Zinfandel."

"Oh good. Too many people start with White Zinfandel and never try anything else. You are bold for stepping out," Olivia applauded him. She reached for a bottle of wine on the rack. "Here, try this South African Chenin Blanc. It's one of my favorites. I know you won't be disappointed." His fingers lightly grazed hers when she handed the bottle to him. Her body tingled from the soft touch.

"Chenin Blanc, huh? All right. I'll try it." He studied the label. "Tell you what. Let me buy a bottle of it for you to show my appreciation for helping me out. No strings attached, of course."

"Well, I won't turn away a free bottle of wine. I thank you.

Definitely, no strings attached." Olivia's face warmed from blushing.

They both laughed and headed to the checkout line. After paying for their items, he handed her the bottle and stuck his hand out to shake hers. "Malcolm. My name is Malcolm. Is it possible I can at least know the name of the lovely lady for whom I bought a bottle of wine?"

Olivia laughed and shook his hand. His gentle yet strong grip held hers a second longer than it should've lasted. "My name is Olivia, and thank you for your generosity. I will definitely enjoy this treat."

"You do that, my sister. I hope I will see you in the wine aisle again. Have a good night." And with that, he strolled out of the store.

Olivia stood for a moment, wishing he had asked for her number. But then she quickly shook away that thought and headed home to have dinner – alone.

CHAPTER 31

"Savvy, I'm telling you. I can't get this man out of my head." Olivia whined. She and Savvy wandered around tasting food and wine at a festival after Savvy returned from visiting her family.

"I can't believe he bought you a bottle of wine and didn't even ask for your phone number. Who does that?" Savvy questioned.

"What if I never see him again? He was cute. I have to admit; I could see myself dating a guy like him."

"Hey. Slow it down. You just got Ross out of your life. Don't you need some time to recover from that craziness?" Savvy warned.

"I know. But, over this last week, thoughts about Malcolm are keeping me up at night." Olivia sighed.

"I'm just saying, be careful," Savvy said.

"I know. I probably won't ever see him again." Olivia sulked.

"Don't worry. You'll cross paths again, I bet."

Olivia stopped and grabbed her friend's arm. "Savvy. I know this sounds crazy. Maybe I'm imagining things. But, see the guy at the next booth with the Frederick Douglas t-shirt on?" Olivia nodded in his direction.

"Where? Which booth?" Savvy looked around and didn't see

who Olivia referred to.

"Stop looking so obvious," Olivia said through clenched teeth. "Over to the left. He has on the jeans which fit just right. Looks like Tupac."

Savvy cautiously peered to her left. Her eyes widened when she spotted the guy. "Yes, I see him. He's a cutie. What about him?"

"That's Malcolm. I can't believe he's here," Olivia squealed. She almost spilled her wine from her glass.

Malcolm looked in their direction and showed pearly white teeth when he smiled. He walked through the crowd toward them while swirling a glass of wine.

Olivia exhaled. His appearance took her breath away. He was as fine as the night they met.

"Olivia, right?" He stopped in front of her with his gorgeous smile still on his face.

She swooned with warmth when she saw his hypnotizing eyes and stuttered. "Y-yes. I'm Olivia. Hi, Malcolm."

"Funny seeing you here. I heard someone say my name. And here you are." Malcolm said. "How are you?"

An electrical current seemed to flow from his body to Olivia's. "I'm good. How was that wine I suggested?"

"I loved it. Because of you, I'm hooked on Chenin Blanc. It's my favorite now. It makes me think of you." He kept his eyes still focused on her.

"Um, hello. Excuse me you two." Savvy broke the moment. "Let me introduce myself since my friend has turned into a zombie. My name is Savvy, and I already know, you are Malcolm. So nice to meet you."

Olivia and Malcolm laughed. Malcolm shook her hand. "It is nice to meet you, Savvy. I got lost in the moment after seeing Olivia again. I met her a week ago at the grocery store. I've been kicking myself all week because I didn't ask her for her phone number. Wow. Here she is and as beautiful as she was that night."

Olivia's cheeks became warm with a blush. "You wanted my number? Why didn't you ask me for it?"

"I don't know what I was thinking. But, look at God. He brought us together again." Malcolm said.

"Yes, look at God." Savvy chimed in. "You know what? While you two get reacquainted, I'm heading to another booth for more wine." She nodded at Olivia. "I'll see you in a little bit, missy. Nice to meet you, Malcolm." She strutted off to let the two of them talk.

Malcolm and Olivia were paralyzed while looking at each other. Olivia laughed and dropped her head. "I'm sorry for staring. I was just talking about you to Savvy right before I spotted you."

"No need to apologize. I've been talking about you to my boys so much; they are tired of hearing about the beautiful woman in the wine aisle," Malcolm said.

"No way," Olivia said.

"Well, before I miss this opportunity again, may I please get your phone number?" Malcolm whipped out a pen and a napkin. "There's no way I'll make the same mistake again."

Olivia chuckled. "There's no way I will let you leave without it." She wrote her number on his napkin. She noticed her hand shaking with excitement.

"I don't want to keep you from your friend. I'm actually out here with some of my clients who I need to locate. Can I call you tonight?" Malcolm asked.

"I was hoping that you would. You certainly can," Olivia responded.

"I look forward to talking again. Perhaps, we can plan some

time to crack open a bottle of Chenin Blanc together," Malcolm suggested.

"I would like that very much," Olivia said.

"Okay, I'll talk to you later then." Malcolm's eyes lingered on Olivia. He took her hand and gently placed his lips on it in a kiss. Olivia's body weakened from his touch.

"Talk to you later." Olivia sighed.

He walked away, glancing back to smile at her, before disappearing into the crowd.

Olivia didn't notice the people around her as she soaked in all she could about this encounter. She wished later was already here, so she could hear his voice again.

***

Malcolm and Olivia never lost touch again and started a fiery love affair. They couldn't stand to be away from each other and spent every day together.

Olivia made a point to spoil Malcolm every chance she could. He was a sports fanatic, and she made sure he had front row tickets on the fifty-yard line when the Philadelphia Eagles played the Dallas Cowboys. Nothing but the best for Malcolm was Olivia's motto.

They both had adventurous spirits and took numerous vacations where they could enjoy being active. During their short dating period, they hiked mountains in Phoenix, skied in Vail, and surfed in Hawaii.

Olivia spared no expense to make sure they had the best vacations. Since Malcolm worked in network marketing, she understood he didn't always have a steady amount of money coming in. She decided to handle everything to ensure they would have a high-quality life together. She figured his financial situation would change, and he would be able to spoil her one day.

Olivia sent postcards to Savvy from every place they traveled. She expressed her excitement on her trips by writing about all they were doing. Sometimes, Olivia mailed two postcards at a time to be a continuation of the first one. She always ran out of space from capturing every moment in their adventures.

There was no question they were in love. Anyone around them could feel the magic and electricity that flowed between them. Malcolm accepted her for who she was and made her feel like a queen. The only time she didn't get his full attention was when he watched sports.

Except for one time. Malcolm asked Olivia to marry him at a Super Bowl party with all of their friends. Of course, she said yes.

PART 4

BREATHE AGAIN

CHAPTER 32

2000

The weather on the island of St. Lucia couldn't have been more perfect for a wedding. The temperature was seventy-four degrees with a cool breeze coming off the North Atlantic Ocean. The sound of waves crashing to shore along with the laughing calls of seagulls filled the air.

Savvy and Olivia enjoyed early morning massages in cabanas on the beach. They now lazed around the resort pool sipping on Piña Coladas.

"So, are you relaxed, Bride-to-be?" Savvy asked Olivia and snuck a glance at her friend lounging in the chair next to hers.

Olivia lifted her Tiffany sunglasses and flashed a big smile at Savvy. The contrast of the bright yellow bikini on her dark skin made her appear ready to model for a magazine. She felt comfortable with her weight and size. "I am relaxed, happy, and jittery all at the same time. Savvy, I can't believe my wedding day is finally here."

"I know. I'm excited for you and Malcolm. You are going to be such an elegant bride," Savvy exclaimed.

"Well, thank you for treating me to a fabulous massage on the beach. My therapist had the strongest hands, which is exactly what I needed. I think he found every knot in my body and held on to them until they were worked out."

"My massage therapist was sexy. I wish I could put him in my suitcase and bring him to San Antonio. Did you see his amazing dreadlocks? He gave me a glimpse of heaven," Savvy sighed.

"Girl, you're too funny. Sounds like he worked out more than merely a few knots on you," Olivia joked.

"Yes, he did. If only I could keep his hands on me for the rest of my time here," Savvy giggled.

"Hey, maybe you should slip him your number. Live a little, right?" Olivia winked at Savvy.

"Just like Terry McMillan's book, *How Stella Got Her Groove Back*. Maybe I need excitement in my life." Savvy drifted away into the thought.

"Girl, your mind disappeared with whatever is in your head."

"It sure did. Anyway, now that my mind is back, you're quite welcome for the massage. I got what I needed out of it like you did," Savvy laughed. "Thank you for asking me to be your bridesmaid. I know you could've picked anyone. It's a privilege and an honor to stand beside you to witness you marrying the man of your dreams."

"Savvy, you don't know what it means to me to have you here. There's no one else I would even have considered. If you couldn't be my bridesmaid, I would not have had anyone at all. You're the best friend ever, and I'm getting teary-eyed thinking about the fact you're still in my life after all of those crazy years." Tears welled in the corners of her eyes.

"Stop with all of the mushy stuff, will ya?" Savvy laughed. "Let's finish working on our tans and get you back to your room to get dressed for this evening."

Olivia giggled. "I never thought I would purposely lay in the sun to get a tan. Malcolm loves my chocolate skin. He's going to be happy to see how dark I am after laying out here for hours."

"You haven't seen Malcolm since last night's dinner, right?"

"There's no way I'm going to start off with bad luck in my marriage by having my soon-to-be husband see me before the wedding. We agreed he would stay on the other side of the resort at another pool with his friends and family."

"Good. I'm sure he and the family are recuperating after the party the resort staff threw for all of us last night. Five-star service. I can't believe we're even awake right now with all of those yummy rum punches we drank," Savvy said.

"Don't remind me. Ugh. I don't want to see another one ever in life." Olivia groaned at the thought. "Now, a Piña Colada, I can definitely do."

Savvy lifted her glass, and they toasted. "Here's to you, Olivia. The Bride-to-be."

"Cheers," Olivia laughed, and they took a sip before lying back in their lounging chairs. Olivia closed her eyes. *I can't believe Malcolm and I are about to become Mr. and Mrs. Who would've thought someone wants me to be their wife. I truly don't deserve him.*

"What are you chuckling about?" Savvy asked.

"Did I laugh out loud?" Olivia snickered and covered her mouth with her hand. "I'm reminiscing about how Malcolm and I bumped into each other at the food and wine festival. It had to be the best day of my life. We've had a lot of fun together."

"The two of you are like magnets. My goodness, I couldn't get your attention anymore after you spotted each other. Talk about serious chemistry."

"He drew me in like a moth to a flame."

"Well, I must say, you both have something special together." Savvy smiled at her friend.

"I love the fact he accepts me for who I am. Malcolm hasn't

asked me to change a thing about myself. He's dependable and isn't a liar. It's crazy thinking about the fact we are getting married and haven't dated for long." Olivia sighed. "But when you know, you know. I can't find anything wrong with him at all. I adore my in-laws to be, and they treat me better than my own family does."

"You've been blessed, and you deserve it, Olivia."

"I agree, Savvy. After dealing with all of my stupid relationships in the past, it's a relief to have a real man finally. He's educated, healthy, great looking, has an awesome body, loves his family and me. What more could one ask for?" Olivia beamed.

"Exactly. You couldn't have designed this relationship any more perfectly even if you had created it yourself."

"There is one thing I would change though," Olivia said and raised herself in the chair to face Savvy.

Savvy squinted at Olivia and lifted the brim of her beach hat to see her better. "What would that one thing be, missy?"

"I wish he had a better job. I mean, money is no big deal since I make an excellent salary. I must say, it would be nice if he could do something other than network marketing," Olivia explained.

"From what I remember, he's with a good company, right? I hear people can make a whole lot of money with some of those opportunities," Savvy said.

"I guess, however, his pay isn't consistent. I mean, there are some months when he doesn't have any money coming in. I don't know how he can live with inconsistent income. You have to be a great salesperson to do those jobs," Olivia elaborated.

"I still don't see what the problem is," Savvy said.

"A person has to get out early each day and be persistent about chasing after the business. I don't know if it's the right job for him. I won't worry about it now. Nevertheless, I definitely plan to help him put in resumes with a few Fortune 500 companies. We can land him a great career in marketing, which is what he majored in when he attended Tennessee State University."

"Now, Olivia, don't go pushing Malcolm to do something he doesn't feel passionate about. The last thing you want is a man to be in a job he hates. Please, don't hound him about making more money. You make more than $250,000 a year with your job. Not to mention the fact you get additional paychecks from speaking engagements and writing articles. You two are going to be fine," Savvy said.

"Savvy, don't worry. I won't nag him. But, you know, I bought my own wedding ring since he couldn't get me the one I wanted. He didn't have money for a two-carat diamond, and it's important to me to have that size or bigger. It isn't a big deal. However, I have visions of us doing more together financially."

Savvy's mouth dropped open. "Olivia. Did you buy your own ring to have a bigger one? Are you serious? How did we go from discussing how he's the perfect man for you, to focusing on insignificant, materialistic stuff? You have four cars between the two of you. You already have an amazing house with a pool in a historic neighborhood. Your concerns about money are moot. They don't matter, okay? Geesh. You're making me mad listening to you whine." Savvy shook her head.

"I know, I know. We'll be fine with what we have, I guess." Olivia lowered her head in shame.

"You better believe it. By the time we all leave this island, there's no looking back. Do you understand me?" Savvy scolded her.

"Yes, ma'am. I understand," Olivia replied sheepishly.

"Good. Now let's head to our rooms and get ready. Is the

resort staff taking care of your hair and makeup?"

"Yes, they have everything covered from A to Z. I still want you to come to my bridal suite. We can get ready together," Olivia said. They began to gather their beach bags and put on their cover-ups.

"Okay, I'll bring my stuff to your room. In the meantime, I want you to think about what a wonderful man you're about to marry in a few hours. Promise?" Savvy stood from her chair and looked Olivia in the eyes.

"I promise forever. We'll be perfect together," Olivia replied when they walked away from the pool.

Her mind shifted to her trifling family for a moment. She couldn't believe that none of them were here to witness her big day. They made every excuse in the world to keep from coming.

She thought her father would've come since they spent time together after her hospital incident. However, he was reluctant to travel to St. Lucia without her mother. Olivia knew it was more of the same, controlling nature of her mother.

Olivia didn't care about her sister not being there. It would be just like her to try to make the whole trip about herself with her needy ways. Thank God she didn't come.

Her parents made a big to-do for her sister's wedding a year ago and even paid for it. Her mother's reasoning for not paying for Olivia's was the fact she was a psychologist. She felt she had enough money to pay for her own. According to her, Sheree struggled to make ends meet with her hair salon salary. However, Olivia knew her sister made a good amount of money from charging a lot for weaves and braids. She didn't manage her finances well and always cried wolf about being broke.

Olivia didn't mind paying for her wedding, yet it hurt knowing they chose not to attend. They probably wouldn't even attend her funeral when she died.

Olivia shook her head to get the negative thoughts out of her head and think about her soon-to-be husband instead. There was no question they belong together.

CHAPTER 33

The wedding turned out to be the perfect display of love anyone could ever imagine. Everything turned out the way Olivia and Malcolm planned. Their intimate group of nineteen family members and friends partied all night long.

Savvy caught the bouquet when she dove to the ground and wrestled with one of Malcolm's drunk aunts. The dirt marks on her dress didn't matter when she stood victoriously, holding the torn apart bouquet in the air.

Olivia laughed and enjoyed Savvy's theatrical performance. Having her for a bridesmaid blessed her special day in many ways. The fact her family did not show up, turned out to be the last thing on her mind. *I am married to the man of my dreams, forever. No one can ever take that away from me.*

She and Malcolm agreed Olivia would keep Maxwell for her last name since she wouldn't want her patients to become confused. Taking on his last name, Turnipseed didn't excite her. Dr. Olivia Turnipseed sounded funny. Although she wasn't interested in having kids any time soon, the last thing she wanted, was for bullies to make fun of their children and call them baby turnip seeds.

After everyone left to go home a few days after the wedding, Olivia and Malcolm stayed in St. Lucia for their Honeymoon for a week. It turned out to be the most magical way to start their lives off together.

When they returned to San Antonio, Malcolm moved his things into her house. They settled into a husband and wife life of discovery.

Six weeks into their marriage, Olivia became nauseous and dizzy when she began preparing breakfast for the two of them. She grabbed a cup of water and after taking a few sips, went back to working on the food.

Malcolm strolled into the kitchen and wrapped his arms around her waist from behind.

"Hey, babe, everything smells fabulous. Do I smell bacon in the oven?" Malcolm asked, feathering kisses on the back of her neck.

"Yes, it is. Unfortunately, the smell is making me nauseous. Can you finish cooking the eggs? I think I'm going to be sick." Olivia quickly dropped the spatula and ran to the bathroom on the side of the kitchen. She barely made it to the toilet to throw up.

Instantly, her stomach began to calm down. She grabbed a washcloth and welcomed the stinging of the cold water she splashed on her flushed face. Malcolm stood in the doorway with his forehead wrinkled in concern.

"Babe, are you okay? Do you want me to take you to the doctor or anything?" he asked and rubbed her back gently.

"No, no. I'm fine. It's probably something I ate last night. You know I had peach cobbler and ice cream after dinner. I think it must have settled wrong. I wonder if I'm lactose intolerant? Anyway, I feel better already," Olivia reassured him. "Come on, let's get back to the kitchen where I can finish making your breakfast."

"Are you sure? Maybe you should go lie down."

"I promise you; I feel much better. I'm actually starving

now." Olivia took Malcolm by the hand and led him into the kitchen. "Let's eat. I have pancakes keeping warm in the oven to go with the bacon and eggs. I can't wait."

They devoured the food and relocated to their bedroom to devour each other with love.

Two weeks later, Olivia found out she was pregnant.

CHAPTER 34

"So, your doctor has confirmed it? I'm going to be an Auntie. Oh, Olivia. I'm happy for you and Malcolm," Savvy exclaimed. They relaxed in the wicker rocking chairs on her deck in the backyard. The cool and breezy wind made the unrelenting San Antonio heat bearable.

"Thanks," Olivia responded dryly.

"Thanks? Why aren't you excited? You're about to be a mama." Savvy studied her friend. She poured two glasses of homemade lemonade on ice from a glass pitcher.

"Savvy, we just got married. I wasn't expecting to barely have a few weeks together with only the two of us. This pregnancy changes everything. I'm mad at myself for not taking precautions when we were on our Honeymoon."

"How does Malcolm feel about having children already?" Savvy sipped her lemonade.

"Oh. He's excited and started looking around for a crib and car seat already. I feel bad I don't share his enthusiasm. He wants at least two to four kids. That's never going to happen in my opinion," Olivia exclaimed.

"You're kidding, right?" Savvy asked.

"Do you know how much damage is done to a woman's body after giving birth? You gain weight and get ugly stretch marks. I'm not ready for all of that yet," Olivia whined.

"Wow. I had no idea you had concerns like that. You used

to talk about wanting children. I thought the two of you would be on the same page about having kids before you got married."

"It may sound crazy to some people, however, I'm not ready to sacrifice my lifestyle. I mean, what about me? When a baby comes into the world, it's all about them. When will I work out? When will I get to travel and enjoy things with only Malcolm and me? When can I shop for myself? When will I get enough sleep? I don't know if I can deal with this right now." Olivia began to sound frantic.

"Okay, okay, try not to get stressed out. Believe me, although I don't have kids, I can tell you, you will adjust. Have you noticed there are moms in the world who have great lives? You'll find other ways to do things, although it may be tough sometimes. Plus, you have an amazing husband who will tag team with you in taking care of the baby. All hope is not lost," Savvy said.

"I know. That's what I keep telling myself. I don't want to get fat to the point Malcolm can't stand looking at me. As you know, I recently got my body back into shape. The last thing I need is to have to deal with being overweight."

"With the way you work out, it won't be a problem for you to continue to exercise during your pregnancy. Since you're healthy, you'll probably lose weight quickly anyway, especially if you breastfeed. Stop worrying, and enjoy the fact a miracle is growing inside of you right now. You're the vessel for a beautiful baby. You both have been given a gift. You're growing a Turnipseed inside your body," Savvy laughed.

Olivia couldn't help but to chuckle and calm down.

"What would I do without you, Savvy? You always know what to say to me. I get anxious about stupid stuff. I guess my hormones are out of whack right now, which is probably why I'm emotional."

"I understand, my friend. I'll be here along the way. Of course, I'll be the best Auntie ever and will help in any way needed. I can't wait to find out if you're having a boy or a girl. I can throw a baby reveal party for you and Malcolm. It'll be fun. This is exciting."

"Whoa, Trigger," Olivia laughed.

"Can you tell I'm overjoyed?" Savvy squealed.

"Completely," Olivia said sarcastically.

"I will not curb my enthusiasm. You need to get ramped up."

"I know. I will eventually. I guess," Olivia said, uninterested.

"By the way, on a totally different subject. I've been meaning to ask, how are things with you and Malcolm regarding your concerns about his job? Did you keep from nagging him?" Savvy studied Olivia's face closely looking for clues.

Olivia patted herself on the stomach and sipped on her lemonade. "Yes, I haven't even brought it up. Now, I have this to focus on instead."

"This? You're referring to the beautiful baby you two have been blessed with, right?" Savvy questioned.

"Yes, of course. What if our baby comes out ugly?"

"Oh, my goodness, Olivia. What has gotten into you? Both you and Malcolm are knockout gorgeous. There's no question, you'll have a child stunning enough to be in magazines." Savvy huffed in disbelief at Olivia's question.

"I hope the baby doesn't come out dark like me. Their life will be easier not having to deal with their skin color being like mine," Olivia said sadly.

"Oh, come on. Are you kidding me? That crazy thought again? You were supposed to be done saying damaging things about yourself when you started dating Malcolm. He likes dark skin," Savvy fussed.

"I know. I can't help it."

"It's time for you to stop thinking your skin has to be light. I know your parents put those ideas in your head. Can you please use your own psychology education on yourself? You have to stop indulging in negative thoughts," Savvy scolded.

"It's easy for you to say. You're such a pretty, brown color. You probably never had to deal with the same issues I did."

"We're all different shades of color. God has done amazing work in developing many stunning shades and complexions. Why question what He has designed? Please don't raise your kids to feel bad about dark-skinned people. If you don't appreciate the Lord's creation, it would be insulting to Him."

"I never thought about it from a spiritual perspective. I wish you'd been around to tell me this years ago," Olivia said.

"Well, I'm telling you now. Today is day one for you to straighten out these thoughts in your head. Start living like you know you're beautiful both inside and out. You're fearfully and wonderfully made," Savvy responded.

"Did you go biblical on me?" Olivia questioned. "Yeah, you're right. I need to follow my own advice and not let others define who I am. I'll do my best to raise this baby to appreciate everything about who they are, and how they look."

"You definitely have to get a grip on these insecurities. Many children mimic their mothers when it comes to how they see themselves. If you communicate your issues about your looks, they will do the same. You must make sure you're not saying damaging things about your body image. Do you know what I mean?"

"Yes, I know exactly what you're saying. When I think about my mother, I realize she always wears makeup too light in color for her face. Although she has light skin, she wants to pass for white," Olivia said.

She continued, "As a teenager, she made me use bleaching cream to try to lighten my skin. Did you know that can cause the development of cancer cells? I could've died or ended up infertile from my own mother trying to make me light-skinned."

Savvy's mouth dropped open. "Are you serious? What a horrible thing to do to a child."

"My mother wouldn't let me play out in the sun. She told me if I got too dark, I would blend in with the night. She claimed she wouldn't be able to find me after the sun set. My sister got involved in making fun of me, and they both called me Kingsford. It wasn't until I got older when I figured out, they were comparing my skin color to coal," Olivia said. She was getting angry thinking about the way they used to torture her.

"That's downright mean," Savvy exclaimed.

"I don't ever want our child to experience what I did. It's painful. I definitely won't put him or her through the same thing."

"Your family is cruel for that. You're attractive, and it's sad they can't appreciate you the way the rest of us do. Your family needs professional help. Don't let me hear you saying crazy stuff about yourself again. Understood?" Savvy flashed a look to let Olivia know she was serious.

"Yes, ma'am," Olivia answered. "It's amazing how things from our childhood can scar us for life. I don't even realize what I'm saying sometimes. It's been a part of my DNA forever. Today is a new day for me. I'll make sure I change this destructive way of thinking before our baby is born."

"Believe me; I'll put you in check if I hear anything sounding close to badmouthing yourself." Savvy shook her finger at Olivia.

"Savvy, I need you in my life to bring me back to reality from time to time. You have a way of putting my head back on straight. Everyone needs a friend like you." Olivia finished her drink, stood, and hugged Savvy tightly. "Girl, you put your foot in that lemonade. It tasted delicious. I could've drunk the whole pitcher myself. I'm feigning for it like a crack addict feigns for drugs. What do you put in it?"

"Grandma's ancient Negro recipe," Savvy said slyly. "If I tell you, I'd have to kill you."

"Well, it would be worth dying for. Okay, I better get going. I didn't realize how late it is."

"No problem. I need to get to Hard Body Fitness to get my boot camp workout in." Savvy stood to open the back door for them to go inside.

She escorted her through the house to the front. Olivia turned to Savvy and took both of her hands into hers. "Thank you for getting me off the ledge again. What would I do without you?"

"Girl, stop sounding all sentimental. Sometimes, you think too much about things. Now get out of here, and get home to that husband of yours." Olivia walked to her car laughing and blowing kisses to Savvy.

CHAPTER 35

"Hey, Liv. I'm in the back," Malcolm called from the backyard. Olivia headed through the kitchen and out the sliding door to the covered patio.

Malcolm wore an apron on top of his Michigan State University T-shirt. She could see his clothes perfectly matched with green shorts, and green and white sneakers. The grill appeared overloaded with steaks, chicken, ribs, and vegetables. He was cooking enough food for a football team.

She loved his handsomeness with his MSU baseball hat turned around backward. He expertly flipped the steaks and closed the lid on the grill. He walked to Olivia to give her a tight bear hug and a juicy kiss on her lips.

"Hi, baby. You smell like smoke. Good enough to eat." Olivia kissed him back.

"Call me Chef Malcolm. I'm making a gourmet dinner for my baby mama."

"Boy. You're too crazy," Olivia laughed. "I know those steaks are going to melt in my mouth. I can't wait and neither can this bundle in here."

"How's my little one doing?" Malcolm rubbed her stomach with his big hands. His eyes sparkled with joy. He leaned toward her and planted a kiss on the top of her belly."

"From what I can tell, Mama and baby are doing fine. By the way, Savvy said to tell you hi." Olivia sat on the outdoor sofa and raised her feet onto the glass coffee table. Her ankles were swollen and tight in her shoes. She slipped them off to get comfortable.

"What's my girl Savvy up to? You should call and tell her to come by for some of my famous BBQ."

"She said she's heading to the gym to get her workout in. I'm sure she'll be interested next time if we let her know earlier. By the way, you sure are cooking a lot of meat. Are we having company over?" Olivia asked when Malcolm headed back to the grill to check on the food.

"Yeah. You know Michigan State is playing Ohio State today. I invited a few of my Frat Brothers to hang out to see the game. Sorry, I didn't mention it earlier. Joe's wife put him out of the house for a bridal shower she's hosting. He and Rodger planned to watch the game there. He called and asked if they could come here instead. I hope you don't mind baby."

Even though she wasn't really in the mood for company, she said, "No, not at all. I know how you are about your football. I'll get my plate and will stay out of the way. I don't think me and the baby want to be around all of you screaming at the TV," Olivia laughed and stood to go into the house.

One thing she knew about Malcolm, was the fact he had to see every sport in existence. He started watching players and keeping stats from their high school years all the way through their professional careers.

Football, basketball, soccer, and baseball kept him glued to the TV most days. Since he completely absorbed himself with the games, there were times Olivia existed like a sports widow.

She did her best not to complain. The times when she joined him to check out a game, he got extremely intense and frustrated about the players. It wasn't fun anymore for her. It would be better for him to watch with his friends instead.

"I'm going to relax upstairs. Let me know when I can come to get a plate. By the way, there's beer in the refrigerator in the garage for you and the guys."

"Thanks, babe. You're the greatest," Malcolm said. They heard the doorbell ring. "Can you get that for me?"

"Sure, no problem." Olivia headed to the front. She peeped through the window and opened the door with a smile. Joe and Rodger stood on the welcome mat loaded with bags of chips and cans of beer.

Rodger was tall and lanky like a basketball player. Because of his baby face, you would never know he was in his late 40's. Joe was short and had to look upward at Olivia.

"Hey, Liv. Penny says hi. She said y'all need to get together soon," Joe informed her when she bent to hug him.

"It's been a while since we've gone out. Please tell her hello for me," Olivia replied.

Their wives were good friends of hers. They didn't get together much since they had active teenagers. The parents stayed busy juggling their crazy schedules.

"Liv. Whassup girl." Rodger followed Joe to a table to place the food and beer on, before hugging her. "Thank you for letting us watch the game here."

"Oh, no problem. Malcolm is out back. You know the way. He's burning up the grill getting ready for y'all and the game. You know Michigan State is gonna win this one." Olivia teased him and tapped his Ohio State hat on the rim.

"Girl, please. And by the way, it is The Ohio State University winning the game today," Rodger declared and straightened his hat.

"Naw, man. She said it right," Joe chimed in. "MSU is about

to put a whuppin' on you Buckeyes."

"You wanna put some money with that trash, you talkin' man?" Rodger gathered the chips and beer and headed toward the patio.

"You know it, my brotha," Joe laughed and followed him outside.

Olivia chuckled at their banter. The trash talking continued with Malcolm when she headed upstairs.

Olivia stopped in her tracks when she walked into the bedroom. There were several shoeboxes and shopping bags on the floor. Looking closer, there were six pairs of new sneakers, four baseball hats, and three T-shirts for Malcolm's favorite college and professional teams.

Malcolm was spending too much money on sports gear. He wasn't even making enough to shop like this. *I'm the one footing most of the bills. He knows his income isn't steady for him to buy this crap.* She stared in disbelief at each item. Her neck warmed from anger. She had to talk to him about this or he was going to drive them into the poor house.

She blocked out Savvy's voice in her head, warning her about not nagging him about his job. *Something had to change, especially with this baby on the way. I'll give him a few months to kick this habit. Otherwise, I'm going to put my foot down and get him straightened out.*

CHAPTER 36

"Olivia, are you seriously interrupting my game right now to say this mess to me?" Malcolm snapped. He reclined in his stadium chair in front of the TV in the man cave. He was dressed from head to toe in San Antonio Spurs paraphernalia to watch them play the Chicago Bulls.

"Yes, I am. There's never a good time to discuss this with you." Olivia stood firmly in front of the TV with her swollen belly blocking the screen.

"Woman. You're about to get yourself hurt if you don't move from in front of this TV. You see I'm watching the game. You made me miss an important play. Move out the way," Malcolm yelled and tried to look around her to see the television.

"I know you didn't raise your voice at me, Malcolm." Olivia squatted to snatch the remote control from the table and turned the TV off.

"Noooooo," Malcolm screamed and jumped from his chair. "Woman. You've lost your frickin' mind. I can't believe you turned the game off. Give me the remote." Malcolm lunged to grab it from her hand.

Olivia waddled away from him and swung her arm behind her back. "You better step away from me and have a seat. We're going to have a conversation about all the money you're spending on sports paraphernalia right now. You're always glued to the TV. I need peace of mind about what's going on. The sooner you calm down, the sooner you can get back to your stupid game."

Malcolm glared at her and reluctantly sat back in his chair. He poked his lip out and pouted like a kid who lost his dog.

Olivia took a deep breath and stared at Malcolm squarely in the eyes. "Now, like I said, we need to talk about all of the money you've been spending on clothing and shoes. Malcolm, you have T-shirts, sweatshirts, jerseys, jackets, hats, shoes, you name it, for all your favorite teams. We don't have room in our closet or drawers for anything else. I can appreciate your passion for sports. However, you've been ordering new stuff every week.

"Olivia, you're exaggerating. I'm not buying stuff every week," Malcolm snapped.

"Oh, yes you are. I've seen the credit card statements and every single dime you're spending. It's ridiculous, Malcolm," Olivia snapped back.

"Are you spying on what I'm spending?" Malcolm asked. His brow furrowed in anger.

"I don't have to spy. I can see everything you bring in this house and all the deliveries for this crap. It's too much money and too much stuff. Considering you aren't bringing in a decent paycheck, I pay for all of this. I'm sick and tired of it." The baby kicked in her stomach, and Olivia's heart began pounding rapidly. It took her breath away, and she steadied herself by hanging onto the back of a chair.

"Really, Olivia? Do you want to play that card? You think you're better than me cause you're earning more money?" Malcolm stood and started pacing the carpeted floor. "You knew when we got married; this business is extremely hard. I put a lot of effort into my work."

"Malcolm, I'm not saying I'm better than you. We're not in competition with each other. We must start thinking about our future together financially. We're going to need our money for the baby. We only have one more month to go before the baby gets here, and we still have a ton of things we need to buy for her." Olivia tried to soften her tone to diffuse Malcolm's anger.

"Okay, fine. Be like that. I can never do enough for you. You make it seem like I'm not contributing anything to this household. Do you think you're the only one paying the bills in here? I mean, what else do you want from me Liv?" Malcolm scowled.

"Look, Malcolm, this hasn't been easy for me to bring up. I've been trying to figure out the best way to say this to you for months. It's been impossible since you always have a game on. I didn't want this to turn into an argument. We need to do some planning. Perhaps we need to consult with a Financial Advisor to help. Savvy told me about a reputable company called J Maur Wealth Advisors. Let's simply schedule a consultation to see what we can do."

"I ain't talking to any kind of Financial Advisor, Liv. We don't need anyone in our business looking at our money. We don't have a money problem, and that's that. Now, I'm done talking, and you need to give me the remote." Malcolm glared at her and stuck his hand out.

Olivia froze and stared in disbelief at the man she loved. He glared back at her, and they locked eyes in competition with each other. The baby began shifting positions and brought about a sense of anxiety.

Suddenly, Olivia screamed and threw the remote on the wall causing the back to pop off and the batteries to fall out. Malcolm scrambled to put it together to turn the TV on.

Without another word, he plopped onto the recliner and started cursing at the basketball players since he missed the Bulls scoring several more points over the Spurs.

Olivia's back tightened when she left the theater room in the agony of defeat. She placed both hands on her hips to ease the pain. The baby began punching and kicking around in her stomach like a boxer, which took her breath away.

She stopped in the hallway to inhale and exhale slowly. She rubbed her stomach to try to calm the baby down. Taking deep, calculated breaths, she slowly treaded downstairs and gripped the handrail to stay balanced.

In a daze, standing on the last step, something wet trickled down her legs. She looked down and saw a puddle of water pooled around her slippered feet. *No. No. It's too soon. She's not due yet. This can't be happening. I'm not ready.*

"Malcolm. Help me. I think my water broke," she yelled up the stairs. She clung to the stairwell and sunk to the second step in pain. One last scream brought Malcolm running downstairs to her with concern spread over his face.

"I got you, baby. It's gonna be okay. I got you," Malcolm comforted her and helped her stand.

"We've got to go now, Malcolm. Our baby is on the way. It's too soon. I'm scared. I'm so afraid," Olivia cried.

CHAPTER 37

Savvy inhaled the delightful fragrance of the bouquet of twelve pink roses. She knocked gently on the door. Once she heard Malcolm's voice calling out for her to come in, she slowly entered the room.

In the dimly lit room, Savvy saw Olivia holding a tiny bundle wrapped tightly like a burrito against her chest. She squealed with joy.

Savvy hugged Malcolm and handed the flowers to him before tip-toeing to the bed with tears of happiness gathering in her eyes.

Olivia's face appeared radiant despite any pain she experienced from giving birth. She adjusted the bundle in her arms for Savvy to see the baby's sweet face.

Savvy gasped and peered at the most angelic, baby girl she'd ever seen. Her skin is the color of mahogany. Curly, mink black hair framed her face. Tiny, perfect bow lips opened in a yawn. Her beauty overwhelmed Savvy when her light brown eyes fluttered open.

"Oh, Olivia and Malcolm. She is gorgeous." Savvy exclaimed, wiping tears from her face. "How are you doing, Mama?"

"Savvy, I can't express how happy I am right now. I've

totally forgotten about the pain. She's perfect in every way. You know, I've already counted every toe and finger." Olivia placed a tiny, pink, cap which had fallen off the baby's head, back on. She lifted her toward Savvy. "Come on, Auntie. Come hold your niece, Simone Imani Turnipseed."

"Me? Hold her right now? She's tiny. I'm afraid I'll hurt her." Savvy backed away from the bed.

"Girl, please. She clearly survived being squeezed like a tube of toothpaste coming into this world. You won't hurt her. Hold the back of her head with one hand and her body with the other. You'll do fine. You need to get used to it since you'll be babysitting for us."

"Okay, okay. Let me wash my hands first," Savvy said nervously and walked to the sink. After drying off, she headed toward the bed and reached to hold Simone gently. The baby began cooing and settled into the crook of her elbow. One of her tiny arms popped through the top of the bundle. A pink mitt covered her hand, which started punching into the air like a boxer.

"I'm going to nickname her Laila Ali since she's throwing these punches," Savvy laughed. She sat on the leather love seat and cuddled Simone.

"I'll be the one doing the boxing on any knuckleheads trying to date her." Malcolm turned from watching the TV above the bed to gaze at Simone with love in his eyes. "They'll wish they'd never laid eyes on her once I get my hands on them."

"Well, aren't you planning way ahead for her future boyfriends?" Savvy laughed and adjusted the cap on Simone's head, which kept falling off her silky hair.

"You got that right. They better think twice before they come her way. I ain't taking no mess," Malcolm replied.

"Baby, you have plenty of time to get ready for that since

we're only on day one," Olivia teased.

"So, give me details. How much does she weigh? How long did it take?" Savvy asked. "I sure hope you got here in time to get an epidural. Forget all-natural births."

"You better believe it. I screamed for it by the time they got me checked in. There's no way I could've had this baby without it. I would've locked my legs together and kept her inside," Olivia laughed.

"Our baby girl weighs 7 pounds, 3 ounces, and is 17 inches long. She came out right on time to make me miss the end of the Spurs game," Malcolm joked.

"Savvy. He would've put a TV on top of my forehead if he could have. He wanted to name her Donovan after the former Philadelphia Eagles Quarterback. Can you believe that nonsense?" Olivia joked back.

"That would've been a perfect name for a girl or boy, and you know it. Donovan Imani Turnipseed," Malcolm defended his idea.

"Boy. You need to stop playing. She's too adorable to be called Donovan," Savvy chimed in. "Simone Imani is a perfect name for this princess of a baby.

"I wasn't expecting her to come out when she did. I became nauseated and asked for Malcolm to bring me a trashcan. When I thought I needed to throw up, she shot out like a torpedo instead. Thankfully, the nurse stood in front of my legs. She had to catch her in her arms like a football," Olivia exclaimed.

"We already know she'll have the energy of her mama. That's for sure. She's beautiful like her too." Malcolm smoothed Olivia's hair back from her forehead before kissing her softly on the lips. Anyone could see how happy they were about the birth of their first child.

"I'm happy for both of you. I can't believe she's here

already. We haven't even had the baby shower yet. She wasn't due for another four weeks, right?" Savvy asked.

"Right. She couldn't wait to get here. She kicked around in my stomach a lot throughout my pregnancy. I was extremely scared when my water broke. I wasn't expecting everything to happen fast like it did. Now, I'm glad she arrived early. It seemed like she did aerobics in my belly every night once I laid in bed to go to sleep." Olivia shook her head.

A woman wearing pink scrubs with brightly colored clogs knocked twice and entered the room. She smiled and greeted Savvy, "Hello there, I'm Kathleen, the lactation consultant."

"Hi there, I'm Savvy, Olivia's best friend."

"It's nice to meet you." She turned to Olivia. "Olivia, it's time for you to nurse Simone again."

"Well. That's my cue to leave. I'm going to get out of the way and let you nurse my niece." Savvy stood slowly and cradled Simone on one arm to pass her back to Olivia.

"Savvy, thank you for coming by and thank you for the lovely flowers. Malcolm had you on speed dial. We knew you'd want to be here right away."

Savvy hugged Olivia and Malcolm before kissing Simone on the forehead. "Congratulations and I love all of you. Please let me know if there's anything I can do. Don't hesitate to call me to help. Welcome to the world, Simone Imani." Savvy glided out the door like she'd seen heaven.

CHAPTER 38

"Savvy, I'm tired," Olivia complained. She placed her elbows on the teahouse table, propping her face with her hands.

Savvy stood above Simone's baby carriage and lifted her into her arms. The baby had on a lavender baby layette with purple flowers. An oversized purple bow headband wrapped around her curly hair. Her tiny booted feet and mitted hands punched around. She cooed and focused her eyes on Savvy.

"Well, that's the life of a new mother, you know? Have you and Malcolm figured out a good routine for the two of you?" Savvy settled into her chair with Simone and took a sip of her cinnamon tea.

"Well, that's the problem. You would think after three months, we would've found a routine that works for both of us. The problem is, when Simone cries, we both wake up. Going back to sleep is hard. Both of us are extremely tired the next day. It isn't any good for him or me."

"Wow, I never thought about that."

"Yeah, me either. I think I have a solution though." Olivia took a bite of her blueberry muffin. "We need to rotate with one of us sleeping in the guest bedroom. When Simone cries, Malcolm can go feed and change her and not wake me up. We'll switch responsibility each night. One of us has got to get sleep to function each day."

"Do you mean you would sleep in separate beds in different rooms?" Savvy asked.

"Exactly."

"I don't know, Olivia. I mean, your idea is an interesting approach, yet, I don't think you should get in the habit of sleeping apart from each other all of the time," Savvy explained.

"It's only until she can sleep through the night. It's not like we ever feel like doing the nasty anyway. I can't stand for him to touch me since I'm still nursing Simone. He thinks these Ta-Tas are for him, which is out of the question." Olivia pointed to her breasts. "Oh, and by the way, after I wean Simone off, I will definitely be getting a breast job. These things will hang like Snoopy's nose the way they'll sag."

"You're too funny." Simone stirred in Savvy's arms and drifted to sleep.

"But I'm serious, though. Malcolm is already saying he wants to have another one right away. I'm barely getting some of this weight off now. Nursing is helping me to get rid of it fast. I've been working out twice a day to rush the process." Olivia patted her stomach. "Having a baby ruins your body and men don't seem to understand. I'm serious about getting my boobs done."

"Well, don't go overboard with the workouts, Olivia. Plus, you don't need to do anything to your breasts. You can't tell you recently delivered a baby. You're already smaller than me, and I haven't had any. Don't forget your previous addiction to exercise. Remember what you learned when you were in treatment for your eating disorder years ago," Savvy reminded her.

"You don't forget a thing, do you?" Olivia asked in disbelief. "Don't worry, I'm eating healthy, and I'm not working out like I did when I had my problem. I still go to my quarterly eating disorder meetings, so I'm good. I feel like I'm being chastised by my mama." Olivia rolled her eyes.

"Great. We're not going down that road again. Do you hear me?" Savvy shook her finger at Olivia and rocked Simone in her arms.

Olivia answered, "Yes ma'am. I want to make sure Malcolm doesn't start looking at any of these women who are more fit and trim than me. I have to get my body back in shape quickly. You know how men are."

"You have a good man, Olivia. I don't think you have to worry about him," Savvy reassured her.

"Yeah, you're right. I think I would be more likely to cheat on him way before he would even think about doing that to me. He definitely isn't that kind of guy," Olivia agreed. "My biggest issue is, he should get another job to help out with our bills."

"Tell me what's going on. You've been complaining about Malcolm needing a different job since before the wedding. Are you still paying for everything? Please tell me you are not." Savvy said.

"He's still binge shopping for sports paraphernalia. I foot the bills with my money. He won't even use his own to buy diapers for the baby," Olivia exclaimed.

"Why are you still even saying mine and his? You two are married, and you shouldn't be territorial about that," Savvy scolded Olivia.

"This is a big problem. Not to mention, he can't seem to do anything right with Simone. I write out a checklist of things for him to do with her, and he never finishes the list. The way he holds her and plays with her, makes me cringe every time he picks her up. He acts like she's a football. He's too rough with her."

"I've seen the way Malcolm picks Simone up, and there's nothing wrong with how he holds her. Do you seriously write out a checklist for him and expect him to follow it to the letter?"

Words began to shoot out of Olivia's mouth rapidly. Her nose flared with frustration, and she balled her hands into fists. "Yes. If I didn't, he wouldn't know what to do. He can't even put a diaper on straight, Savvy."

"Hey. Hey. Calm down. Where's all this nonsense coming from? You're trippin' right now, and making mountains out of molehills. I think you need to stop overreacting and realize Malcolm is doing the best he can with Simone. Don't forget, he's new at parenthood, too. Can I get you to breathe?" Savvy put a hand on Olivia's shoulder.

Olivia took several deep, cleansing breaths in and out. She closed her eyes until her shoulders drooped in relaxation. Savvy noticed her transform from a look of peace to her forehead wrinkling with concern. Her eyes opened in distress. "Savvy, I'm a horrible wife and mom. I don't want to be all alone in raising Simone."

"Stop expecting Malcolm to be perfect. You're doing a much better job than you think you are, and you're not alone. He'll help if you let him. I know it can't be easy right now. You're not a bad wife or mom. I think you two need to sit together, pray for guidance, and have a conversation about what you need from each other."

"I hear ya girl. I hear ya." Olivia sighed. "There's something else I need to tell you, though."

Savvy stared at Olivia waiting through her pause.

"I'm pregnant again. I didn't want this right now." Olivia wrung her hands in her lap.

"Already? Are you sure?"

"Yes, I'm sure. I started acting absent-minded, and my stomach has been unusually upset. When I missed my period, I bought a pregnancy test not thinking it would be positive. Well, it was. You know I called my doctor immediately without even telling Malcolm. I visited her, and she confirmed it." Olivia fought back the tears.

"That's wonderful. You two don't waste any time. The kids will be close to each other in age and can be best friends. It's not going to be bad like you think it will be. Stop making this sound like doom and gloom."

"You don't understand, Savvy. My body is still out of shape from Simone. I'm furious with myself for giving in to Malcolm one night and having sex with him. The one time we got busy doing the do since I gave birth, and we have another baby on the way."

"Well, that explains your rollercoaster emotions. Your hormones are all out of whack, not to mention, you haven't been having enough sex to relax your nerves. You better realize this new Turnipseed growing inside of you is another blessing."

"But what about me? It's my body getting all stretched out, not Malcolm's. It's my life dominated by diapers, burp cloths, spit-up, crying, feedings, and sore arms. It's me, not him. All he does is stick it in me, and I'm the one who suffers for nine months. He gets to keep on having fun. I'm the one who can't have a drink. I'm the one who gets fatter and fatter. It's me, and no one cares about me Savvy." Olivia frantically spilled out her frustrations and tears fell from her eyes.

"Olivia, stop it. You're not doing you, or the baby, any good with this stress. Breathe right now. In and out slowly." Savvy took small breaths, hoping to get Olivia to follow suit.

Olivia followed Savvy's instructions again and finally calmed down. She grabbed a napkin off the table to wipe the tears from her face.

"Look, I know you're worried about the money. However, you're doing better than most with your practice. I think you two should meet with the financial advisor I recommended. They can help y'all develop a budget and make smart investments for your kid's future. Also, I think you should seek out counseling at church. It wouldn't hurt to get help from someone with credentials after their name who can advise you on this situation. There are some things both of you need to lay out on the table before it's too late," Savvy suggested.

"Once again you say exactly what I need to hear. I always feel better after we talk. You make me see things differently. I'm going to suggest these ideas to Malcolm and figure out what we can do. At the rate I'm going, I'll destroy our marriage if I don't get a grip."

"You can do this Olivia. Anything is possible if you stop being anxious about everything, and talk with God instead. Trust me, He will answer, and He will take care of you. You believe me, right?" Savvy asked.

"Yes, I do believe you, and I have to get back to going to church. I need to be reminded to leave my problems at the altar," Olivia said.

"Good. I'm glad you recognize God's grace. Oh, my goodness. I didn't realize what time it is. Girl, I better get out of here. I have a date tonight with the cutie pie I told you about." Savvy finished her cup of tea and stood to place Simone back in the carriage.

"Oh yes. You better get going, and you must give me the juicy details tomorrow. Thanks again for listening to my problems. Go have yourself a good time. I love you, Savvy." Olivia hugged her tightly.

Savvy hugged her back, "I love you more, Olivia. Now go home to your husband. You two can figure this stuff out. And by the way, give your man some booty."

PART 5

HOLD UP

CHAPTER 39

2011

"Come on kids. Hurry up and get in the car. We don't want to be late for your swimming lessons," Olivia yelled from the garage.

"Mom, I can't find my goggles," Simone whined.

"They should've been in your cubby by the back door. Go back in and look again," Olivia sighed with frustration. They went through this every week, and it was beyond frustrating how they could never get out of the house on time. "Tell your brother to get out here. Now."

"He's still on the computer," Simone tattled.

"What? Tell him I said, don't make me come in there and snatch him out," Olivia shouted.

"Christian. Mom said to get your butt out here," Simone yelled from the doorway.

"Stop saying the word butt, Simone," Olivia scolded. "If you both aren't in the car in one minute, we're not going."

Both of them came running out of the house.

"I wasn't on the computer." Christian jumped into the backseat.

"Yes, you were," Simone replied and buckled her seatbelt.

Olivia glanced in the rearview mirror and saw him ball his little fists up as he yelled, "No, I wasn't."

"Were too," Simone replied to irritate him.

"Stop it. Both of you. That's enough," Olivia snapped at them and backed out the garage. "Next time, we won't go if you aren't ready on time. Understand?"

"Yes," the kids said in unison.

Olivia took a deep breath. Malcolm needed to be taking the kids to these expensive swim lessons. She always ended up driving them while he was out golfing. She was tired of playing chauffer while he got to chill.

Fifteen minutes later, Olivia rushed the kids into the gym. After talking with some of the other parents, she found a spot on the bleachers to watch Christian and Simone swim.

"Hey, Mom," Christian yelled while balancing carefully on the diving board. "Watch me jump. Are you lookin'?"

"Yes, baby. I see you," Olivia replied enthusiastically. She smiled, her anger at them earlier, dissipating. She was happy to see how well they were doing in swim class and couldn't believe that Malcolm thought they were a waste of time.

Christian bounced on the board slightly and gracefully dove into the water. He surfaced quickly with a smile on his face. "Did you see me, Mom?"

"Great job, honey," Olivia cheered and stuck her thumb in the air. "Beautiful dive. You are awesome."

Christian swam to the edge of the pool to join Simone and the other kids listening to the swim instructor. Olivia's mind floated away to thinking about her crazy existence.

Life became a whirlwind eight years ago with Christian August Turnipseed's entrance into the world. Like Simone, he also had mahogany-colored skin, and a head full of jet black, curly hair.

Although neither child turned out golden-skinned like Malcolm, Olivia loved their complexion. She finally came to terms with her issues about being dark-skinned. Her children were beautiful, and it wasn't just her who thought so. They often got stopped in public by strangers commenting on their beauty.

Her parents and sister never bothered to travel to San Antonio to see the kids. After all these years, Malcolm hadn't met her family. He suggested planning a family vacation to visit them, however, out of spite, Olivia refused once her mother made excuses for not coming to help her after Simone's birth.

Although disappointed, she decided to stop wasting time trying to force a bond between her parents and children. Olivia figured her mother would be unhappy to see they were dark-skinned. She didn't know how she would react if her mother said one negative word about her kids.

Olivia made a vow to herself to never treat her children the way her parents treated her. She showered them with love in every way possible. She made sure the kids had exposure to every type of activity possible to keep them competitive with others. Simone took gymnastics, swimming, basketball, tennis and piano lessons. Christian excelled in karate, swimming, soccer, tennis, golf, and played the drums. Malcolm loved bragging on his "well-rounded" kids, even though he could never be bothered to take them to lessons.

Olivia wished Malcolm would spend more time with the children. He showed more interest in watching college and professional sports versus throwing a football around with Christian in their backyard or attending any of the kid's games. Olivia grew weary of making excuses to the children whenever they questioned why their daddy never showed for games or performances.

It's pathetic I had to be the one to teach our son how to catch a football instead of Malcolm. Why am I always going to the games by myself or with other parents?

Any time Olivia raised this subject with Malcolm, he shrugged it off and told her to stop making a big deal about it. How could she not make a big deal? He just didn't get it.

Ten years of marriage had passed. On the surface, they had the kind of life many longed for. They had four cars, an exquisite home in an upscale neighborhood, high society friends, and memberships in exclusive clubs. Rubbing shoulders with the rich and famous had been Olivia's dream. Now, it had become her perfect reality.

Socially, they attended many "see and be seen" events in town. Olivia had a designated closet packed full of designer gowns for the various black-tie affairs and galas they attended.

A local magazine featured Olivia as a Rising Star in the community. As a well-known, sought-after psychologist, she'd received awards and recognition from a variety of organizations.

Her rapidly growing practice led her to acquire another office. She hired eight additional practitioners to manage the increase in patient load.

She continued her program for women who were dealing with eating disorders and self-image issues. Helping others avoid what she experienced for many years, became her life passion.

Despite having a crazy schedule with the kids, she and Malcolm were enjoying the benefits of being a wealthy family in San Antonio due to her success.

In the meantime, behind the scenes, Malcolm didn't accomplish much with his network marketing. It seemed to be every other year; he switched to another company to chase a rabbit into another dreadful hole.

Olivia had morphed into being a constant nag about Malcolm's shortcomings when it came to his financial contributions to their marriage. And over the years, his spending habits still hadn't improved.

They constantly argued about the bills, and it often ended with Malcolm storming out of the house or Olivia closing herself off in the bedroom. They were fine financially due to Olivia's practice, yet, she became frustrated with the fact her paychecks paid for everything instead of his.

Olivia snapped out of her deep thoughts when she realized the kids were no longer in the water. She made her way down to the locker rooms and waited for the kids to exit. Children swarmed around looking for their parents. The noise from their excited chatter filled the room.

Simone skipped out of the girls' room with her braids still soaking wet and dripping on her clothes.

"Mom. Did you see me float on my back?" Simone's eyes were wide with excitement.

"I'm proud of you. You've come a long way, baby." Olivia hoped her face didn't give away the fact she didn't notice Simone floating.

Christian ran out from the boys' room with another kid Olivia recognized from previous weeks.

"Hey, Mom," Christian exclaimed. "This is Jeremy. Can he come over and play Super Mario with me on my Nintendo? Please?" The boys jumped around in excitement.

"Hi, Jeremy. Nice to see you," Olivia spotted his mother and waved across the room. "Today won't work, but let's see about next week. We can even stop out for pizza afterward if your mother says it's okay."

"Cool," the boys said in unison. They high-fived, and Jeremy ran off.

"All right, we gotta go kids. We need to grab lunch before I drop you guys off. I have my hair appointment in a little bit, and I don't want to be late." Olivia hurried the kids to the car.

"I get to sit in the front," Simone yelled.

"No, you don't. It's my turn," Christian shouted and pushed Simone away from the front door.

"Nope. I called it first," Simone taunted and elbowed him in the ribs.

"Mom," Christian whined. "She rode in the front on the way here. That's not fair." He folded his arms, stuck his bottom lip out, and burrowed his eyebrows into a mean scowl.

"Hey. Stop it." Olivia grabbed both kids by their arms and pulled them close to her. "Simone in the back. Christian in the front. Both of you had better act like you have some sense in your head. I'm tired of all of this fighting back and forth. I am not in the mood for it today. Do you hear me?"

"Yes, Mom," the kids uttered and took their seats.

"Goodness. Y'all are getting on my nerves. Also, why are you both so ashy to the point you look gray? Didn't I tell you two to take showers after swimming? My goodness, I can smell the chlorine on you," Olivia scolded. "As soon as we get home, take a shower before you do anything else and put on some lotion."

"But Mom, what about my hair?" Simone asked.

"I'll do it later. Just rinse it to get the chlorine out. How many times do we have to go over this each week?" Olivia shook her head in frustration and drove to pick up sandwiches.

You would think our kids didn't have any home training. Maybe if their daddy took some time with them, I wouldn't have to lose my mind dealing with this nonsense. Something has got to change. Otherwise, I'm running away.

CHAPTER 40

"Hey, girl. Whatchu up to?" Olivia asked Savvy. She balanced the phone between her ear and shoulder. She tucked her freshly relaxed hair behind her ear and picked up two potholders. The smell of baked Cornish hens filled her nostrils once she opened the oven door.

"Hey, Liv," Savvy replied. "Not much. I'm sitting on the back porch painting my toenails. I've gone too long with chipped polish. I thought I could stretch out another week before I get a pedicure. However, my nails look raggedy."

"Girl, me too. It's been forever since I've had my nails done. The nail tech will need to use a chainsaw to work on my feet. I haven't had time to go," Olivia complained. "One of these days, I'll have to make myself a priority. What do you think about having a spa day with a couple of our friends?"

"Oh, yes. Count me in," Savvy agreed.

"By the way, did you hear about President Barack Obama running for re-election? I'm so excited," Olivia squealed.

"Yes. I'm praying for four more years with President and Michelle Obama. I know it hasn't been easy being the first African-American President in the White House. I love them," Savvy exclaimed.

"Me, too. If he wins again, we have to go to the

Inauguration like we did in 2008."

"We sure do. I still remember how peaceful everything was in such a large crowd. The galas were off the chain. We must be there. You should bring the kids."

"Not a bad idea. It will be a great historic moment for them. Let's make it happen."

"Sounds good to me."

"Hold up a second. I need to pull this food out of the oven. I'm standing here talking to you with the door open. Let me put my phone down, so I don't drop it." Olivia clunked the phone on the counter. She placed the Cornish hens, then the macaroni and cheese, on placemats on the dining room table before closing the oven.

She put her phone back to her ear. "Okay, sorry about that."

"No problem. I know you're cooking something delicious. I would invite myself over to eat, but I need to run a few errands." Savvy said.

"No hot date tonight? I've been meaning to ask you if the dating scene has improved around here?" Olivia asked.

Savvy groaned, "Girl, no. One of my frat brothers even told me, he can't think of anyone in his fraternity worth introducing me to. He claims they are all players."

"Now, that's ridiculous. Not one?"

"No, not one. Then, you know I joined the Singles Ministry. I thought, surely, I would meet someone since our church is huge."

"Don't tell me you didn't meet one potential guy."

"Nope. Everyone is either too old, goofy, or not of interest to me."

"Hey. I just realized, we never talked about your internet date in Dallas." Olivia recalled.

"That's right. I never did tell you about how that fiasco with

Leonard turned out. I think when I called you, you were busy with the kids at swim practice. I totally forgot we didn't talk about it."

"Right. Leonard Wesley Boykin. I remember because I made you text me with his full name and license plate number. This is the one you met on the Rattler Roundup internet site, right?" Olivia asked.

"Yeah. Never again." Savvy said.

"Uh oh. What happened?"

"Girl, this had to be the grossest date I've ever been on."

"What do you mean by gross?"

"Well, you know he flew me to Dallas to go to a Mavericks basketball game."

"Right. He gets major points for being generous and creative."

Savvy reflected, "Exactly what I thought, too. I mean, no man has ever spent money to fly me somewhere on a first date."

"You said you know some of the same people from FAMU, right?"

"Right. So, I didn't feel concerned regarding my safety since we had several conversations on the phone the last few weeks. Of course, I checked him out with our mutual friends."

"Okay, what's the problem? What made this date gross?" Olivia pressed.

"When he arrived at Love Field airport, he met me at the curbside in a light blue, two-seater, convertible BMW with cream colored seats."

"I remember from your text message. More points for having a fly car."

"So, he gets out of the car to open the door for me, and he hands me this big bouquet of white roses. I thought it was thoughtful of him to bring flowers," Savvy continued. "His pictures on the dating website didn't lead me to think he would be short and nerdy though. He told me he favored Emmitt Smith on the Dallas Cowboy's team. Imagine my disappointment to see he resembled Bishop T.D. Jakes instead. I'm not saying T.D. Jakes is ugly. Nevertheless, Leonard wasn't what I expected from his pictures. I actually think Bishop Jakes is handsome. He just doesn't look anything like Emmitt Smith, you know?"

"Yeah, nerds are good these days. Keep going," Olivia pressed impatiently.

"I have to build the story Olivia," Savvy laughed. "Anyway, when he handed me the bouquet, he got clumsy in trying to hug me at the same time. The flowers crushed in between us and some of them fell onto my chest. So, he started apologizing and tried to wipe them off my breasts. I had to tell him it's okay, and I could get them off myself. He got really embarrassed and kept saying sorry. Thankfully, they didn't ruin my dress."

"Okay, okay. Get to the good part."

"Well, once we got the flowers off my dress, he opened the door for me, and we finally got into his car. I noticed he had on a long-sleeved, black, Dallas Mavericks T-Shirt and it had something white on the sleeve. I figured some of the roses must have smeared on his shirt or something," Savvy said.

"Okay. Move on please."

"So anyway, we headed to the American Airlines Center for the game. I noticed he kept sniffing and sneezing constantly. I guess he must've been allergic to the flowers. It got to be extremely bad with him sneezing everywhere in the car. I kept turning my head toward the window and praying he wouldn't spray me in the face. He began having an allergy attack," Savvy recalled.

"Yuck. Now, that's gross."

"Tell me about it. Well, next thing I know, his nose is running terribly bad. He wiped his snotty nose across the sleeve of his shirt," Savvy exclaimed.

"No, he didn't," Olivia yelled into the phone.

"Yes, he did. That's the white stuff on his shirt. This grown man just finished hugging me with that arm. Oh, my gosh. I wanted to throw up." Savvy gagged on the phone.

Olivia started laughing. "I wish I could've seen your face."

"Oh, and it gets worse," Savvy continued. "So, we get to the game, and he insisted that we get ice cream before we sat in our seats. He swore they had the best in town. Do you know I couldn't even eat it without gagging? The white color reminded me of the dried snot on his shirt. Oh my gosh, I can never eat vanilla ice cream again. I'm getting sick thinking about it."

"Did you say anything to him?"

"I did. After he wiped his nose for the umpteenth time on his shirt, I finally asked him if I could get him some tissues for him to use. Do you know he said, no thanks? Can you believe that? It took everything in me to not leave him there and catch a cab back to the airport," Savvy said.

"Oh, Savvy. I'm sorry it turned out badly for you. You're better than me. I would've left and told him he is a hazard to the health of other people. A grown man doing that mess ain't right."

Savvy chuckled. "I can laugh about it now. It sure wasn't funny at the time. Nevertheless, I made it through the game, back to the airport, and safely back home. He keeps calling, so I told him I didn't think we were compatible."

"I would say you definitely have nothing in common in any way, shape, or form. Tell the man to go to an allergist and get his allergies treated."

"Enough about me. How are my niece and nephew doing?

You know it is time for them to come hang out with Auntie Savvy. I will spoil them rotten."

"Girl, you can come and get them anytime. You know they love seeing you. All they ask about is Auntie Savvy this and Auntie Savvy that," Olivia laughed.

"I'm the best auntie in the world. Maybe I can come to get them on Sunday."

"You know what, they're going to SeaWorld on Sunday with one of our neighbors and her kids. How about you get them the following weekend? You can have them stay with you for a slumber party if you don't have a hot date," Olivia offered.

"Girl puh-leeze. No hot dates for me anytime soon. Let's put it on the calendar. I'm going to let them eat and drink anything they want. Sugary sodas, cracker jack popcorn, ice cream, cookies, you name it," Savvy laughed.

"Noooo. You'll totally destroy everything I've put into place. You know I don't allow that stuff in this house," Olivia pleaded.

"Hey. I'm the auntie, and that's the way it is."

"I see I'll have to put them on a juicing diet to detox when you bring them home. Ugh."

"Girl, you're too funny. You know how Auntie Savvy does it, and I ain't changing no time soon."

Olivia groaned at the thought of her kids eating like crazy. "I know, I know. I guess I can let them off their food routine for a night of fun."

"On a different subject, how's Malcolm doing?"

"Girl, don't get me started. That man has pushed my buttons to the nth degree. If he seemed like a cheating kind of guy, I would have my suspicions." Olivia placed tomatoes and cucumbers on a bed of romaine lettuce in four salad bowls. She placed them on the dining room table along with the other food.

"Suspicions? Why would you even say that? What do you

think is going on?" Savvy asked.

"Well, he's spending more time away from the house, buying new clothes, and even cologne. He's acting differently, and I can't quite put my finger on it. Extremely unusual behavior." Olivia placed four plates on the table along with silverware, napkins, and glasses of water. "It seems like all we do is argue about stupid stuff, and we can't seem to communicate anymore the way we used to. Thankfully, we only sleep in the same bed three times a week."

"Wait a minute. Did you say you still sleep separately? Please tell me that isn't the case," Savvy said. "I still can't believe you guys did that the entire time the kids were babies."

"You heard me right. I mean, we still get together and have sex. He seems freakier in bed these days. He's been asking me to try different positions and some stuff I don't do, you know. I can't imagine where he gets these ideas. It's possibly from watching movies on TV or something."

"Hmmm, that's interesting."

"Anyway, I got used to not having to listen to his loud snoring every night. I keep telling him; he needs to have a study done to see if he has sleep apnea. It's like living with a bear. I have too much to do each day to be missing out on a good night of rest. I got spoiled by having the bed all to myself when the kids were young," Olivia admitted.

"It has been ten years. You need to get back in the bed together. Every night, Olivia," Savvy said. "I don't think it's healthy for a husband and wife to be apart like that. I know you're thinking, what do I know since I'm not married, right?"

"No, not at all. I get what you're saying. I'm telling you, it has nothing to do with the issues we're having. Our problems are all financial and not the fact we don't sleep in the same bed. Trust me," Olivia said.

"Okay, okay, if you say so. Let me ask you this. How often are you making love?" Savvy inquired.

"Wow, aren't you the Dr. Phil. I thought I'm the psychologist around here," Olivia joked.

"Seriously, how often?" Savvy persisted.

"Maybe once every other month or so. Something like that," Olivia said flatly.

"Are you kidding me? You can't be serious. Every other month?"

"Give or take. What's the big deal? We're super tired every night, and the kids keep us busy. I mean, he would probably like for us to do it more often. With all the financial stuff, I'm not turned on anymore. It's hard to be in the mood when he gets on my nerves," Olivia explained.

"That's not good. I think you need to find a way to keep your husband satisfied. I'm not saying he's creeping out there or anything. The problem is, you aren't giving him enough booty. Plus, you two keep arguing, and he leaves the house mad. I would be cautious about a clean-up woman lingering around to comfort your man. You know what I mean?"

"Well, I appreciate your concern. Malcolm is nothing like Dwain, Ross, or anyone else I've dated over the years. I know I tend to end up with men who are cheaters. But this time, I know in my heart, I don't have to worry about him cheating. He isn't that kind of man." Olivia explained.

"Uh huh." Savvy sounded doubtful.

"He wouldn't disrespect me for not putting out. He loves me too much, and he worships the ground I walk on. I never even see him looking at other women. He gets mad when he hears about other guys messing around on their wives. He's a God-fearing man, who I know will honor our vows."

"I see," Savvy said.

"Plus, by being in San Antonio, he definitely ain't looking at any Hispanic women here. He's not a racist, but he can't stand seeing interracial couples. He said it goes against the principles of the Motherland. He always says *black people need to be with black people.* I don't need to worry about him cheating. Period," Olivia said confidently.

"If you're so sure about him being faithful, then what were you talking about when you said you have your suspicions about him?" Savvy questioned.

"I said, if he seemed like a cheating guy, then I would have my suspicions. But, I'm trying to explain to you, that he's not like that."

"But what about everything you just said about how he's acting differently? What do you think he is doing?"

"Oh, forget what I said about that. I'm just complaining about him getting on my nerves. He's probably having an early mid-life crisis. Once we work our financial issues out, then I'm sure everything will improve." Olivia stated.

"Well, if you think you two are fine, I'll leave it alone. Hey, I got to get out of this house and get to the grocery store. Tell everyone hi for me." Savvy said.

Olivia frowned when she looked at the clock. "Yeah, I need to yell for the kids to come to dinner. I thought Malcolm would've been home by now and he's not here. I need to give him a call. Have a good night my friend. Bye,"

"Bye, Liv," Savvy replied.

CHAPTER 41

Olivia held the phone in her hand, thinking about Savvy's concerns. "Malcolm knows everything I've been through with Dwain and Ross. I believe in my heart; he would never hurt me the way the two of them did. He's my husband, and a father to our children. He's better than they ever will be." She mumbled and punched in Malcolm's cell phone number. His voicemail answered.

Confused, she laid the phone on the table. "Now, that's strange. He always answers my calls."

Memories of calling Dwain and Ross flooded Olivia's mind. She remembered how they both were with other women whenever she couldn't reach them. "No way. I'm not about to make myself go insane by thinking those negative thoughts." Olivia shook her head to clear her mind. "He had better have a good excuse for being late though."

Olivia headed to the bottom of the stairwell. "Simone. Christian. Dinner's ready," she called to the kids. The rumble and tumble of their feet running indicated they heard her loud and clear.

"Yay. Mom, I'm starving. I'm gonna pass out from hunger," Christian yelled, running past her to the dining room.

"Me, too. Why did we have to wait this long for dinner?" Simone chased after Christian to try to beat him to the table.

"Hey. Go wash those dirty hands before you sit down," Olivia yelled at the kids when she entered the dining room. They raced to get to the bathroom and back to the table.

"I get the big Cornish hen," Simone yelled.

"No, you don't, it's my turn for the big one," Christian argued.

"No, it's not."

"Yes, it is."

"Is not."

"Is too. Mom," Christian whined.

"Y'all, stop arguing or else neither one of you will eat anything," Olivia scolded. Christian sulked, and Simone smirked and threw her arms up in victory.

Olivia sat at the table. She searched her cell phone screen for a missed call from Malcolm. *Where could he be right now? He didn't mention he would miss dinner tonight.*

"Who wants to lead us in grace?" Olivia asked once the kids settled into their seats.

"I'll do it, Mama." Simone bowed her head. "Dear Lord, thank you for this yummy food Mama has prepared for us to eat. Let it be nourishing to our bodies, and thanks for letting me get the big Cornish hen tonight. In Jesus name. Amen."

Olivia laughed. "Child. You're too funny and thank you for saying the grace. Christian, what Bible verse do you want to say before we eat?"

Still upset about the Cornish hen, Christian cut his eyes at Simone and mumbled, "Romans 2nd chapter, 8th verse: But for those who are self-seeking and who reject the truth and follow evil, there will be wrath and anger."

"Mom. He's being mean. Don't be wishing wrath and anger on me," Simone complained.

"Christian. Quit using scriptures to get back at your sister.

That's not very nice. Stop worrying about the food. The Cornish hens are all the same size. Now let's eat," Olivia said.

"Hey Mom, where's Dad?" Christian asked with his mouth full of food.

"Christian, stop talking with your mouth full," Olivia responded when they heard the key in the back door and Malcolm strolled in on cue.

"Daddy," Simone screamed, running from her chair to Malcolm for a hug.

"Hey, baby girl. How's my princess doing?" Malcolm hugged her back, lifting her off the ground to twirl her around.

"Don't spin her too much Malcolm. She's eating and will get sick if you keep doing that," Olivia warned.

"I'm fine, Mama. I love it, Daddy." Simone giggled when Malcolm spun her around one more time before putting her down. Smiling, she wobbled with dizziness back to the table.

Malcolm walked into the dining room to ruffle Christian's miniature afro and give him a fist bump. "Hey, big man. Are you getting enough to eat, son?"

"Yeah, but Simone got the biggest Cornish hen. I should be the one with the largest piece. I need more protein for my muscles." Christian flexed his puny arms. "See Dad. Aren't they big now? I've been doing pushups like you told me to."

"Yes, son. I can see they are bigger. Keep it up, and you'll be strong like me before you know it." Malcolm flexed his bicep muscles, which bulged under his new shirt. Christian eyes grew huge in admiration of his Dad's arms.

Olivia noticed Malcolm put his keys on the counter and started to walk toward the stairwell. "Aren't you going to eat?" she asked, a little taken aback that he hadn't even kissed her like he normally did when he got home.

"Oh, no, honey. I got together with the boys. We stopped

out to get wings and beer after we played golf tonight. I meant to call you. The time got away from me," Malcolm said and headed upstairs.

Stunned by Malcolm's answer, Olivia jumped from the table and followed him to the stairwell. "You've been gone since the crack of dawn. It's been more than twelve hours since you left."

"Yeah, it wasn't planned. One of my boys is going through some things. He needed to talk and get it off his chest. You know I had to be there for him. What's the big deal?" Malcolm paused on the stairs and turned around to glare at Olivia.

"What's the big deal? I can't believe you asked me that question. Malcolm, the big deal is you stayed out all day long. You haven't spent any time with the kids. You could've at least had the decency to call to let me know you were going to miss dinner. I didn't know if something happened to you or what. When I called you, I got your voicemail. Why didn't you let me know?"

"Woman, will you get off my back? How many times do I have to tell you, it wasn't planned? I needed to be there for my boy," Malcolm snapped before turning away. She started following him up the stairs. "Why do you have a nervous breakdown about stupid stuff? I ain't one of the kids. I don't have to tell you every single thing I do. Now, I'm going to shower. I'll come downstairs when I'm done."

Olivia stopped in her tracks on the stairs, hurt from his tone of voice and chosen words. Her heart now fluttered from brokenness at that moment. She couldn't think of any more words to say when he walked into the bedroom and slammed the door.

CHAPTER 42

The sun broke through the horizon. The sky turned a brilliant reddish-orange color. Olivia longed for the ray of light in what seemed to be the darkness of her life. She lounged in a chair on the veranda in her yellow silk robe. Chirps of the birds in the otherwise peaceful, early morning, interrupted her deep thought about the argument with Malcolm the night before.

Everyone else remained asleep when she arose to meditate and plan her week. She decided not to bother the kids about going to church since a ball of anxiety remained clenched in her chest from Malcolm's words.

She took a few sips of her lukewarm, strong, black coffee and wondered what needed to happen to get her marriage back on track.

Olivia rested her head on the back of the chair and closed her eyes. She began analyzing Malcolm's behavior. *Perhaps I should think of him as one of my patients and evaluate his actions.*

First, it's ridiculous he refuses to go with me to any type of marriage or financial counseling. For some reason, he thinks it opens the door for people to meddle in our business. Just because I know a lot of professionals in the industry, doesn't mean our family secrets would end up publicized. My goodness. I can't believe his solution for everything is; I need to stop nagging him and get off his back.

Let me think this through. Is there anything Malcolm has done to show he even cares about the family and me anymore? I guess he's taken on more responsibility by suggesting he handle paying the phone bill each month. Hmmm. That ain't much, but I guess it's something. Oh yeah, he did begin managing the reconciliation of our bank account since I hate balancing a checkbook. He probably only wants to do it to keep me from getting on him about how much money he's spending.

But why is he away from home more now? He's leaving the house earlier in the morning and staying out later each night. I know he claims he's working on building his business, but, is he really spending this much time at networking breakfast meetings and evening happy hours? Perhaps I could believe it if I witnessed the fruit of his extra labor in the form of a paycheck. If only something consistent would come in. Then maybe I will develop confidence in his business and know our future is secure.

Olivia recalled a conversation one morning when she entered the bedroom…

Malcolm was fixing his tie in the mirror and whistling. She hadn't heard him whistle in years.

"Good morning." She sniffed and walked toward him. "What's that smell? Is that cologne?"

"Oh. Hey. It sure is. Do you like it?" He glanced at her reflection.

"It's a bit strong, but it smells nice. Since when did you start wearing cologne again? I thought it messed with your allergies?"

"I must've grown out of it. Maybe, the stuff you were buying me had the wrong combination of scents." He finished with his tie and gave himself a look of approval in the mirror.

"Where are you going so early? You beat me getting up today. I sense a high level of energy." Olivia observed.

"Ginseng, baby. You should try it. I have an important breakfast meeting with a potential client. Great way to start the day with new money coming in." Malcolm turned away and put his wallet in his pants pocket.

"Is that a new suit? I haven't seen this one before." Olivia stepped closer and rubbed his arm. "Malcolm, I can tell this is expensive. Why are you buying more clothes?"

"Baby, you know I have to be on point from head to toe if you want me to bring in the dough."

Olivia huffed in exasperation. "What a lame excuse. Just another reason to keep shopping with money you don't have."

As soon as the words left her mouth, she knew she hurt Malcolm to the core.

"I'm out." Malcolm left the room without kissing her goodbye.

Olivia raised her head and opened her eyes. Now the sun's radiance fell across her lap.

"Could Malcolm be cheating on me? Is that why he's treating me the way he is? No. Stop it. I have to stop thinking the worst. It's making me mad again. God gave me a good man. We have to just work through our problems," she mumbled.

Olivia breathed in deeply through her nostrils, taking in the cool, morning air and letting it out slowly. She repeated this breathing exercise five times. The sound of Malcolm's alarm clock buzzed when she let go of her final breath. She stood from her lounger and slipped on her slippers. She leaned her head back and extended her arms to the sky in an awakening stretch. She was ready to face another day.

CHAPTER 43

Olivia stepped through the sliding door into the guest bedroom. Originally, she planned to follow Savvy's advice and sleep in the same bed with Malcolm. However, after their argument last night, she'd spared him from being punched in the throat while he slept by sleeping in a different room.

After showering, Olivia put on a pair of jeans, a yellow t-shirt, and her white slippers to wake the kids.

"Christian," she knocked on his bedroom door. "Are you up?"

"Yes, Mom. I already took my shower. I can't wait to go to SeaWorld." His excitement permeated through the door.

Olivia laughed. "Well, all right. Glad you are ready to go. I'm going to check on your sister."

"I'm downstairs, Mom. I already ate cereal," Simone's voice floated from the kitchen. "By the way, Dad left for the golf course."

"Okay, thanks for passing on the message, dear." Olivia sighed and headed downstairs just when the doorbell rang.

She opened the door and smiled upon seeing her neighbors, Rhonice and Dion. They had become great friends. Their kids were the same age as Simone and Christian. They played well together and spent time between the two houses like family.

"Good morning," Olivia said.

"Good morning, Liv," they replied in unison.

Christian nearly tumbled down the stairs. "Hi, Mr. and Mrs. Hudson. We can't wait. Are we leaving yet? Where's Marley?" Christian jumped around bubbling with excitement.

Rhonice laughed. "Marley and McKenzie are in the car. Grab your water shoes and let's get going."

"Okay. Come on, Simone. It's time to go," Christian yelled down the hall while frantically putting on his shoes. Simone ran out from the kitchen and hugged the Hudsons.

"Hi, Mr. and Mrs. Hudson. Will we get to see Shamu?" Simone squealed in anticipation.

"Of course. We'll see whatever shows you want to," Rhonice replied.

Dion laughed and spoke as if he were sharing a secret. "Hey, kids. I'm going to make sure we ride all of the big rollercoasters."

"Yay," the kids squealed. "Bye, Mom."

Olivia hugged them quickly. "Bye. Make sure you don't run off and get lost in the park. Put your hats on. Be on your best behavior and no arguing," Olivia instructed.

"Yeah, Mom. We will. Stop worrying," Christian shouted back and ran after Simone to the car. "Hey, Marley and McKenzie. Here we come."

"Can you tell they're anxious to get there?" Rhonice laughed. "We'll keep them hydrated and fed. You'll have two kids brought back to you at the end of the day. They'll be in one piece, although they might be soaking wet."

"Thank you two for taking them with y'all. I owe you." She smiled and waved at the car when they backed out of the driveway. They honked their horn and drove off.

Olivia entered the house and closed the door. They would

be gone until evening. A lazy day lounging around the pool with a good book and several mimosas are what she needed. Malcolm would be out late since the guys usually go to a cigar lounge afterward on Sundays. She appreciated having the home to herself instead of dealing with him.

Thinking about which swimsuit to put on, she decided to head to the kitchen to find her champagne to add to orange juice. A bagel with cream cheese, smoked salmon, and capers sounded like a good breakfast today.

When passing the office, a blinking light on the computer caught her eye. She stopped and peeked in. A faint humming sound came from the desktop.

She walked to the desk, leaned over the computer, and wiggled the mouse. The screen showed more than a game.

Olivia widened her eyes at the sick display before her. In disbelief, she turned her head and shook it to clear her mind. She hoped what flashed before her wasn't real. *What in the world is Christian using this computer to look at? I'm going to beat his behind when he gets home. He knows better than to look at this nastiness. I'm telling his daddy, and he's going on punishment forever.*

When she refocused on the screen, she read the top of the page. A dating website called *Large Luscious Latina Ladies Love Black Men* displayed in front of her eyes. It showed Malcolm had been chatting with a woman online. He didn't exit the site before leaving the house to hang out with his friends.

Olivia's heart pounded in her chest, and blood rushed to her ears. She placed her hand on the desk to keep herself from falling.

She slumped into the office chair without taking her eyes off the screen and began scanning the words on the page.

Malcolm and this chic, Carmen, were going back and forth about how they were looking forward to meeting this weekend at a restaurant in the Pearl Brewery. That was one of Olivia's favorite places. It's where she'd taken Malcolm for Father's Day last year, and he'd claimed that he didn't even like the food.

Olivia's hand shook when she clicked on the mouse to view Carmen's profile in detail. The woman had to be at least 400 pounds. Skimpy, sheer red lingerie, stretched as though it were too tight on her body. Heavy black mascara and blue eyeshadow painted underneath high arched eyebrows, gave her the appearance of a clown. To top it off, her makeup didn't conceal her acne covered face.

The woman knelt in a doggie style position on a king-sized bed, showing a red lacy thong lost in her behind. She gazed seductively at the camera with her red painted fingernail stuck in her pouty, cherry colored lipstick mouth.

Her profile said that she was a five-feet-one inch tall, twenty-two years old, and had three children all below the age of six. The youngest was two years old. Her favorite hobby was watching reality TV and going to the movies. She'd never lived anywhere outside of San Antonio. It appeared she finished high school and was a stay-at-home Mom.

Olivia unconsciously bit her fingernails. Her heart pounded wildly against her chest wall in shock. Unsure about what she'd possibly see, she reluctantly clicked to view Malcolm's profile. What he wrote about himself horrified her.

First, his picture was one she'd taken of him when they were on South Beach in Miami. He wore turquoise swimming trunks, and casually laid back on a beach chair. His flexed chest muscles glistened in the sun. It was her favorite picture because he smiled at her with his eyes filled with passion. This had to be one of their best vacations with only the two of them.

Secondly, his profile read he was single, thirty-three, no kids and never married. "He's forty-three years old, married, with two children," Olivia yelled in disbelief.

Malcolm wrote that he was a marketing executive for a Fortune 500 company. He listed several travel destinations he claimed to have gone to, including South Africa, Paris, Belize, and Egypt although he'd never been to any of those places.

Tears pooled in the corners of Olivia's eyes. Her hand shook vigorously in her attempt to direct the mouse to click on additional chats Malcolm had with other women.

Several pages of women with the same type of features filled his pages. Grossly overweight, heavy makeup, and at least two to four kids. Olivia clicked on one of the profiles, and a long string of conversation, which dated back four months, popped onto the screen.

She started reading.

HEY, BABY, IT'S MARIAH.

HEY, SWEETHEART.

I MISS YOU.

I MISS YOU TOO.

I CAN STILL SMELL YOUR COLOGNE ON MY CLOTHES. I KEEP SMELLING THEM AND THINKING ABOUT YOU.

I KNOW HOW MUCH YOU LIKE IT. I'M GLAD IT KEEPS ME ON YOUR MIND.

I WISH WE HAD MORE TIME TOGETHER YESTERDAY.

YEAH, ME TOO. SORRY I COULDN'T GET OUT OF MY MEETING.

THAT'S OKAY, BABY. I KNOW YOU WORK HARD FOR ME.

YOU GOT THAT RIGHT. WHEN CAN I TASTE THOSE SWEET LIPS AGAIN?

ARE WE STILL ON FOR THURSDAY MORNING?

YOU KNOW IT. I'LL GET YOU AT 6 AM, AND WE CAN GO TO THE RIVERWALK HOTEL. I KNOW HOW MUCH YOU LOVE BEING THERE.

I CAN'T WAIT. I'M SHIVERING JUST THINKING ABOUT YOU TOUCHING ME AGAIN.

I'M GOING TO DO SOME THINGS TO YOU THAT WILL MAKE YOU SCREAM, GIRL.

BABY, YOU KNOW I'LL DO THE SAME TO YOU.

I'LL CALL YOU LATER. I LOVE YOU MORE THAN YOU COULD EVER KNOW.

I LOVE YOU TOO.

Love? He told her he loves her? He called her sweetheart? Olivia stared at the screen. She couldn't move.

Olivia struggled with the thoughts going through her mind. *Once again, just like Dwain did to me in college, my man is cheating on me with light-skinned, Hispanic women. I'm not good enough because I'm dark-skinned?*

Her brain flooded with conversations she and Malcolm had recently. These messages explained why he decided to change his workout routine time to the morning instead of the evening. He claimed he needed to leave at 5:30 am to travel to the gym and get in his exercise in before work.

Olivia blinked her eyes slowly, and more revelations crossed her mind. This woman, Mariah, was someone he'd obviously been seeing for a while. The other chic, Carmen, was who he was about to meet in person for the first time this weekend. How many others are there? How long had this been going on?

"I've done everything to stay in tiptop shape after the kids were born, just to keep him happy. He's cheating with these women who haven't worked out a day in their lives?" Olivia screamed.

On top of that, Malcolm acted as if it killed him to be around interracial couples. He's sleeping with Hispanic women. He always said he'd never found them to be attractive.

The tears splattered her cheeks, spilling onto the keyboard from the thoughts consuming her.

Rage replaced Olivia's tears. Red dots formed in front of her eyes, and her head throbbed at the temples. She jumped from the chair and ran up the winding staircase two steps at a time to their bedroom.

Slinging the bedroom closet door open, she pulled out Malcolm's nylon bag of clothes to be dry cleaned. Frantically fumbling with the bag, she dropped to her knees on the hardwood floor without wincing from the pain.

She started pulling his clothes out to check every item. After searching through the first pair of slacks, she didn't find anything. She threw them aside. In the next pair, she wiggled her fingers around in one of the back pockets and felt a piece of paper. Pulling it out, she read that it is a parking lot receipt for the St. Andrew's hotel from two Thursdays ago. She checked the time stamp, and it read 11:07 AM.

Olivia drew in a sharp breath, recalling that day perfectly. That was the day she'd asked Malcolm to meet her at the school for a conference with Christian's teacher at noon. He'd arrived late, and his hair was wet. He smelled like something sweet and not like the soap at the gym, but she didn't say anything so they could focus on the discussion with the teacher.

Olivia continued to dig through his clothes and grabbed a pair of jeans. She tore into the front pockets and found nothing. In the back, she found a yellow receipt from Farmington's Steakhouse.

There was a purchase of three glasses of White Zinfandel, three margaritas, four appetizers, and a dessert during Happy Hour. Malcolm loved margaritas with Grand Marnier, and she noticed there were three extra shots of Grand Marnier on the receipt.

Olivia fell from her knees and sat on the floor exhausted with emotion. She leaned her head against the wall and closed her eyes. This was the same night that Malcolm claimed he needed to work late. Olivia had been furious because he'd promised Simone that he would be at her game, and he hadn't shown up.

Olivia held her pounding head in deep thought. Her temples throbbed from anger building inside her mind. Simone kept scanning the stands that night. She had such a look of disappointment. She cried the entire car ride home after the game.

Olivia slammed her fist into her hand repeatedly with each recovered thought. Malcolm had been in the shower when they'd made it home after the game. Even though Olivia had gone off on him, he'd ignored her, walked down to Simone's room, promised her they'd go for ice cream later, then came back, got in bed and started snoring like he didn't have a care in the world.

Olivia struggled to swallow the lump in her throat caused by her repulsion with Malcolm. She hadn't experienced pain to this extent since she'd been beaten up in college by Isabella and the other girl. At this point, she would prefer the physical injury instead of the emotional damage to her heart.

The urge to run to the kitchen hit her. Olivia needed to regain the control she'd lost in that moment. *I can eat everything in the pantry. I know something will help. Maybe, I need to gain weight to get him to love me. I need to be what he wants me to be. I'm too skinny and black. He's cheating because of the way I look. I gotta do something.*

Defeated, she began to sob uncontrollably. Olivia weakly pushed herself onto her feet and leaned against the wall to keep from falling. Her stomach wretched and she fought the desire to vomit. With her arms wrapped around herself, she began to rock back and forth in agony. "No. No. Oh, God. Please. Please. Take this away from me. Wake me up. Don't let this be real.

Why? Why? Why is this happening? I've done everything You told me to do. This isn't fair. I can't live like this. I'd be better off dead. Just kill me now God. I don't want this. Please help me," she wailed. Tears poured from her eyes with the screams leaving her lips.

CHAPTER 44

Savvy toweled off after finishing her workout at the gym. Her cell phone rang in her purse. She fished it out and noticed Olivia's name on the screen.

"Hey, Girl. Whassup?" Savvy asked breathlessly and wiped her face.

"Savvy. Savvy. I can't believe this. I can't believe this is happening," Olivia cried into the phone.

"Olivia. What is it? I can't understand you. Calm down." Savvy tried to comprehend her words.

"It's Malcolm. I can't believe this." Olivia continued to wail on the phone.

"What happened to Malcolm? Has he been in an accident? Is he okay?" Savvy questioned. "Try to breathe and tell me what's going on."

Olivia gulped and took a few deep breaths. "I wish he had been in an accident. It would've been better than this."

"You don't mean that. Tell me, what happened."

"I found out Malcolm is cheating on me with at least two women," Olivia exclaimed.

"Are you sure?" Savvy asked. "Why do you think he's cheating on you?"

"I read it on the computer. He's been on a dating website called Large Luscious Latina Ladies Love Black Men. He has a profile where he claims to be single with no kids. He's been seeing one of them for at least four months and is about to meet another one this weekend." Olivia wailed without taking a breath.

"What?" Savvy put her fingers in air quotations. "Mr., I am the King of African-American pride, himself? He doesn't even like seeing interracial couples. I remember how furious he was at the Fiesta parade after seeing a black man with a white woman standing in front of him."

"Exactly. And he knows how much it bothers me to see a black man date a Hispanic woman ever since my incident in college," Olivia cried.

"Yeah, I remember those crazy girls who jumped you. Wow. I didn't realize that's why you can't stand seeing Hispanic women with black men. Of course, living in San Antonio, there are a lot of mixed couples."

"Well, now, he's denied his family, lied about his age, his job, and is having sex with someone else. I don't know what to do." Olivia started to cry again. "What if he gave me an STD? What if I have HIV or AIDS? What am I going to do Savvy? I might die."

"Look, Olivia, are you sure he wasn't just messing around on the computer?" Savvy asked.

"No. I searched through his clothes and found receipts for a hotel and Happy Hour at times he supposedly would've been at the gym or working late. He even missed Simone's basketball game to be out with this trick."

"No, he didn't," Savvy exclaimed. "Okay, okay. Try not to get worked up again. Where are the kids and Malcolm right now?"

"The kids are out with the Hudson's at SeaWorld. Malcolm is supposedly out playing golf with the guys." Olivia choked on her words.

"Okay, I'm coming over right now. We can figure out what's going on."

"No, please don't come over. I'm a mess. I need some time to myself," Olivia pleaded.

"I don't think you should be alone. I'm on my way," Savvy stated firmly.

"I need to absorb all of this in. I called you to hear your voice but, I'm okay," Olivia said, sounding like she was trying to compose herself.

"Are you sure you don't need me to come by right now? I'm leaving the gym at this moment, and I can swing by on my way home."

"Please, Savvy. I appreciate you offering to come over. Give me time alone today, and you can come by tomorrow once I clear my head. I love you for being there for me." Olivia sniffled.

"Okay," Savvy said hesitantly. "I'm going to call and check on you. Please, don't do anything crazy. We don't need another incident like what you did to get back at Ross. Okay?"

"Don't worry. I think I want to get in the bed right now and get rid of this headache. It hurts so bad." Olivia sighed. "Just say a prayer for my family. I don't know what is about to happen to all of us."

"Of course, I'll pray for you and the family. I'm furious he did this to you. I know you wanted to believe in him. He had better hope I don't see him on the streets right now." Savvy fumed. "I know you are torn apart inside, and I'm sorry you are going through this. I feel like I need to be there with you. Is there anything I can do?"

"I don't think so. I'll let you know what I find out when I talk to him. I'll call you later," Olivia said wearily.

"I love you, my friend. Don't do anything crazy. Please call me for anything."

"I will. Bye." Olivia sighed.

"Bye," Savvy said and ended the call. *Dear Lord, please let this all be a misunderstanding. I figured he might be cheating, but not like this.*

Savvy sat in her car and thought about going to Olivia's house anyway to check on her. Since she seemed adamant about needing time to get her head together, Savvy decided to go home instead. That ended up being the biggest mistake she could have ever made.

CHAPTER 45

The coldness of the washcloth on Olivia's eyes did nothing to erase the visions of all she'd seen on the computer screen. Olivia lay restlessly in bed. Her stomach lurched, and her mind spun like a merry-go-round. *This is a nightmare. I'm going to wake from it at any moment.* Unfortunately, this situation was real and not a dream.

After speaking to Savvy earlier, she called Malcolm eight times. Nothing except his voice message reverberated in her ear. After the last attempt to reach him, she screamed and hurled the phone across the room. The screen cracked when it hit the wall and fell to the hardwood floor.

Darkness from outside her window seeped into the room and her body. *How long have I been in this bed?* Her body ached when she rolled over to squint at the digital clock, which showed 8:09 pm. She groaned once she realized the number of hours since her discovery of Malcolm's infidelity. The kids would be home soon. She had to pull herself together.

The washcloth dropped to the floor when she used her wobbly arms and pushed herself up to a seated position. Her legs became like heavy logs when she dangled them on the side of the bed. She eased her feet into her slippers. Pain pounded her temples, causing her to clutch her head quickly. Her head felt like it was about to explode and her stomach growled, reminding her that she hadn't eaten anything all day.

Suddenly, an alert dinged from her phone indicating the delivery of a text message. Olivia stood and staggered to where the phone lay on the floor to see if it had come from Malcolm.

She tried to decipher the message through the cracked screen. The text was from Simone:

Mom. Can we spend the night with Marley and McKenzie? Having a blast. Mrs. Hudson said we're going to have pizza. Can we come get our sleeping bags and PJs? Pleeeeeaaaassse Mom.

The Hudson's yard adjoined to theirs with a gate allowing access between the yards. The kids could come in through the back door and get their belongings.

Olivia absentmindedly typed a text message back.

Sure babe. No problem.

She called Malcolm's number again, and again, did not get an answer.

How can he do this to me? After all, I've done for him. I've been taking care of him all these years, and this is how he treats me? I hate him from the depth of my soul. I hate him.

Olivia stumbled out of her room. She clung to the railing to keep from falling downstairs. She made her way to the wet bar and hung on to the barstool. A bottle of vodka sat on the counter with the top off. Did she really drink a half a bottle of that stuff earlier? No wonder she felt like a train hit her. She drank it on an empty stomach, too. That's why her head felt like it was split open.

She groaned and leaned on the counter to keep her balance. Against her better judgment, she snatched the bottle and took a big swig from it. The burn of the white liquid flowed through her throat and into her grumbling belly.

The grandfather clock in the living room read 8:46 when

she heard the garage door opening. She could hear the engine of the Escalade as Malcolm pulled in.

She staggered to the kitchen and flopped onto a chair after turning it to face the door to the garage. Her hands were clammy and cold, yet her body burned like a sauna inside.

It seemed like a slow-motion picture when she heard Malcolm whistling and jingling his keys. The click from the sound of the door unlocking vibrated throughout the house, along with the ticking of the clock.

The door opened, and Malcolm stopped whistling abruptly when he noticed Olivia glaring at him.

"Hi, baby," Malcolm said with surprise on his face. His gym bag hung on his shoulder and he held his cell phone in his hand.

Olivia didn't respond to him. *Why is his hair wet? I smell honeysuckle. He smells like he just showered with someone else's soap. That's not a golf shirt he's wearing. Why does he have on a dress shirt instead? He never puts on clothes like these when he's out with the guys.* She glared at him with her arms crossed. The tapping of her foot on the floor matched the ticking of the clock in the quiet room.

"Olivia, are you okay?" Malcolm slowly placed his bag on the floor and his phone on the kitchen island. He kept his eyes on her. "You don't look well. Have you been drinking?"

Olivia stood slowly and stared at him. "How dare you ask me if I've been drinkin'," she slurred. "Where've you been?"

"Olivia, you know I've been out playing golf with the guys. Afterward, we hung out to have drinks and cigars at the cigar club." Malcolm peered at her with concern in his eyes. "It's the same as always, Olivia."

"You lie," Olivia yelled. She jabbed him hard several times in the chest with her finger. "Why's your hair wet?" She smacked him upside his head.

"Ouch," Malcolm yelped and put his hand to head. "Why

did you hit me?"

"You're a liar," she yelled at him. "Tell me. Why's your hair wet when you only had drinks and cigars?"

"Olivia, I decided to get a workout in before coming home. I stopped at the gym and took a shower when I finished. Why are you trippin'?"

"Oh. You were at the gym, huh? After a full day of golf, drinks, and cigars. You expect me to believe you worked out?" Olivia narrowed her eyes to make them thin slits on her face.

"Look, I don't know how much drinking you've been doing. You need to stop questioning me like this, woman," Malcolm said angrily.

"Why didn't you answer your phone?" Olivia asked through clenched teeth. "I called you a million times and kept getting your voicemail."

"Babe, my battery must have died. I didn't even notice you were calling me," Malcolm tried to explain.

Just at that moment, Malcolm's phone rang. They both stared at it, and then at each other. Time seemed to stand still.

Suddenly, Olivia ran to the phone and snatched it from the counter. Malcolm jumped toward her and tried to pry it from her hands.

Olivia managed to pull away from him with a death grip on the phone. She ran into the bathroom in a panic. She managed to slam and lock the solid oak door before Malcolm rammed into it. The door didn't budge open.

"Olivia. Give me my phone," Malcolm yelled and pounded on the door. The door shook but remained closed.

Olivia ignored him. She stared at the missed call from Mariah. His battery read it had a charge of seventy-eight percent. With her hands sweating and shaking, she hit the call button. A woman answered the phone saying, "Hey, *Papi*. I miss you already, baby."

"*Papi*, huh? You want to speak to *Papi?* This. Is. His. Wife. Now you listen to me, you whore. Don't you ever call this number again," Olivia screamed into the phone, and ended the call. Malcolm was so bold; he even put the woman's name in his contact list.

"Olivia. You better give me my phone. Open this door."

Olivia ignored Malcolm and frantically examined the apps on his phone. She flicked each page with her thumb until she found his picture gallery and clicked on it.

Jumping out at her were naked photos of five morbidly obese Hispanic women. They were all in X-rated positions showing every nook and cranny of their bodies, which burned her eyes.

Olivia gasped out loud in shock when she found six nude pictures of Malcolm. They were selfies he had taken in their bathroom mirror. He wore his new designer underwear, pulled low around his hips, while he held his erection in his hand.

Dropping to her knees and landing on the soft bathroom rug, she held the phone with trembling hands, overcome with the horror of seeing her husband like this. Although she dreaded coming across anything else, she couldn't fight the urge to search through his phone for videos. When she discovered one and pressed play, Olivia heaved seeing Malcolm having sex with two women in a threesome.

She dropped the phone on the tile floor like a hot potato, repulsed at what she saw. She leaned above the toilet and gagged with nothing coming out. The sound of Malcolm pounding on the door became hollow and faded away as though she were in a tunnel.

Completely spent with emotion, Olivia grabbed the sink to

pull herself from the floor. She tried to steady herself back on her feet. However, the room spun constantly. Tears splattered her cheeks into the oval, brass sink bowl. Slowly raising her head, she caught her reflection in the mirror. The puffy, red-rimmed eyes looking back did not seem to belong to her.

The risk of passing out finally dissolved. She reached her hand out to the brass handle to turn on the water. The cold liquid stung her like tiny bumble bees when she splashed her flushed face four times. She blindly reached for the flowered hand towel on the rack to dry off.

Her body weakened with despair. She couldn't stop shaking. She breathed in deeply and exhaled to get herself together for what she had to handle. *What am I going to do?*

Suddenly, her mind snapped back into the present situation. She heard the pounding again. Olivia grabbed the phone from the floor, quickly opened the door and screamed, "I hate you." She threw the phone with all her might toward Malcolm's face.

He fell backward and blocked his face with his hands to keep it from hitting him. He caught the phone with his left hand right before it landed on the floor. His face sagged with guilt in realization Olivia was on to him. He noticed she'd called the number back.

"Baby, it's not what you think," Malcolm tried to explain.

"What do you think I think Malcolm? Huh?" Olivia asked him, eerily calm. "Do you think I think you've been cheating on me with some whores since you've been on the Large Luscious Latina Ladies Love Black Men dating website? Or do you think I must be thinking about how you lied about being single and not having any children? Or thinking about how you lied about your age and your job? Or thinking about how you're meeting with this chick, Carmen, at hotels when you're supposedly working out in the morning? Or thinking about the trick, Mariah, you met with today? Or perhaps I'm thinking about the receipts I found in your pants for a hotel and happy hour? Or am I thinking about how you missed our daughter's basketball game since you were out screwing your ho? Or am I thinking about all of the naked pictures of women and videos of you having sex with them on your phone?" By now, Olivia had worked her way to yelling in his face with spittle flying from her mouth.

Malcolm's face fell, realizing Olivia knew everything he'd done. "Look, Baby, I can explain."

"Really? You think you can explain? You think you can justify bringing your nasty body into our bed and putting me at risk for an STD?" Olivia raged.

"It's only a game. You don't think I would mess around with Hispanic women, do you?" Malcolm asked, trying to recover. "You know how I feel about anyone being with someone outside of our race. One of my boys wanted me to check out his profile on that website. He's interested in some girl. That's all, baby."

"Shut up. Shut up and get out of my face. How dare you lie to me," Olivia yelled and pounded her fist on the table. "I saw the video of your friggin' threesome!"

"Baby, I'm sorry," Malcolm pleaded. "The truth is we haven't been having sex the way I need to. I mean, we sleep in separate beds most nights. A man has his needs, you know? Please forgive me. I didn't mean to hurt you."

"Didn't mean to hurt me? Or you didn't mean for me to find out?" Olivia's throat became raw with pain, which didn't stop her from yelling. "After all these years, I can't believe you would do this to me. You even had enough nerve to expect for me to be perfect like a model. These women are all jacked up. You bastard."

Olivia grabbed a bourbon glass from the counter and threw

it at him. He dodged out of the way, and it smashed on the wall behind him. The force of her throw left shards of glass embedded in the plaster. Shattered crystal spread across the floor in dangerous pieces. "I hate you. Do you hear me? I hate you," she screamed at the top of her lungs.

"Liv. Please, listen baby. I promise you; I didn't have unprotected sex. I wouldn't do that to you. You have to believe me, baby," Malcolm begged.

"Don't you ever call me baby again. You are dead to me."

Olivia had enough of looking at him. She grabbed her car keys from the counter and ran to the door, which led to the garage.

"Olivia. Where are you going? You shouldn't go out like this." Malcolm approached her.

"Get. Away. From. Me." Olivia said in a low voice, narrowing her eyes, which would kill him if they could. She stuck her index finger out in his direction in a threatening manner to curse him.

Malcolm backed away with his hands in surrender. Olivia opened the door to run to her car. She either had to get far away from him or kill him.

CHAPTER 46

In a daze, Olivia climbed into her Mercedes. Tears began springing from her eyes until she couldn't cry anymore. Exhausted and defeated, she didn't know what to do.

Voices chattered in her head. *Start the car. All I have to do is sit here in the garage with the door closed until I die from carbon monoxide poisoning. This can be my sweet escape from this cruel world. Perhaps my brother and grandfather were better off than everyone else once they ended their lives.*

She held her head in her hands, rocking back and forth, trying to shake the voices out. "No. No. I don't deserve this. After all, I've done for him and the kids. I've emptied myself, and this is what he does to me. No one loves or cares about me. I can't keep living my life like this," Olivia yelled and pounded her fists on the steering wheel.

Clinching her eyes tightly, she tried to quiet her mind. *It would be so easy just to end my life. I can make Malcolm suffer forever once I'm dead.*

Opening her eyes, she leaned her head back and gazed toward heaven in desperation. "Please God, forgive me for whatever I do."

Although she prayed for forgiveness, Olivia's heart hardened at the opportunity for a way out of her situation. She slowly stared to her left and focused on the wall of the garage. A jumbo, red gasoline container with a yellow spout, sat on the floor next to the lawn mower. She tilted her head to the side staring blankly at the can.

Olivia slowly opened her car door and got out to move toward the gasoline container in a hypnotized state. When she picked it up, the fluid sloshed back and forth inside. She could tell from the weight; it was almost full.

Put the container down. Don't do this. Ignoring her thoughts, she carried the canister to the door leading into the house and opened it. Malcolm was no longer in the kitchen.

The room seemed to get bigger. It appeared hazy like a dream world where things did not seem to be real. Olivia slowly walked across the floor to the kitchen junk drawer. She placed the gasoline canister near her feet.

Olivia opened the drawer and dug through it frantically, tossing items out, until she found her candle lighter. She flicked it on and off, staring at the flame in awe, to the point that she almost forgot where she was. A familiar sensation prickled her skin. It reminded her of the feeling she had when she burned Ross's jersey.

Olivia lifted the canister and walked slowly to the stairwell. She floated in a trance toward the master bedroom. She heard the shower running behind the closed bathroom door. The thought of him washing away his whore's scent, caused red spots to flash before her eyes.

The sound of Malcolm whistling, drifted to her ears, driving her anger to a higher level. *I mean nothing to him since he seems to be at peace enough to sing in the shower.*

Olivia jumped into action. She opened the spout on the container and splashed gasoline all around the bedroom and in front of the bathroom door. Splotches of the liquid landed on their Vera Wang comforter and pillows and soaked into the rugs on the floor. The intoxicating smell made her giddy and nauseous at the same time.

Olivia stopped long enough to examine the lighter in her hand. She became aware of the feel of it at that moment. Clicking it on and off several times mesmerized her with the flickering flame.

Maybe I should lie in our bed and light the gasoline. I can end it all for both of us. Perhaps I can do like my grandfather did when he set his house on fire. My parents wouldn't even miss me since I don't matter to them. I know Simone and Christian love me, but I'm good for no one now. If I leave Malcolm, they will hate me for breaking up our family. This is the only way I can have peace.

The sound of Malcolm's whistling pierced her ears and annoyed her with the thought of him not having a care in the world. *Oh, he thinks he can be happy now? Nah, he is going to die. I'm going to live. I'll raise the kids by myself since he's denied all of us with his cheating.*

She took a deep breath and lit the trail of gasoline in front of the bathroom. Olivia left the bedroom, closed the door, and walked calmly down the stairs.

Olivia retraced her steps to the garage. She sloshed gasoline around the four cars. After placing the canister on the floor, she lit the trail of liquid with the lighter. She closed the door, before coolly walking back into the house.

Olivia made her way to the foyer and stared up the stairs. Smoke slithered out from beneath the master-bedroom door.

As if she were having an out of body experience, Olivia observed herself step out into the still night in her slippers. She closed the door behind her, and nonchalantly strolled down the driveway to the street. Once there, she made her way to a point where she could still see her home. In anticipation of what would happen, she sat on the curbside with her hands folded on her lap.

The dinging and vibration of her cell phone startled Olivia out of her trance. She grunted and dug it out of the front pocket of her jeans to read the text message. The swelling of her eyes from crying earlier made it difficult to make out the words. She squinted, and her eyes darted back and forth across her phone screen reading the words repeatedly,

Hey Liv. I thought the kids would be right back to my house after grabbing their sleepover stuff. Let me know if they're coming for pizza. We're waiting on them. Rhonice.

Blood drained from her head, causing her to swoon. Her heart raced and pounded hard against her chest.

The crackle and pop of Spanish roof tiles snapping drew her eyes to her house. Thick plumes of black smoke pouring like water from the master bedroom window, blocked the moon. Flames flickered with fury, devouring the stucco walls.

The ground tremored from the rumble of the fire. She heard a roar from the expanding blaze. The red, orange and yellow monster swallowed the Kiowa and Tuscarora crape myrtle trees lining their perfectly manicured yard like fuel.

Olivia's dry lips released a gurgled moan of regret from her throat, which turned into a hoarse, blood-curdling scream penetrating the air. "No, no, no! Somebody, please help me. Oh, my Lord. My kids are in the house. Please, somebody, help me please!"

Her lungs struggled to breathe due to the heaving of her sobs, which burdened her chest. With tears pouring from her eyes, she pushed herself from the curb where she sat.

She tripped into a run toward what had now developed into a ferocious, merciless blaze engulfing all she loved. The intense heat on her face threatened to cook her from the inside and made her turn away, coughing from the acrid smell of burning wood.

Olivia stumbled on a rock, stubbed her toe, and lost her footing. She fell hard on her hands and knees to the asphalt and ripped her jeans from scraping the ground. The fall embedded pebbles in her palms, causing her to howl in pain. She grabbed her leg and blood dripped onto her fingers.

Ashes stung her eyes and nose. Olivia tried to crawl toward the house, which shot out glimmering embers. The heat from the fire forced her to rise from the ground. She staggered back to the middle of the street, away from the house.

The smell of penetrating smoke and Olivia's screams drew her neighbors from their homes.

Her neighbor, Maurice, suddenly appeared in front of her with his eyes bugged wide open, seeming bewildered and terrified. "I called 9-1-1."

Olivia stared at him without registering what he said after that. His mouth opened and closed. However, in her horror, she couldn't understand his jumbled and muffled words. Finally, they poured clearly into her ears.

"Olivia, are you okay? Where's your family? I called the fire department, and they should be here any minute now. Olivia? Olivia?" Maurice grabbed her shoulders, shaking her hard. She kept staring at him blankly with her eyes spilling tears.

Olivia's attention shifted away from Maurice toward the house. She was shocked to see her husband, Malcolm, stumble out of the front door. Flames were on the back of his robe, and he cried out in agony.

She breathed in sharply when she noticed Christian and Simone tucked beneath each of his arms. Covered in soot, they gasped for air and coughed violently.

Maurice ran to help them and other neighbors, Robert, Faye,

Antoinette, Leon, and the Hudsons, joined him. They shouted to push Malcolm onto the ground to put out the fire on his robe. He rolled around, screaming and writhing in pain. Leon quickly removed his shirt to beat the flames.

Malcolm's blackened robe hung in tatters from the fire once smothered. Their neighbors helped him stand and move along with the kids further away from the house.

Suddenly, Christian broke away from the group and ran across the cobblestone driveway toward the house wailing, "Mama. Where's Mama? Mama!"

Robert chased and grabbed him by the waist when he reached the front door. He quickly carried him downhill to the other end of the street. Christian continued screaming and crying for her, with his arms stretched toward the home.

Olivia refrained from running to him. She put her hand to her mouth, sobbing at the sight of her son trying to save her.

A fireball erupted from the garage into the dark sky and illuminated the atmosphere. Olivia's hands burned from the unforgiving heat when she shielded her eyes from the bright light.

The force from the explosion pushed her further away in the opposite direction from her family. Debris and ashes began falling all around the neighborhood causing her neighbors to scream and scurry to find cover.

Sirens pierced the air when firefighters arrived. They jumped off their trucks to control the blaze by drowning it with water from their hoses. Black smoke turned white after they extinguished the leaping flames.

Paramedics ran to Malcolm and the kids to help them with their injuries. They were all loaded into ambulances on gurneys and whisked away with sirens blasting throughout the neighborhood.

Olivia shook her head slowly with tears streaking her soot-covered cheeks. *How can this be happening? How can this be my perfect life? How did I get here?*

She gazed sadly at everything going on around her, and quietly slipped away into the darkness.

CHAPTER 47

"Olivia. Olivia," Savvy screamed into the phone. Sunlight peeping through the blinds washed over her. She sat on the side of her bed, frozen in fear. The dead phone tumbled from her trembling hand and landed with a thud on the floor rug.

Olivia's distressed call about Malcolm the previous night came to mind. "I know she was angry, but there's no way she could set her house on fire," she whispered in disbelief. "My friend does some crazy stuff, but she would never hurt her family."

Savvy frantically searched for the remote control on the nightstand. She found it under a book and pointed toward the TV to turn on the morning news. The anchor finished reporting about a stolen ATM on the west side of San Antonio before a breaking story banner popped up.

"Breaking news. A home located in a Bexar County Historic District has been destroyed by fire. The house belonged to a psychologist, Dr. Olivia C. Maxell, and her husband, Malcolm Turnipseed." A video of the home burning flashed on the screen. Savvy screamed and fell limply to the bed. Her stomach cramped in knots and throbbing pain shot through her head.

The reporter continued, "Arson investigators are working to determine if the fire was purposefully set. Firefighters responded to the blaze around 9:30 tonight and the two-story home was already engulfed in flames. Turnipseed and their children were transported to the hospital by ambulance.

"This can't be for real," Savvy said in disbelief.

"Dr. Olivia C. Maxwell is missing, and a neighbor reported seeing her run into a wooded area," blared the reporter.

"I know Olivia didn't do this," Savvy mumbled.

A picture of Olivia flashed on the news. She increased the volume to make sure she could hear correctly.

"Mr. Turnipseed's wife, Dr. Olivia C. Maxwell, is being blamed for starting this fire. The police are searching for her. Mr. Turnipseed is asking for his wife to turn herself in."

Savvy's mouth fell open. "This can't be happening. I must be having a nightmare right now."

Her eyes remained glued to the TV. They showed a video of Olivia's clinics across the city. The reporter talked about her being a leader in the community and an influential psychologist in San Antonio. They interviewed the Chief of Police, who asked for anyone with information about Dr. Maxwell's whereabouts, to contact the police department immediately.

Savvy grabbed her phone from the floor and called Olivia. The message from her voicemail played. She hastily threw on clothes and grabbed her purse and keys to go to the hospital.

CHAPTER 48

The anchor on the 5 pm news didn't bother to hide his disdain as he delivered the breaking news.

"Dr. Olivia C. Maxwell has been taken into custody by investigators with the Arson Unit of the San Antonio Police Department. It was just after 2 p.m. when Dr. Maxwell turned herself in. She has been charged with first-degree arson for setting her own home on fire in one of San Antonio's historic districts last night. Fortunately, her entire family escaped with minor injuries."

"Neighbors who called 911 said the fire started after 9:00 pm," the anchor stated.

"There were gigantic flames and black smoke coming out of the windows," an anonymous neighbor recalled. "Thankfully, we carried her husband and kids away from the house right before there was a big explosion."

Another neighbor came on the screen. "It was scary to watch their house in flames right next door to all of our homes. We were praying for everyone in the house to be okay and hoping the whole neighborhood wouldn't be destroyed." She paused shakily and continued, "You don't think someone you know could do something like this. She's someone I chat with regularly when the kids are playing together. I can't believe she would put everyone's life at risk. It could've been much worse. This kind of thing doesn't happen in our neighborhood."

The anchor continued to talk. Olivia's mug shot flashed on the TV repeatedly along with a video of their burned home. She appeared bewildered with tree leaves stuck in her hair and scratches on her face. Pictures of her and Malcolm in their wedding photo in *Jet* magazine showed throughout the report.

A reporter managed to get into the hospital where Malcolm remained in recovery. When informed that Olivia turned herself in, he replied weakly, "I'm glad to hear that. I ask for privacy for my family. We need to deal with this tragedy. I have no further comments."

PART 6

WAIT, WHAT?

EPILOGUE

One Month Later

"Dr. Maxwell. Why did you set your house on fire? Were you trying to kill your husband and children?"

"Is it true that you thought he was cheating on you?

"Dr. Maxwell. How did you get out of jail so fast after pleading guilty to a felony second-degree arson? Why do you think the judge allowed you to serve only thirty days instead of a ten-year sentence?"

Olivia shrunk behind sunglasses and refused to make eye contact with the swarm of reporters. She was thankful for the clothes Savvy brought to her, along with a large floppy hat, which helped conceal her face. Her first taste of freedom became cannibalized by the eager public fishing for details. She clung to Savvy's arm for support.

Her attorney stepped between her and the mob of people to make a statement. Her silver dreadlocks wrapped into an enormous French roll on the top of her head gave her a look which demanded respect.

"Excuse me. Are you her attorney? Can you tell the public why your client is being shown preferential treatment?"

"Folks, please back up and give Dr. Maxwell some space."

"Yes, my name is Jewel Noble, and I am representing Dr. Maxwell. Anyone who knows Dr. Maxwell is shocked by the events which have been reported."

"Attorney Noble, why did Dr. Maxwell start the fire?"

"As you heard during her court case, the fire was a result of a very complicated situation and a history of circumstances which were a product of the relationship. She is a dedicated mother to her children and a highly respected psychologist in our community."

"Attorney Noble. Can you please explain why Dr. Maxwell is not sentenced to prison?"

"Her husband, Malcolm Turnipseed, wrote a character letter to the court asking she not be sentenced to prison. She has served thirty days and paid a fine of $60,000 in restitution for the crime, and will provide community service during her ten years of probation. The probation will be deferred based on behavior. Now, we just ask for privacy. Thank you."

A chorus of "Dr. Maxwell" and "Attorney Noble" followed the trio to the limousine waiting to whisk them away.

As the car moved onto the highway, Savvy hugged Olivia in the back seat. "You are free, Olivia."

"Thank God." Olivia hugged her friend and smiled.

With God's gift of freedom, the daunting task of healing awaited Olivia. She would begin with herself, and then, her children.

The End

Book Club Discussion Guide
Reasonable Insanity

1. What does Reasonable Insanity mean?
2. What is your first impression of Olivia when you were introduced to her?
3. Where do you believe Olivia's standard of perfection originated from?
4. How can women be more accepting of their skin color, size, and shape in order to not be moved to change to please others?
5. What signs of mental illness were reflected in this story? Did you think of Olivia as being mentally ill?
6. What do you think Savvy could have done differently in Olivia's life? Did she do enough as Olivia's best friend? Should she have rekindled their relationship as adults after being pulled into trouble with Olivia during their college years?
7. Why does Olivia have so many failed relationships? What type of man does she attract and why? How did she end up with Dwain, Ross, and Malcolm? Could she have done anything differently in these relationships?
8. Do you know any Black women who have dealt with or are dealing with bulimia? What would you do if you became aware of a friend dealing with an eating disorder?
9. Is Olivia fit to be a Psychologist even though she has so many issues of her own?

10. Why do you think Malcolm cheated on Olivia? Was it justified?

11. Did you understand Olivia's mindset when she decided to burn the house down? What led to her snapping instead of just leaving Malcolm?

12. .Were you surprised at the way the book ended? What do you think is next for Dr. Olivia C. Maxwell?

About Cynthia Freeman Gibbs

Cynthia Freeman Gibbs is a native of Lansing, MI.
She enjoys writing in quaint coffee shops, and is pursuing a
pescatarian/pseudo vegetarian life. After obtaining her M.B.A.
from Florida A&M University, she moved to San Antonio, TX
where she currently resides with her husband. She is active in
the Tobin Writer's Group, Delta Sigma Theta Sorority,
Incorporated, her church, and enjoys volunteering in her
community.

Made in the USA
Columbia, SC
03 October 2018